I0618342

TOUCH OF CORRUPTION

John J. Parkington

Indian Canyon Press
Palm Springs, CA

Also by John J. Parkington
Justice Rendered
Body Parts

ISBN-10: 0983677921
EAN-13: 9780983677925

Indian Canyon Press
Palm Springs, CA

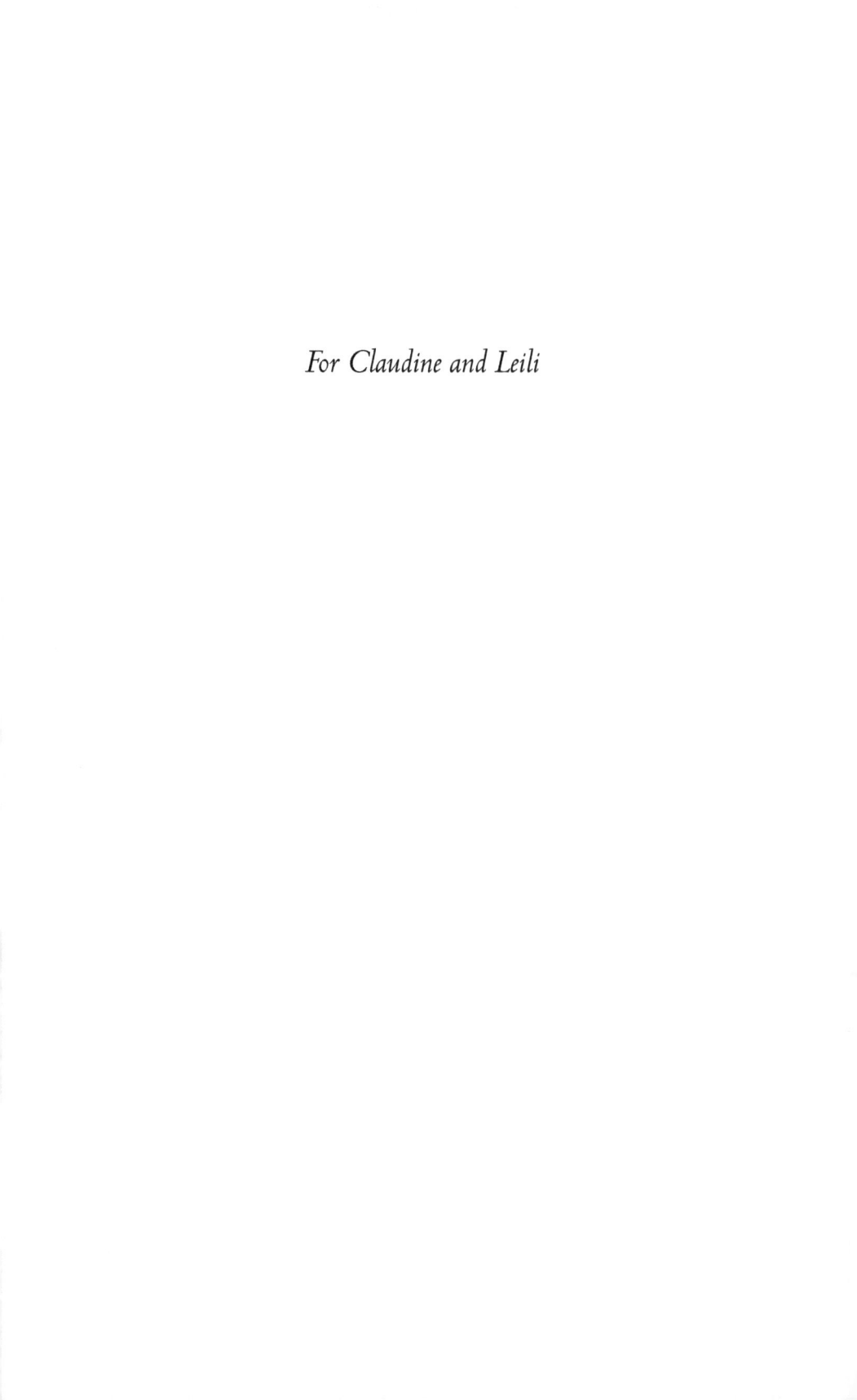

For Claudine and Leili

I

The black Mercedes limousine glided to a stop under the canopy of The Hay-Adams Hotel, one block from the White House. A black doorman, attired in white shirt, black tie and slacks and a bright red vest, hurried to open the right rear passenger door. He bid good afternoon to Senator Bradley Bullman, "Bull" to friends and one of the most powerful U.S. Senators on Capitol Hill. The Senator exited his limo and strode hastily to the hotel entrance to escape the sticky July humidity.

Bull wore one of his custom-made navy blue pin-striped suits, complemented by a 3-ply white cotton dress shirt, silk floral Brioni tie and black Bruno Magli slip-ons. Standing an imposing six foot four and deeply tanned with wavy gray hair, he was always quick to flash his trademark white teeth. Long gone were his days as a Georgia State halfback, but he kept fit with regular workouts in the Congressional Gym. Though sixty-two, he could easily pass for a man ten years younger.

Bull walked through the hotel, acknowledging gestures of recognition from friends and rivals alike. He came to a halt at the elevators, the doors of which carried the hotel's insignia. In his right palm, he discreetly carried a card key to the Presidential Suite. It afforded guests unparalleled views of the White House, Lafayette Square and St. John's Church. Not merely an insider's favorite, the Presidential Suite had been a one-of-a-kind space in the most powerful city in the world for nearly a century. Leading world statesmen occupied this suite when lucky enough to snag reservations. The space encompassed a living room, dining area with working fireplace, bedroom and one-and-a-half baths. The Frette Italian linens, intricately carved plaster ceilings and canopy bed, antique furnishings and precious Persian carpets all contributed a sense of regency.

Well earned, Bull thought, after his twenty-one years in the U.S. Senate, following four as a Representative. He held little interest in his private, inherited wealth, compared with the massive power he wielded over national and international policies that affected the daily lives of billions.

The hotel routinely served as a venue for business and political meetings. No one would think it odd to see a distinguished Senator on premise, particularly Bradley Bullman. He glanced at the gold Patek Philippe Nautilus on his wrist—2:03 PM.

Once in the elevator and alone, heat built in his groin. His mouth watered in anticipation, and he unconsciously licked his lips. *Dakota…I can't wait to get my hands on your sweet little ass.*

• • •

Two minutes before Bull boarded the elevator, a uniformed bellman knocked on the Presidential Suite's door. Sara McElvy, *AKA* Dakota, answered in a sheer, white baby doll, embroidered with tiny red roses encircling the neck and hemline.

"Please give this envelope to Senator Bullman as soon as he arrives," the bellman said. "It's of critical importance." He left abruptly, leaving Dakota holding the standard #10 white business envelope, sealed and blank on both sides.

How's he know Bull's coming? she wondered. Sara closed the door, paused a moment to study the envelope again and placed it on the wooden Civil War era table in the foyer. *Hope this isn't like the one I gave Hillier last week. Guy pissed his pants, cried like a baby and slinked out of the room.*

Dakota's attention was drawn to her reflection in the gilded-framed mirror over the table. An exotic and sophisticated woman of thirty-seven. Five foot nine with a narrow face, natural D-cup breasts, brunette hair pulled in a tight ponytail and shaved genitals as the Senator ordered. She giggled and set about making Bull's favorite drink—a double Jack Daniel's on the rocks. His standing expectation upon arrival.

• • •

Senator Bullman stepped from the elevator and felt his feet sink into the plush hallway carpet as he headed to the suite. He thought about the $8,000 cash fee he gave Dakota every other Thursday. *Not bad, considering the room is probably two G's a night.* For the past three months he'd seen Dakota, Bull didn't realize others employed her to encourage his perverse interests.

He paused at the suite's door and swiveled his head right and left. *Hallway empty.* Bull slid the card key into the electronic lock, entered and quickly closed the door. After twisting the bolt lock with a practiced hand, he roughly embraced

Dakota, gripping her ass. "Mmm, you're soft and warm. ...What's that I smell? Gardenias?"

"It's a new eau de toilette." She extricated herself from his powerful hold and handed him his drink.

He guzzled it down, feeling the warmth flow through him. "Turn around. I wanna look," he said, licking his lips.

Dakota made a slow 360 degree turn with her hands clasped behind her head. Her baby doll did little to hide what she would soon share with him.

The Senator removed his suit coat and flopped on the living room couch. He loosened his tie and began unbuttoning his shirt. "Strip baby. You know the drill."

"Bull, a hotel bellman came by a few minutes ago..."

"Not interested. I wanna see your naked butt. And I hope you've been saving up." He chuckled and massaged the growing bulge in his custom-pleated trousers.

"The guy left an envelope for you. Said it was critical."

"Huh?" His mind went on alert.

"I'll get it." She walked to the antique foyer table, picked up the envelope and carried it by its corner to the Senator.

"No one knows I'm here. Who's it from?"

"Beats me."

"What's in it?" A few beads of perspiration formed on his brow. His eyes darted from Dakota to the envelope and back.

"Don't know. Bellman handed it to me and said you need to check it out."

Bull handled the envelope by its edges as if it was infected. He turned it over, examining the blank front and back. *What's this? Who could know I'm here? Should I open it? ... Now? ...Later? No, now. Get it over with, whatever the fuck it is.*

Dakota stood statuesque in front of the Senator while he slipped a thumb under the envelope's flap, opened it and removed a single typewritten sheet. Bull plucked reading glasses from the breast pocket of his suit jacket and examined the page.

Senator Bullman,

As Chairman of the Senate Committee on Banking, we order you to halt all regulatory changes to the banking industry for one year. This is no request. It's a demand. If the enclosed photograph is insufficient to convince you of our hold on you, we have hundreds more, including audio-video recordings of your deviant behavior.

Fail to comply and we will give the pics and recordings to the media.

Bull didn't budge for several ticks. *Is this a joke?* He yanked the photograph from the envelope. It showed him lying naked on his back, spread eagle in the room's canopy bed. Wrists tied with white silk cloth to the headboard, ankles to the footboard. His recognizable face and well-known toothy grin in full view. Dakota was squatting over him, facing away from the camera, defecating on his chest.

Bull's mouth opened and closed soundlessly. His hands trembled as he crumpled the envelope and its contents. His face grew hot. Leaping awkwardly to his feet, he lunged at Dakota, standing four feet away and wringing her hands. "YOU FILTHY BITCH!"

She backed away, but not far or fast enough. Bull landed an open-handed slap that sent her careening off balance toward the dining area's Louis XIV table. Dakota fell and struck her left temple hard on its corner. She slumped to the floor.

"WHO'S BEHIND THIS? ANSWER ME!"

No response. No movement. Her eyes were open, but she wasn't breathing. A trickle of blood oozed from her left ear and nostril. Bull put two fingers against her neck, then an ear next to her left breast—no heart beat, no reassuring sounds of life.

Twenty seconds later, stunned and hyperventilating, he turned away from her lifeless body. Bull crawled across the glossy parquet floor onto the century old floral-design Persian carpet in the living room. Mind racing. Thoughts incoherent. He sat on the carpet, arms around his shins, rocking back and forth. Petrified with fear. A minute passed. The suite's telephone rang, puncturing the silence and jarring the Senator.

What should I do? It rang six times and stopped. He sucked in a deep breath and released it. Seconds later, his cell phone began clanging. On the fourth ring, he answered, voice croaking, "Yes?"

"Look what you've done you *fool*," a man's disembodied voice said. "She was an ignorant tool, but a useful one. You'll pay *dearly* for this."

"Wh…who are you?" Bull looked haltingly around the elegant room for physical evidence of the male voice on the phone.

"The one who *owns* you. Pick up your jacket, the letter and photograph and leave. We'll sanitize the room and deal with the body. Do you understand?"

"No, I mean yes, but…" Tears streamed down Bull's cheeks.

"Go about the rest of the day as you normally would. Understand?"

"Yes." He spotted Dakota's dead eyes and whimpered, "I didn't mean to…"

"What you *meant* to do is irrelevant. I video recorded it all. A woman named St. John will contact you at your office tomorrow morning. Be available. Clear?"

"No, I…I can't. I mean, I'll try, but…"

"COMPLY! Or suffer the consequences. Oh, and drop the fee on the foyer table when you leave. Now get out." The line went dead.

Dazed, Bull scrambled to his feet, pocketed his phone and picked up his jacket. He folded it over his forearm and shoved the letter and photo in a pocket. Without even a glance at Dakota's corpse, he placed an envelope containing eight grand on the foyer table, left the suite and took the elevator to the lobby. He ignored colleagues as he left the hotel. Bull fast-walked two blocks up Pennsylvania Avenue and caught a taxi to his four-story row house in Georgetown. His wife, Melissa, had reminded him to be home by 7 PM—sober. She expected ten for a catered dinner at 8:00.

Entering his home unseen, Bull thought, *How the hell can I halt banking reform? Shit, I leaned on those pricks for months to drive change. . . . What about Dakota? Will that guy really take care of. . .? Dear god, I've fucked up.* He rushed to the bar, grabbed an unopened bottle of Jack Daniels, a glass and bucket of ice and ran upstairs to his bath to hide out until dinnertime.

2

Carrie Linden marched through the crowded hallways of Northwestern Memorial Hospital on East Superior Street in Chicago. The cool fluorescent lighting and antiseptic smells amplified her tension as she headed to Room 423. Carrie had received an urgent call from a nurse, informing her a patient named Brenda Butler lay in the burn unit. During conscious moments, Brenda had repeatedly cried out for her.

The two had last met three years ago at the Chanel fragrance counter in Neiman Marcus on North Michigan Avenue. The time before was college graduation fifteen years earlier. Their brief visit in Neiman's left Carrie with the impression Brenda led the life of a pampered lady of leisure. A gorgeous black woman, five foot ten with short hair and smooth, unblemished skin that gleamed like marble in the store's lights. Everything about Brenda suggested she lived large—her Armani attire, Prada purse and matching shoes and the names on the sales bags she toted. Though Brenda had always carried herself with distinction, she'd radiated elegance.

Carrie remembered feeling embarrassed during their Neiman's encounter. At that time, she struggled to overcome a drinking problem. Her appearance and hygiene had suffered. And she'd barely dug out of her psychological hole when, with hair unwashed for days and no makeup, she bumped into gorgeous Brenda.

Their meeting was cordial. Carrie gave Brenda her business card, but Brenda revealed little about her life. Instead, Brenda had focused their brief conversation on Carrie's success as an investigative reporter for the *Chicago Tribune*.

At the burn center nurses' station, Carrie asked permission to visit Brenda. A nurse made her don a surgical cap and gown, ear loop face mask and latex-free gloves.

Carrie paused at the door to Room 423, straightened the green smock that now covered her violet-colored linen dress and took a deep breath through the mask. She tiptoed into the dimly lit hospital room and stepped quietly to the foot of Brenda's bed. A cool white light on the wall above the bed illuminated the room. A strong medicinal smell permeated the air.

Brenda lay on her stomach, head turned from the door toward the curtained window. A plastic sheet hung above and over her body, which was naked to the waist. Her once silken, bronze skin displayed multiple charred black patches. An IV bottle dangled from a steel pole near the bed with a tube running into Brenda's arm. Multiple wires from her body connected to monitors. A catheter tube led from Brenda under the sheet to a half-full urine collection bag, which sagged, hanging on the side of the bed.

"Brenda? It's Carrie. I'm here," Carrie whispered as she rounded the end of the bed to face her erstwhile friend.

Brenda's left eye opened part way. The other was dark and swollen shut. A tear from her good eye streamed down her nose, hung for a second and dropped onto the pillow. The good eye closed. Brenda made no further response.

Carrie raced to the nurses' station, tearing off the hospital garb on the way. "I'm Carrie Linden. Someone please tell me what happened to Brenda Butler."

A pudgy, forty-something-year-old man with thinning hair and a sparse brown beard and dressed in green scrubs stood. He set aside a folder crammed with forms and said, "Ms. Linden? I'm Dr. Paul Goretski. Let's step into a room to talk."

He shut the door to the empty patient room they'd entered and said, "Ms. Linden, I'm in charge of Ms. Butler's care."

"Call me Carrie." She sat on the edge of the hospital bed, eyeing the burn doc and taking in frequent, short breaths.

He leaned his back against a blank wall and folded his arms across his chest. "Ever since Ms. Butler arrived into emergency, she's asked for you and only you...when she's lucid, that is. I know you by reputation. I'm an avid reader of your column. Seen you on TV too. What's your connection with Ms. Butler?"

"I'm an old college friend. Haven't seen her in years. Beyond that, there's little I can tell. I don't even know where she lives. ...She was estranged from her mother, but that was years ago. No father or siblings to my knowledge. What happened?"

"You're not family, but we can't locate any relatives. She's been so insistent about seeing you I'll share some details with you. Maybe you can help us help her. ...We learned Brenda's name and address from her driver's license. EMS dropped off her clothes and purse from the hotel."

"For crying out loud what happened to her?" Carrie pleaded.

Goretski inhaled deeply. "Two nights ago, someone called 911 just after nine, directing EMS to a room at The Drake. The hotel desk clerk who let them into the room later told police he'd often seen Ms. Butler at the Drake. She was found lying naked on her stomach, wrists and ankles bound to bedposts with burns on her back."

"Holy hell!" Carrie put hand to mouth. ..."How bad is she?"

"Ms. Butler sustained burns on roughly forty percent of her back. The big problem is the degree of her injuries. She suffered full thickness burns. You're probably more familiar with the term third degree burns. Don't know what Ms. Butler does for a living, but I can guess. A few times she's said, 'He used his cigar on me.'"

"Oh my God!" Carrie's eyes widened. She involuntarily flinched at the horror.

"I don't know who *he* is, but four of the burn marks are consistent with what could have been a cigar. We found bits of tobacco in the wounds." He grimaced having repeated it again. "Also there were traces of an incendiary fluid on her back."

"SHIT! ...Sorry." She swallowed as she tasted bile rising in her throat.

"It likely accounts for the majority of her burns. When the EMS techs found her, she'd been gagged with her panties. ...Fortunate for her attacker I suppose. Those burns would have made a Navy Seal scream. The cops investigated, but no one reported seeing or hearing anything. No fingerprints, except for Ms. Butler's, and she won't name the creep who did it. They've got no leads.

"We're temporarily treating her burns with an enzymatic ointment. That's a type of topical disinfectant. She's also being pumped full of antibiotics to ward off infection, and we're medicating her for pain. Her burns extend down to the third layer of the skin, the subcutaneous tissue. No muscle damage, but she'll require skin grafts. We'll perform autografts..."

"That's her own skin, right?" Carrie asked, remembering her harrowing experience with the black market for human organ and tissue transplantation.

"Right. We'll take grafts from her unburned skin, such as her buttocks and upper thighs, to cover the damaged area. Before the grafts, we'll remove all necrotic tissue...skin that's dead because it can't get sufficient blood flowing to it."

"Ugh." Carrie closed her eyes and shook her head. "Will she be okay?"

"She'll live. But the grafts will result in a good deal of permanent scarring."

Carrie winced. The tears that had built now overflowed and rolled down her cheeks. Using her right index finger like a windshield blade, she swiped them away.

"We'll operate in a day or two, depending on her condition and ability to authorize surgery." Goretski rubbed his eyes and pinched the bridge of his nose.

"What about her face? It looked swollen."

"She sustained a beating too. Nothing was broken, and the swelling will subside. She'll have a few problems when this is over. One is the disfigurement on her back and the areas we use to harvest the grafts. I don't know how it will affect her, uh, profession. …She'll likely suffer post-traumatic stress too. Psychotherapy could help."

"What can I do?" Carrie asked, fists clenching and unclenching.

"It may be inconvenient, but you could spend time at her bedside. Ms. Butler will be here for weeks, and she keeps asking for you. You're presence might provide comfort. Maybe you'll learn about her family or the animal who hurt her."

Carrie mentally paged through her schedule. "I can do that. If I learn anything, I'll let you know. You keep me posted too."

They exchanged business cards and left the room.

During the taxi ride to her downtown brownstone apartment, Carrie made a mental list of what she'd need to tend to Brenda and simultaneously work—laptop, cell phone, chargers and research materials for an article on illegal immigration. As a self-employed syndicated columnist and TV personality, no longer at the *Tribune*, Carrie worked from anywhere she could connect to the internet.

When she exited the cab, her stomach turned thinking about Brenda's burns. Upon entering her large two bedroom apartment, she recalled the bottle of Jameson Irish whiskey, gathering dust under her kitchen sink. She shook the alcoholic urge from her mind and proceeded to gather her work materials.

I'm gonna find out who hurt Brenda and make the sonofabitch pay. …Wish I could call Michael.

3

Two days had passed since water flooded the sub-basement of the luxury Chevy Chase, Maryland condominium. The mid-rise building comprised forty residential units, all with values in the mid-seven figures. A plumber made the needed repairs, but the sub-basement housed a private storage closet for each unit. Whatever wasn't elevated off the concrete slab sat, for two days, in a half-inch of water. The property manager notified all owners to inspect their stored items for damage.

A week earlier, Michael Taylor had completed renovations to his kitchen—the one area of his three-bedroom, four bath condo unit, which the former owner hadn't tackled. He'd solicited ideas for the kitchen redo from Carrie when they'd been lovers, and he merely implemented them. His inexpensive furnishings in plain view of the new gourmet kitchen stood out like flea market eyesores. Previously, he'd paid no attention to his furniture. In fact, if not for the urging from his accountant and financial advisor, he never would have even thought to purchase such an expensive residence.

Michael grimaced when he read the notice about the flood. Between the commotion of the kitchen project and his heavy client load, he'd forgotten the property manager's warnings not to store anything directly on the concrete slab.

This evening, he visited the sub-basement, which had a musty smell to it. When he opened his storage closet, he saw water had seeped up the sides of three cardboard boxes, etching wavy dark lines five inches up and around each of them. He'd stored nothing else in the bin. Two boxes contained remnants of his mother's estate. After she died, Michael disposed of her life traces, except for the contents of these two boxes. Personal memorabilia occupied the third, smaller box.

One by one, he humped the boxes up to his condo and placed them on the warm Rosa Verona-colored marble floor in his circular entrance foyer. Michael pulled up a cheap, brown naugahyde-covered footstool and sat. His attention went first to his personal box. It contained letters, cards, dinner napkins, ticket stubs and photos, all with one thing in common—Carrie Linden.

Gazing at the photograph of Carrie hugging and kissing him, he imagined the beautiful blond, her five foot eight height and nice curves. Her unpretentious, down-to-earth manner and her endearing smile. Michael's muscle memory of Carrie in his arms made him catch his breath. He loved this smart, independent and successful woman. Previous women in his life wanted to change him in some material way, his workaholic habits or inexpensive attire. Carrie accepted him as he was.

But he couldn't tolerate her proclivity to get embroiled in dangerous situations involving killers and organized crime. Her escapades routinely threatened her life, his and those of friends. The irony was he loved her for it too because her obsession and impulsiveness for bringing justice to evildoers had saved countless lives.

They'd not spoken in ten months since her last reckless adventure. Michael's private investigator, Max, check on Carrie monthly. In addition to Carrie's risk orientation, which Max interpreted as a death wish, she periodically fell off the wagon when overcome by stress. A few times, Michael had found her dead drunk.

Michael refused to accept the proposition of marrying a woman with an active substance abuse problem, no matter how much he loved her. He'd grown up, parented by a single alcoholic mother. Michael swore he'd never live under the same roof again with a drunk. Years ago, he'd beaten an addiction to Alprazolam, more commonly known as Xanax, for severe anxiety attacks by learning to manage the physiological symptoms of anxiety without the use of meds. His mother's drinking and erratic, often life threatening behavior laid the foundation for his underlying psychological problem. *Why can't Carrie control her addictive urges?*

The storage box had suffered the brunt of the water damage. Michael set his salvaged items aside and broke down the small box for disposal.

He turned his attention to his mother's possessions, now his. This walk back in time at once brought smiles and frowns as the items in the boxes stirred childhood and young adult memories. A little monkey carved from soapstone from the Montgomery County Annual Fair thirty years ago. Candles used for a Thanksgiving dinner she once hosted when sober. A box containing a few pieces of costume jewelry. The Coach purse Michael gave her for Christmas years earlier. And more...

Michael's mother, Jeannie Taylor, had spent three decades as a waitress in cheap eateries. He'd applied himself in school and worked his way up from borderline poverty. The criminal law practice he'd founded in Bethesda upon graduating Harvard Law became an overnight success. At thirty-eight, Michael had achieved wealth.

Along the way, he supported Jeannie—a little during junior high and high school with his earnings from a newspaper route and then as a stock boy and cashier at Giant Foods, more from bartending income during his years on academic scholarship at the University of Maryland and Harvard, and fully after his law practice took off.

While sorting Jeannie's effects, Michael found a small, green metal tin full of letters, tied with twine in bunches. The same person had addressed them by hand to Jeannie, dating to Michael's infancy. A Las Vegas, Nevada postmark showed on each envelope. He counted one hundred letters in chronological order, one every three months, from the month he was born until the year after he founded his law practice.

Michael ran his fingers through his thick black hair. This discovery raised questions. A lot of questions. He'd lived with the impression his mother's life was an open book to him. But she'd secretly corresponded with someone for over half his life.

He quickly rummaged through Jeannie's other belongings and organized them into three categories—a few keepsakes, items for Goodwill Industries and a trash pile. After breaking down the waterlogged boxes, he walked to the kitchen and grabbed a Diet Coke. He ferried the tin of letters to his home office desk and began reading.

At the end of the first letter, Michael cried. At two in the morning, exhausted, he finished reading the last one. "All My Love, Tony" appeared at the end of each letter. He rubbed his deep blue eyes, now bloodshot. Suddenly Michael began weaving in his chair. Dizzy, disoriented and short of breath, he summoned the will to stave off a panic attack, something he'd spent years learning to control. The attack quickly vanished. Taking his mind off the letters, he listened for a moment to the distant wail of an ambulance, racing south toward the District of Columbia.

Emotionally spent, he picked up the sole photograph enclosed with one of the earliest letters. He shook his head slowly and breathed through his open mouth as he studied the photo at length again.

A young Jeannie Taylor stood arm and arm with a boy in front of the Washington National Monument. Their attire signaled a spring day in D.C. What most disturbed Michael was the name, written in pencil in Jeannie's hand on the photo's reverse—Tony Amici. One of Jeannie's familiar hand drawn hearts appeared on each side of the name. His brow furrowed. His mind raced, thinking of all the implications.

4

Senator Bullman's executive secretary stuck her head in his spacious office.

"Senator, a Ms. St. John is here, and she *demands* to meet with you. *No* appointment. I told her you're booked solid, but the woman's quite rude."

Bull looked up from a donor's letter and saw his reflection in the plate glass of a framed photograph of his wife. The bags under his eyes bulged more than usual. His complexion was ashen. Following several hits of Jack Daniel's in his home bath, the boring dinner party with four glasses of wine and a snifter of brandy afterwards, he'd stayed awake all night, cold sober, tormented over Dakota and the trouble he was in.

"What's next on my agenda?"

"A meeting with Representative Gordon Davis about a consumer study."

"Reschedule Davis, and send in the St. John woman." *Gotta get this over with.*

St. John strutted into Bull's office, and his secretary closed the heavy wooden door after her. Despite the sexy image he'd conjured for a woman with the last name St. John, if that was her real name, he instantly sized her up as a tough dyke. A rectangular-shaped female, fortyish, with short-cropped hair and scant make-up, wearing a masculine looking khaki-colored business suit, white shirt and paisley tie.

"Senator, I believe you're expecting me," she said.

Bull slumped in his chair. "Dreading more like. Who the hell are you people?"

"Not anyone you want to fuck with." Without invitation she plopped down on a cherry wood Chippendale side chair across his desk. This will take only a few minutes, if you focus on what *I* have to say. Let's first walk down memory lane."

St. John retrieved a thin laptop from her briefcase and placed it on the leather insert in Bull's desk, angled so he could view the screen. She keyed a video clip. A highlight from one of his action adventures with Dakota filled the screen. His voice both audible and recognizable with a genuine smile, which was normally counterfeit.

"Oh sweet Jesus." He leaned forward. His face fell into his palms, elbows on his desk. "Stop it. Now. Stop. . . .I'm gonna be sick." Sweat formed on his brow.

St. John closed the file and slipped the laptop into her briefcase.

Lifting his head, he growled, "Have you no decency?"

"HA! You're asking *me* about decency? What a fuckin' laugh. Look. We have many of these clips. Just one of Dakota dropping a hot Cleveland steamer on your chest will sink your political career. Far worse if we release the recording of your last rendezvous. You now have proof positive of what we've got on you."

"What happened with, uh, uh. . .?" Bull put a hand to his throat, gasping.

"She'll be found. Away from the hotel. No connection with you, unless we release the video of her demise."

"Oh my god. . . .What about her, uh, family?"

"Don't concern yourself," St. John said with a smirk on her face.

"Wha. . .what are you going to do?" Droplets of perspiration streamed down the middle of his back. He licked his lips. His breathing picked up.

"Nothing. . .so long as you play ball, you bad boy. You *will* delay for a full year the banking industry reforms your committee is working on. Otherwise. . ."

"Everyone will think I'm nuts! I've been pushing hard for change, twisting arms, calling in favors. I'll look like an idiot."

"You'll look far worse if MSNBC or Fox News gets one of these videos."

He pulled his handkerchief and wiped his brow. "Is. . .is that all you want?"

"For now. . . .Get this straight. We *own* your political ass. *Permanently.* We won't ask you to kill anyone, though you've already done that."

"Christ." Bull's stomach sank as if he plummeted down an elevator. Cold sweat soaked the pits of his blue oxford shirt. Perspiration dribbled down his temples.

"All you need to do is speed up or slow down certain legislative activities in which we have an interest. We may direct your vote on particular bills too."

"Who's the '*we*' you keep referencing?" he asked, trying for the upper hand.

"None of your fuckin' business. But you do have a choice. You wanna remain *Senator* Bullman? Wanna stay out of prison for *murder*? Then comply."

"You're asking me to betray my constituents and to violate my oath of office. You could make me look like a flaming liberal one day and a die-hard conservative the next. I'll lose credibility. I'll lose power and influence. What good will that do?"

"Like I said, you have a choice. Your first decision point comes this afternoon. Throw a monkey wrench in banking reform. Live to be a Senator a while longer."

After a pause, head hung low, he said in a hushed tone, "All right. I'll do it."

St. John stood to leave. "Three other things, Bull. And pay attention."

Using his hanky, he mopped the sweat from his temples and under his eyes.

"First, you'll receive orders in future by cell phone. Second, continue to meet twice a month with a new girl—same fee, new place. You'll be told who and where. Uh, don't kill this one. Third, don't involve the authorities. Remember the videos."

She turned and swaggered out of his office.

Bull checked his watch—10:12 AM. The St. John meeting had taken fourteen minutes. He stepped to an antique cart with wheels, which served as his office bar. Hands shaking, he poured and downed a double shot of Jack Daniel's without pausing to appreciate the liquid's aroma. Bull poured another. At 1 PM, his banking committee would convene. He paced back and forth over his large silk and wool Isfahan carpet. At 10:30 he phoned Senator Stewart Cross.

"Stewart? Bull here. Need your help."

"Hey buddy, always willing to help," Stewart replied.

"I've heard from two top execs, representing a coalition of major banks. They've volunteered to enact the changes we want within a year if we back off."

"That's good news if they actually perform. We'd be heroes in the public eye."

"If what they do doesn't meet our expectations, we can revive reform in a year. Drill them an even bigger asshole than we planned."

"HA!"

"For now, help me table reform." Bull sucked in a breath, crossed his fingers and looked out his west-facing window at The Capitol Reflection Pool.

"It'd save us a lot of work. Which banks are in the coalition?" Stewart asked.

"Uh, Stewart...I need you to trust me on this one. ...They approached me in confidence. They don't want a protracted public fight and a lot of squabbling within the industry. Let's just say they're the ones we'd like to see lead the way."

"Super. What can I do?" Stewart asked.

Bull inhaled and kept his fingers crossed. "Call *our* committee members, and get them to line up behind my request. I'll call Ed Ellis. His side will be ecstatic. If there's any fallout with our folks or the press, I'll handle it."

"I doubt I can reach even a third of our members by one o'clock," Stewart said.

"No problema. I'm cancelling today's committee meeting."

5

"We've got problems," Jim Ruddock said. "The pols pay handsomely for our services. Most become instantly compliant when we confront them with the demands. But, in one week, we've had three girls land in the hospital and a fourth murdered. I watched that go down on camera at The Hay-Adams. And if I hadn't phoned the Congressman at The Drake in Chicago, the girl would have burned to a crisp."

Tony Amici sat behind his metal desk at EZ-Bonds in Las Vegas, peering over his readers at the large man before him, dressed in a polo shirt and khakis. *A Catholic boy, taught solid discipline by Jesuits. Turned stone cold killer. My kind of guy.*

At six foot three, 235 pounds of rippling muscle and accustomed to violence, little rattled Ruddock. A skilled thinker and problem solver. Articulate too, but today he appeared frazzled. *This isn't good*, Tony thought.

Ruddock began work for Tony anew two years ago after spending ten months in the Nevada State Prison in Carson City for vehicular manslaughter. He'd actually committed a premeditated assassination at Tony's direction. Ruddock forced a speeding car off the road and into a concrete wall. The deceased owed Tony a quarter million dollars from gambling debts but had refused to pay. Tony figured he'd collect through the guy's wife from her husband's two million dollar life insurance benefit. And he did—a win-win for Tony and the wife. The D.A., a close friend of Tony's, knocked the charge down from first degree murder to involuntary manslaughter.

Having successfully completed a series of progressively more challenging assignments, Tony believed he could entrust the then thirty-three-year-old Ruddock with a most sensitive project. The decision had been justified—until now, perhaps.

"And your problem is…?" Tony gave Ruddock a thousand-yard stare. He'd perfected *the look* over time, and he knew it caused the biggest bad asses to shudder and think carefully before responding to one of his queries. Tony imagined Ruddock's sphincter tightening, as he watched the rest of the man's body tense.

"These girls don't grow on trees. It took St. John over a year to recruit the original fourteen. They're beautiful, educated and classy...oh, and willing to fuck for a living or engage in any form of debauchery. The kind of sexual know-how these girls possess and dispense is not expertise easily acquired. ....It's not like we can post a want ad in the *Wall Street Journal* or *Vogue* for replacements."

"And?" Tony prompted.

"And...and..."

Tony picked a tiny piece of lint off his hand-crafted silver sharkskin suit jacket. He watched it float to the faded green sheet of linoleum that covered the floor of his four room storefront building—a small reception area with a peeling laminate countertop and wanted posters arranged on the walls, plus three cheaply furnished offices, the largest of which belonged to Tony. "What do you propose, Jim?"

"We'll find substitutes, but that'll take time and recruitment costs."

"Proceed," Tony ordered. "What other actions do you plan?"

Ruddock scratched his blond brush cut hair and craned his neck as if trying to find anywhere in the office to focus, except Tony's face. "The girls in the hospital have to go. If we don't silence them...well, why take the risk?"

"Look at me, Jim." Tony softened his expression.

Ruddock refocused on Tony's face.

"You've done well with this business. If you feel that's a prudent action, take it. No screw-ups or extra links in the chain. Do it yourself. No traces. Understand?"

"Understood boss. I'm on it."

Tony sauntered over to a gunmetal gray filing cabinet and pushed it aside, revealing a floor safe. Kneeling, he opened it and extracted ten stacks of $5,000 in $100 bills. He closed the safe, repositioned the cabinet and loaded the cash into a small paper grocery bag. Handing Ruddock the bag, he said, "Here's fifty large. That should cover your expenses. I'm confident you'll do what's required."

Tony patted the big man on his muscle-bound upper arm. "You're like a son to me, Jim. Make me proud. Now scat. I've got other business."

When Ruddock left, Tony picked up one of the many pre-paid throwaway cell phones he used for different ventures. He speed-dialed a number in Shanghai.

"Yes?" A man with a Chinese accent answered.

"We've encountered a minor problem," Tony said. "Four key employees are gone...as in never coming back. Their replacement will cost four hundred thousand. I'll need it by next Monday in the usual way."

"You will have it. Anything else?"

"Not at this time." The Shanghai connection ended.

Tony examined his eight-nail manicure and smiled. *This is becoming very profitable. Always considered turnover costly, but more might be better. Hehehe. Good thing I didn't bring Ruddock into the tent on the entire operation. Kid doesn't have the temperament for it.*

• • •

Ruddock closed the aluminum-framed glass front door to EZ-Bonds and crossed South Casino Center Boulevard under the sweltering Nevada sun en route to his midnight blue Cadillac DeVille. He sat in the driver's seat for a few minutes with the engine running and the AC on full, thinking about his furtive meeting with Tony.

EZ-Bonds was a joke on the justice system—a bail bonds business, located up the street from the Clark County Detention Center where most of those arrested in Vegas landed. Tony, a fifty-nine-year-old mobster, ran EZ-Bonds, using it as headquarters, the nerve center, for several nefarious activities. Six days a week, excluding Sundays, Tony sat behind his desk at EZ-Bonds, working disposable phones and holding meetings like the one he'd just left. Every week, on an irregular schedule, a tech geek swept EZ-Bonds' building and phone lines and Tony's autos and home for any forms of electronic surveillance. Only last year, the FBI investigated Tony for the umpteenth time and came up empty.

To Ruddock, Tony was a mobster's mobster. He only cared about three things. First was making money. A close second involved maintaining his dual reputation as the prince of darkness to those who *knew* him and a philanthropist to those who *thought* they knew him. A distant third centered on playing the part of a loving husband. Sundays were "wife days." Tony didn't care whom he leaned on, maimed or murdered to achieve some ends or whose ass he kissed to accomplish others.

Tony enjoyed connections with politicians, officials, entertainers, professionals and union bosses throughout Vegas and beyond. He turned heads with his neatly trimmed salt and pepper hair and distinguished attire, not to mention his eight, manicured fingernails. The pinky and ring fingers on his left hand had been missing for forty years. No one ever asked how or where he'd lost them, and Tony never gestured in ways that would suggest he noticed their absence.

Those who worked for Tony considered him a master puppeteer. A year ago, he encouraged Ruddock to buy a condo in Vegas, but the trust deed would be placed in Jim's *and* Tony's names. Tony would tote the note for Jim at a ten percent fixed rate for thirty years. With trepidation, Ruddock politely declined the offer, recognizing the rip off Tony had proposed. Besides, he *never* wanted to owe Tony money. His two bedroom garden apartment that cost $1,150 per month suited his needs just fine.

He thought it odd eighteen months earlier when Tony asked him to run the blackmail scam on members of Congress. Tony ran street prostitution, call girl operations and many other ventures, a few of which Ruddock knew about. The boss kept him and others in the dark about the full gamut of his affairs. But this business, involving political leaders, seemed out of the ordinary so far as Ruddock knew. The action was far from Vegas. *What's Tony know about banking or energy or national defense? What's he stand to gain? The man's an enigma.*

Ruddock accepted the fact that answers to these questions, shrouded in mystery, would remain so. *This is the life I've chosen—a foot soldier in the darkest of businesses, working for the devil incarnate.* He looked down at his massive hands and shook his head. *Like Julius Caesar said when he and his army crossed the Rubicon, "Alea jacta est." The die is cast.*

Ruddock earned well into six figures a year, but he didn't know how long it would last. His sixth sense told him Tony had likely deceived him in multiple ways and would hang him out to dry the moment any heat came down. *Yeah. Like when I ran that guy off the road at Tony's order and spent ten months behind bars, fighting off jailhouse butt fuckers every day. How else could Tony have remained out of prison all these years?*

6

Ruddock keyed St. John's number on his disposable cell phone.

At 8:05 PM, D.C. time, St. John lay in a bubble bath with her newest plaything—a nineteen-year-old Georgetown University coed with inch long hard nipples and a tongue stud. St. John answered her cell on the third ring. "Whaz up?"

"Find four replacements ASAP," he said.

"Well fuck me twice on Sunday. Where the hell am I gonna find them? I came close to my own funeral when I poached the last two from that Manhattan house."

Leaning against the terminal wall at McCarran International Airport, the last thing Ruddock wanted was an argument with *St. Butch*, as he privately called her. They had no choice, unless they were stupid enough to think they could walk away from one of Tony's operations, let alone refuse to carry out one of his directives.

"Just get on with it. I'm en route to Savannah to put an end to our problem there. Then onto D.C. and Chicago for the same. Would you prefer *that* duty to headhunting? I'll swap with you."

"Fuck you!" St. John hung up.

Ruddock thought about the business. He still didn't know St. John well or how Tony knew her. Tony had given him a list of targeted politicians and St. John's phone number. Then, and for emphasis, Tony had written three rules on the white board in his office. He enunciated each word as he wrote them down:

- *Never let St. John know I'm involved.*
- *Use her to procure talent and hook them up with the targets.*
- *Don't get involved with the talent.*

Tony had turned to him and asked, "Understand?" When Ruddock gave the expected reply, Tony erased the board, and they never discussed the rules again.

Ruddock didn't know where St. John lived, and he didn't care. Was St. John her real name? Probably not. He'd called her eighteen months ago at Tony's direction, met at a coffee shop on Dupont Circle in D.C. and forged a deal. She had connections in D.C. social and political circles and got the job done. Nothing else mattered. His tasks included managing the cash, the surveillance technology and the demands.

A tight operation. Few moving parts—Tony, me, St. John and fourteen girls.

After an overnight in Miami and rested, Ruddock took a mid-afternoon American flight to Savannah, Georgia.

For five days, Ramona Phluger, *AKA* Blaze, had slept in a coma in the ICU at St. Joseph's Hospital on Mercy Boulevard.

Ramona adopted her alias in tribute to her long lot of red hair. The copious freckles that adorned her body had made her bashful as a young girl. But, in her teens, her body filled out in ways that made her a sex object for high school boys and others. Craving acceptance, she fulfilled their fantasies. Ramona came to regard sex as a tool. After an encounter with her father's attorney in the back seat of his Mercedes, the lawyer introduced her to the madam of a Manhattan escort service. That launched Blaze's career in the fee-for-sex industry.

Senator Mary Grendel initially met Blaze for a weekend tryst on Hilton Head Island. After their first encounter, Senator Grendel demanded to see Blaze again.

Ramona complained to St. John. She despised Mary Grendel—an ugly, overweight sixty-year-old hag with frizzy gray hair and numerous body moles and skin tags. As if that wasn't enough, Grendel was also an imperious bitch. Blaze found servicing the closet lesbian disgusting and begged St. John for a different assignment.

Impossible. Once she hooked a target, her assignment was to stay with.

When Blaze couldn't explain to Grendel the demand note she'd handed the Senator and its origin, Grendel slammed a nineteen pound table lamp against her head. If outed, conservative and liberal colleagues would condemn her. Furious at the prospect of being exposed for her penchant for muff munching, she swung the lamp a second time. It broke over Blaze's head, fracturing her skull.

Grendel fled the room and escaped the Hilton Head Hyatt Regency.

Ruddock rushed into Blaze's room, yanked his electronic devices, wiped the surfaces he'd seen Grendel touch and removed the broken lamp. Back in his room, he dialed 911 on his disposable phone to get medical help for Blaze.

As they owned Bullman, they owned Grendel after a call from Ruddock and a visit from St. John. Grendel gave them influence over the Senate Committee on Energy and Natural Resources, which she chaired. She'd instantly begun fulfilling her order to halt her committee's crusade to tighten business practices in the energy sector and to eliminate tax loopholes and subsidies for oil and gas and ethanol companies.

The girls understood the arrangement. Lots of easy, under-the-table cash in exchange for complete discretion, regardless of circumstances. Any medical bills would be covered. St. John informed them in crystal clear language what would happen if they revealed anything to anyone. The warning likely guaranteed silence.

Doctors expected Ramona to emerge from her coma. But Ruddock couldn't count on Ramona keeping her tongue in check once she regained consciousness.

Upon reaching St. Joseph's that evening, Ruddock pulled a baseball cap low on his head and approached the Information Desk. The volunteer gave an update. Ramona had emerged from her coma, and the staff had moved her from the ICU to a private room. He breathed easier. Security for regular hospital rooms didn't exist. Ruddock headed to Room 357.

In and out. Do the job. Don't daudle, hesitate or rush out after. Ruddock's self-talk always helped build steadiness for wet work. He glanced at his Rolex Submariner—6:18 PM. *I'll be on the sidewalk in ten minutes, maybe less.*

Ruddock watched a nurse enter Room 357. The nurse left three minutes later and continued her duties down the hall. Another nurse sat at a distant desk, writing. A third entered a room four doors down. With the hallway otherwise empty, Ruddock pulled on a pair of tight-fitting leather gloves and made his move.

The only light in Room 357 emanated from the partially opened bathroom door. Darkness cloaked most of the room. Ruddock planned to break her neck. That tactic always presented a challenge if the intended victim struggled. An alternative, slicing open her jugular vein, would create a huge mess. Her blood would spurt like an out of control fire hose, and he couldn't guarantee he'd leave the room without being splattered with her life liquid.

Fortunately, Ramona was asleep. Ruddock heard her snoring quietly. He grasped her head with his large hands and gave it a hard, fast twist. The audible snap came, followed by a hiss of malodorous air expelled from Ramona's lungs.

He exited the room and walked calmly to the elevator, removing and pocketing his gloves. A code blue announcement belched from hallway speakers. Nurses reacted to the remote signal from Ramona's heart monitoring device, indicating no beat.

The police would find nothing of forensic value in his wake. Ruddock departed the hospital and hopped into his waiting taxi. He'd given the driver two unmatched halves of hundred dollar bills, the other halves to be paid when he returned to the taxi, which held his black ballistic nylon Tumi bag.

Next stop: GW University Hospital to deal with Karen Weinstein.

Days earlier, Karen, *AKA* Destiny, delivered a demand note to veteran Representative Dale Bennett, Chairman of the powerful House Committee on Appropriations. His order? Direct a higher proportion of tax revenue into defense for those contractors involved in military weapons development and manufacture.

Karen suffered multiple fractures to her leg at the feet of the Congressman before Ruddock could intervene by phone. After Bennett raced from the Four Seasons Hotel on Pennsylvania Avenue in D.C., Karen had the presence of mind to dial 911. While EMS whisked Karen to the hospital, Ruddock reclaimed his surveillance paraphernalia and wiped down surfaces, which the hotel room occupants had touched.

Karen survived the attack and phoned St. John to quit. Asked for her pay. Said she'd keep her mouth shut. Would she?

Ruddock couldn't trust what Karen might say once her money ran out. *Have to lay over tonight. Sleep in and catch the eleven o'clock US Airways to Dulles.*

He checked into the Baymont Inn & Suites, halfway between downtown Savannah and the airport. Having paid a paltry $74 in cash for the room, Ruddock decided to treat himself to a lavish dinner. He and St. John paid their own expenses.

After a quick shower, he changed into tan slacks, a yellow pinpoint oxford shirt and navy blazer. He taxi'd to The Pink Restaurant in the North Historic District.

A small article about the restaurant in the airline magazine caught his eye on the flight from Miami. The Pink Restaurant held historic significance. Sherman's generals dined there during the U.S. Civil War. According to the article, the current owners had refurnished the dining room with a fine array of antiquities, and the establishment boasted an impressive assortment of gourmet southern cuisine.

Ruddock arrived at 7:35 PM. Once inside, he paused to let his eyes adjust to the candlelit dining room. *Nice. If ever I want a romantic dinner, this place would suit.*

After admiring the décor and reviewing the menu, he ordered a Caesar salad, blue crab-stuffed grouper with lima beans and homemade bread, accompanied by a crisp Italian pinot grigio. Key lime pie capped a perfect meal. Though Ruddock engaged in the harshest of criminal activities, his palate had grown accustomed to fine food and wine. Not a subject to discuss with Tony.

Throughout dinner, Ruddock pondered the business he ran for Tony. Each of his fourteen girls, now ten, serviced two to three clients. They'd hooked thirty-five elected officials and directed them to focus their legislative efforts on several pro-business initiatives. Ruddock's goal was to increase the girls' client load to four on average. With fifty-six key members of Congress in their pocket, they'd have a sizable stranglehold on whatever D.C. politicians put on their legislative or regulatory plates.

He couldn't grow the operation bigger for a couple of reasons. First, Tony forbade it. Bigger created greater exposure. More exposure meant an unacceptable level risk. *I never want to see the inside of a prison cell again,* Ruddock thought.

Second, the market for these services was limited to those with an appetite for it and, more importantly, a bankroll to pay for it. Not every member of Congress commanded the wealth to support an $8K per visit semi-monthly habit, though far more than fifty-six could easily be seduced at a significantly lower price point.

St. John orchestrated invitations for the girls to various social gatherings around town that paved the way for introductions to their targets. No one knew who these girls were, what they did or how St. John arranged their attendance. She even organized a weekend sexual escapade for six of the thirty-five, all men, with ten members of the talent pool. *That little adventure cost $25K per john—$45K for those who ordered a two-on-one experience. Whoa, and I recorded it all.*

The operation now grossed $560K per month from semi-monthly fees. The girls currently enjoyed an easy gig at five tricks per month on average.

Not all clients demanded the Presidential Suite at The Hay-Adams. Most were satisfied with a $500-a-night room in a four star hotel. *From now on, Bullman, Grendel, Bennett and that fucker from Chicago will be treated to Motel 6.*

After the girls' $3K per visit cut and $50K for hotel expenses, the operation netted $300K per month. Ruddock set his sights on increasing the net by sixty percent over the next few months. After they issued the demands, the pols had no choice but to continue their semi-monthly affairs, if only to drop off their visit fee.

Ruddock paid St. John $40K a month and kept $60K for himself. *Hmm, with a sixty percent increase in revenue, I'll be dragging in close to a hundred large a month. As Virgil put it, "Audentes fortuna juvat." Fortune favors the bold.*

Ruddock currently remitted the remaining $200K a month to Tony. *Great for someone who bears none of the risk, unless I rat him out.* But he'd never do that, unless he wanted to have his tongue removed with pliers without the benefit of anesthesia and right before meeting his maker on a hurry-up schedule.

Tony determined which politicians to target and dreamed up the demands. Ruddock didn't know how Tony divined the targets or the demands or how he benefitted from the Congressional action or inaction that ensued. He dared not ask.

7

Using her left index finger, the stocky Georgetown coed played with her tongue stud while she used her right hand to push egg remnants around her breakfast plate with her fork. Ensconced in St. John's kitchen, dressed only in their panties and exhausted after a night of sex and a few hits of cocaine, they made small talk. The scent of bacon hung in the air.

The condo sat a block off Connecticut Avenue in the upper Northwest section of the District. A ritzy neighborhood, although not the most expensive. St. John had purchased her two-bedroom two-bath unit six years ago with money from her trust fund and savings. She'd almost paid off the loan with her new-found income. *How'd he find me anyway? Doesn't matter. So long's the bucks keep rollin' in.*

She thought, *Do this another year or so, and I'll quit. Condo will be paid, and I'll have an extra half million or more socked away. With my trust, I'm good to go the rest of my life. Do this too long and I'm gonna get caught. No...no...no. That's not for me. He can just find someone else to play madam. Hmm, maybe I could find a sugar mommy to support me. Too bad this little chick-a-dee isn't wealthy.*

St. John studied the coed and thought about their last night together. *Mmm, delectable. And what a set of nipples! Wish I could turn her out. Someone like Grendel would love her, and that'd solve part of my recruitment problem. Too bad she hasn't the class and expertise for our clientele.*

"How long have you lived in D.C.?" the coed asked, breaking St. John's reverie. With mussed hair and big brown cow eyes, the coed looked up and across the kitchen at St. John. Her nipples dangled above her egg plate.

St. John smiled. "My folks moved here when I was eight. Thirty years ago. Dad was a Senator. Mom was your typical Senator's alcoholic wife. She died when I was twelve."

"Sorry." The coed blushed and looked down at a bit of egg.

"No need to be. I got a lot of attention afterwards, some of it unwanted. But I routinely made the Washington social circuit with my father, which was pretty heady."

"That's so cool. You must know a gazillian power players."

"I got to know most of them and their dirty little secrets," St. John said. "Many took liberties with me. You know, a pinch here, a fondle there."

The coed's eyes widened. "Did you tell your father?"

"Hell no. Once I figured out what the assholes wanted, I began sucking and fucking men, women, Senators, Representatives, their aids, lobbyists and high power attorneys. I did it everywhere...offices, closets, bathrooms, yachts. Hell, a few pulled up in limos at my private school for a little lunchtime action. They paid me too."

"Like...how much?" the coed asked incredulously.

"A hundred for a BJ and two bills for a lay—three for the back door. I never did overnights. But I was kid. I had no idea what underage pussy sold for. If I had, I would have charged ten times what I did. And the bastards would have paid too."

The coed squealed.

"One weekend, I went to Camp David with my dad."

"No shit?" The coed leaned forward, lapping up St. John's story.

"No shit. I gave a Secret Service agent a BJ behind a big ass oak tree."

The coed hee-hawed at the visual image. St. John laughed at the memory too.

St. John began clearing the dishes and cleaning the kitchen.

"My father advanced in status and power. No one fucked with him 'cause I had them all by the short hairs. Dad thought his legislative brilliance propelled him forward when all the time my sexual prowess fueled his success."

"Wow! That cracks me up. You still run with that crowd?" the coed asked.

"Not anymore. But I know most of them, including those who hold the real power. Dad's no longer in office, but he still wields a lot of influence.

"People take my calls, do me favors. I've developed a reputation as a... well, call it a social fixer. But generally those folks shy away from me. I'm just as happy. Gives me more time to be with you, sweetie." She leered at the coed.

The coed gazed at St. John in awe and licked her lips. "I like that just fine. Can I tell you something and you promise not to laugh?"

"What is it, doll baby?" St. John asked, setting a skillet in the sink..

"I was so hot for you when I met you at Checker's. But I didn't think I could get to first base with you. You're just...gee...so fuckin' cool and savvy."

"Sweet cheeks, after last night, do you doubt I'm hot for your ass too?"

"Guess not," the coed said.

St. John knelt on the beige-colored travertine floor, tits sagging and swaying as she crawled under the clear glass table toward the coed's crotch. The coed lifted her legs and hooked her calves around St. John's broad shoulders. St. John pulled the coed's pink lace panties aside, and pushed her face into her crotch. The coed leaned her head back, closed her eyes and said, "Oooh baby, I *really* guess not."

8

Carrie entered Brenda's room the next morning, wearing a green smock over a white cotton blouse, beige slacks and cordovan flats. She'd pulled on latex-free gloves, a cap and a mask covering her nose and mouth. Brenda stared at her with her one good eye, still lying on her stomach with tubes and wires running to and from her.

"Hey sweetie, I'm here for you," Carrie said. She set down her laptop case and approached Brenda's bed. "How're you doing?"

"I screwed up," Brenda said. A tear ran from her eye, and Carrie dabbed it with a tissue she pulled from the box on the white melamine table next to Brenda's bed.

"I don't know what *you* did, honey, but someone else messed up. You're a victim. How're you feeling?"

"I hurt bad."

"Brenda, you've been out of it since they brought you in. There's a Dr. Goretski who's in charge of your care. You need surgery…skin grafts."

Brenda began to sob but quickly contained her emotions as her heaving hurt more physically than the psychological anguish of Carrie's news about surgery.

"They need your approval. The sooner the better."

"How bad is it?" Brenda asked.

Carrie stared at her friend. *How can I tell her the bastard destroyed her beautiful back and she'll have nothing but odd looking patches of skin and scars the rest of her life?* Recovering from her mental pause, Carrie said, "According to the doc, you'll recover. What's important now is to give him permission to operate."

After two nurses attended Brenda and arranged for Brenda to sign the surgery authorization forms, Carrie said, "Now you need to do two more things."

"What?" Brenda asked.

"You've gotta fight to get well."

"I'll do my best."

"And, second, you've gotta tell me who hurt you."

Brenda closed her good eye, but tears leaked from her shut eyelid. She remained silent for ten minutes.

Carrie waited patiently, letting silence fill the air. She caught the unpleasant commingled scent of the ointment on Brenda's back, urine collecting in the bag on the side of the bed and cleaning fluids used to sanitize the room.

When Brenda's good eye flicked open, she said, "Remember college graduation? Most of us struggled to figure out what we'd do next."

"Yeah." Carrie smiled under her surgical mask.

"You knew you were going to the *Tribune*, since your daddy and granddaddy worked there. Rest of us didn't know where we'd end up."

"What's that got to do with what happened to you?"

"I met a man. Said I could make a lot of money. Tax-free. Thought I'd try it once or twice. Next thing I knew I was in 'the life.'"

"What life?" Carrie asked.

"Ah Carrie...you were always so naïve. I became a call girl, a hooker."

"Oh."

"With my looks, I could make ten grand a month if I applied myself. I'd just screw a few extra johns. I was already having sex with guys in college for free."

Carrie turned from Brenda to face the window, which looked out on another downtown Chicago building.

"It was a great life. Clients usually treated me like a princess. Showered me with presents and fees. Easy money. I enjoyed a lot of downtime to do whatever I wanted. ...Don't know what I'll do now. Funny...the johns called me 'Heaven.'"

Carrie turned to face Brenda. "You're haven't answered my question. Who did this to you?"

"Then a woman offered me a chance to make even more money, servicing a handful of regular high rollers. It was supposed to reduce my personal risk."

Carrie bunched her eyebrows and tilted her head.

"Get it?" Brenda asked. "I'd know whom I'd be with on a routine basis. And they were supposed to be very upscale clients. Guess upscale doesn't count for much."

"Oh. ...So the creep who hurt you was one of these regular, uh, clients."

"Yup."

"Give me his name."

"If I do, they'll kill me."

"Who's they?" Carrie asked.

Brenda closed her eye and groaned. "I really hurt."

Carrie asked a nurse to adjust Brenda's pain medication, which was on a periodic drip along with the saline bag that hung from the pole next to her bed.

An hour passed during which Brenda slept. Carrie left to buy a cup of coffee from a Starbuck's kiosk in the hospital cafeteria. Scores of hospital workers, dressed variously in green, blue and tan uniforms, walked past her en route from and back to Brenda's room. She wondered what they all did and what types of patients they cared for. When Carrie returned to Room 423, she tried to review her research file on illegal immigration, but Brenda's revelations kept crashing into her conscious thoughts, disrupting her concentration.

"Carrie?"

"Yeah sweetie. Feel like talking?" Carrie hauled herself from the hospital room chair and stood next to Brenda's bed.

"I don't know their names, but a hard looking lesbian recruited me. Made it very clear they'd snuff me if I gave up any client names. I figured I'd never need to.

"Don't know who was working with the dyke. She arranged intros with the johns at parties. Told me where to rendezvous with them and what to charge. I'd take my fee and leave the rest in the hotel room for pickup. She always reserved and paid for the rooms in my name. I just showed up—routine-like."

Carrie began pacing the small hospital room. None of this would help nail the bastard who'd turned Brenda's once smooth skin into charred hamburger meat. She stopped and said, "Brenda. Tell me who did this. I can arrange protection for you."

"I won't give you their names. Believe me, the dyke and whoever works with her will kill me. I was servicing a few U.S. Representatives and Senators."

"Holy crap! ...Why did that pig hurt you?"

"I was being used to blackmail politicians. A few months after I hooked them, a bellman gave me an envelope to present to each client during a rendezvous. When I delivered the first one, the john read the letter and studied a photograph that came with the note. He cried and begged me not to hurt him or his family. I didn't know what he was talking about. A few days later, I handed an envelope to the man who burned me."

"What makes you think blackmail was involved?"

"My last trick liked bondage. After tying me up, he checked out the envelope. He read a letter, looked at a picture and went berserk. He hit me several times and demanded I tell him who sent the note. Said something like 'how dare you order me and my committee around.' I had no idea what he was yelling about.

"Then he burned me with his cigar trying to force me to confess. I begged him to stop, but he took delight in it. He smoked Cuban cigars and joked about turning my brown ass black with an illegal substance. He kept ordering me to tell him who was working with me, but I couldn't. So he burned me again and again. I could smell my flesh burning. ...It hurt so bad."

Carrie weaved on her feet, listening to Brenda's horrid tale.

"Then he stuffed my panties in my mouth and told me he'd pour lighter fluid on me and 'fire me up' unless I talked."

"Lighter fluid?" Carrie asked.

"Yeah. Guy owned a solid gold lighter he bought when he served in Vietnam. You know, an older one with a wick that you pour lighter fluid in. Had an annoying habit of constantly flicking it open and closed. I felt something wet dribbled over my back. I choked trying to scream. He gave me one last chance to talk, but I didn't know anything, so I couldn't answer his questions. Then he lit me on fire."

"Oh my God, Brenda. I'm so sorry." She crossed her arms, put a hand to her mouth and scrunched her eyes shut. Carrie had to sit to avoid keeling over. *God, this is a nightmare.*

"I heard his cell phone ring. Seconds later he hit my back several times with a pillow. Guess he put the fire out. Seemed like I was burning forever. I thought I'd died, but I only passed out. ...Next thing, I woke up here."

"Bastard!" Carrie said through clenched teeth. "What's this creep's name? We can protect you."

"That's not all. I met some other girls by their aliases over a weekend with a half dozen politicos. They're doing the same thing as me. Said they knew a few more girls. None of us knows who's behind this. ...Stupid, huh? I didn't even realize I was involved in a blackmail scheme until now. ...I've had a chance to think."

The door to the room opened, and Dr. Goretski entered, wearing green scrubs and pulling on gloves and a mask.

"How's my patient today?" He picked up Brenda's chart and read as he listened to her reply.

Carrie took advantage of his presence to leave the room. She shivered thinking about Brenda's story as she ambled down the sterile hallway watching her footfalls hit the light gray linoleum, flecked with blue and green specks. She heard moans coming from some patient rooms, silence in others and occasional announcements over crackling speakers in the hallway. Carrie's mind and body hurt from Brenda's revelations. Reeling from Brenda's tale, she picked up her cell and dialed.

Seconds before his cell phone rang, Michael Taylor had ended a new client meeting in the conference room of his Bethesda law office. "Michael Taylor," he answered.

"Oh Michael, I needed to hear your voice," Carrie said. "Something horrible has happened." She bent over at the waist and began sobbing. "I'm so damn pissed."

"Are you hurt?"

"No," she whimpered, "a friend of mine's been brutalized."

9

Max Foerce walked into a wall of cold air as he stepped from the encroaching summer humidity at 9 AM into Michael Taylor's Bethesda, Maryland building.

Max's grandfather had immigrated to the U.S. from Estonia as a young man. No one ever learned to pronounce his last name correctly. Instead of FO-ER-SAY, they'd say FORCE, though it was still spelled FOERCE. He badly wanted to fit in. So he never corrected anyone, and the pronunciation stuck.

Max's parents named him Maximillian Foerce the Third, but during a thirty year career with the FBI, he acquired another appellation. From the start, his FBI managers handed him some of their toughest cases, and he scored a high percentage of successful busts that led to convictions. Max attacked his work like a junk yard dog after a bone. By the end of his distinguished career, he'd also used his service revolver to kill thirteen bad guys in the line of duty. Close to a record at the Bureau. Though exonerated in every shooting, fellow agents dubbed him "Maximum Force."

After thirty years and multiple citations and commendations as an FBI agent, Max retired and set up a sole proprietorship as a private investigator. At fifty-eight today he still felt youthful and kept fit with strenuous workouts. People found Max an interesting man to behold due to his muscular physique, tan complexion, white thick hair combed straight back and his ice blue eyes. With his FBI pension and, moreover, the highly successful investments he'd made over the years, he didn't need to work.

Max walked and acted with an air of confidence, but not arrogance. Today, he dressed his five foot six frame in a new custom-made cream-colored summer weight suit, accented by a royal blue dress shirt with French cuffs from the Custom Shop, a red-on-red checkered silk tie and a pair of dark navy Ferragamo slip-ons with a matching alligator belt. An interesting physical specimen and a well-attired one too.

A few years back, Michael observed Max testify in a complex murder case. He noted Max's ability to explain complex concepts with authority in ways that never confused and often entertained. People listened to Max's deep baritone voice and remembered what he said. Michael needed a reliable P.I. who could get results, and the two hit it off from the outset. After more than five years together, their solid professional relationship grew into a strong friendship. In some ways, Max thought of Michael as the son he'd never fathered. Max had never married either.

Max bid good morning to the receptionist with a big smile. "He in?"

She nodded and Max proceeded past a dozen other attorneys' well-appointed offices directly to Michael's private space. Michael's criminal law practice had expanded dramatically over the last decade. As Managing Partner, Michael shouldered both administrative and client duties.

Max rapped a hard knuckle on Michael's solid oak door and stepped inside.

"Holy cow!" Michael exclaimed. "If it isn't mister red, white and blue. You know, Max, the fourth of July was last week."

"Well, nice to see you too. I'll have you know, aside from my jewelry, I'm wearing four grand in custom clothing. And it's not white, it's cream."

"If you ask me, *it's* over the top," Michael responded.

"Yeah? Tell that to the parade of people I passed on my way to your office who gave admiring nods. You oughta take a lesson and stop buying those bargain basement duds. I've got a newsflash for you, buddy, it'd be pocket change for you."

"Okay, truce. I've got big problems."

They convened at Michael's walnut meeting table, inlaid with turquoise. Each took a caramel-colored leather chair. "I'm not sure where to start," Michael said.

"First off, how many problems are we talking about?" Max asked.

"Two."

"Let's take them one at a time and each from the beginning," Max said in jest.

"You're too clever. ...The first one involves Carrie."

"Oh no. Not *Ms. Deathwish* again. Now what?" Max asked.

Michael told him the story Carrie shared with him about Brenda Butler.

"Huh. What else is new? Those who seek to have things their way have been corrupting those who are supposed to govern for centuries. I can't tell you how many times the FBI has run corruption investigations on those occupying high office. Most led no where. Stop worrying about it. Our forefathers wisely set up lots of checks and balances to prevent a few corrupt politicians from bringing down the system.

"You know how medical research has shown we all have cancer cells in our bodies though only some us suffer full blown cancer? That's what being a U.S. Representative or a Senator is like. They're all touched by corruption, but only some of them succumb. Enough of this. It isn't Carrie's or your problem, my friend, and I'm glad I could solve this little matter for you. I'll send you my bill. What else you got?"

Michael leaned back in his chair, stretched his arms and shoulders and slowly pulled his fingers into his palms, hearing his knuckles crack. He released them and said, "Has anyone ever told you that you can be a real…you know what I mean?"

Max shot his French cuffs and calmly adjusted the perfect half-Windsor knot in his tie. "I *can* be a real asshole, but this isn't me being one. I'm merely trying to prevent you and especially your crazy former girlfriend from diving down some unproductive rat hole 'cause one hooker was in the wrong place at the wrong time. Lots of prostitutes are killed every year. She was lucky to survive the life she chose."

Michael blew out the breath he'd been holding and pinched the bridge of his nose. "It's not only about this one girl, although Carrie wants justice for her friend."

"Nice friend she's got there," Max said.

"I'm serious, Max. This appears to be an orchestrated effort to compromise many members of Congress simultaneously. That's huge."

"Same answer. Leave it alone. You two will get all tangled up in your underwear with this, instead of focusing on what you're supposed to be doing for a living. And there's one other thing. This can be a *very* dangerous pursuit. This stuff goes on all the time. Drop it. Let the cops handle it."

"I'll have another talk with Carrie…*Mr. Tough Guy.*"

"I'm glad to have been of service. What's problem number two?"

Michael stood and began pacing and glancing out his window.

"Hmm, guess you've got a real problem after all," Max muttered.

As he paced, Michael told Max about his mother's letters from Tony Amici, whom Max knew from numerous FBI reports and a black market human body parts ring that he'd helped Carrie and Michael break up almost a year ago.

When Michael finished his tale, Max nodded his head slowly. He stood up, put a hand on Michael's arm and, in a gentle voice, said, "Get your jacket."

"What?"

"Just humor me," Max said. "We're outa here."

They rode in silence in Michael's silver Jaguar XK8 convertible to the Hyatt Regency Bethesda, a dozen blocks north on Wisconsin Avenue. Upon entering the hotel, Max led him to Morton's steakhouse and asked for a private booth.

"I'm sorry, sir, but we're not open for lunch," the maitre d' responded.

"We're not eating—yet. Just give us a booth and bring us two short glasses and a fresh bottle of eighteen year Glen Livet."

Once seated and each having tossed back a shot of single malt scotch, Max said, "I'm going to recap what you think problem number two is. Don't talk. Listen.

"The lord of the criminal underworld in Las Vegas is your biological father. Maybe he is; maybe he isn't. Let's assume he is for sake of discussion.

"Amici provided financial support for you and your mother throughout your youth. Gave you a red bike at thirteen, paid the gas bill, helped with college expenses, maybe even put a word in with the admissions folks at Harvard, and some other stuff."

Michael's stared as Max poured him another inch of the topaz-colored scotch.

"The prick funneled clients your way when you started your law practice. Maybe he accounted for you breaking even your first year in business.

"And likely knowing your involvement in smashing what was, without a doubt, *his* human body parts ring last year, Amici had some miscreant hurt your crazy girlfriend and almost got the two of you and poor old Melvin Grimes killed. Me too! By the way, I checked in with Melvin a week ago. He's doing fine.

"Have I got the story about right?" Max asked.

"Yeah." Michael tossed back another shot, and Max followed suit.

"Good. So listen up." Max fixed Michael with a piercing look. "It's not your fault Tony's sperm found Jeannie's egg. You're not accountable for any of his financial support you may have benefitted from. Be grateful for having received it. You folks were poor as church mice, and you might not have survived otherwise.

"I know you've felt bad about not knowing your father. To discover his identity at this point and the fact he's such a fucking demon has got to be shocking. But you aren't Tony. He's morally bankrupt. Vacant. You're not. The two of you are worlds apart, and that's likely your mom's influence. Be happy about that."

Tears welled up in Michael's eyes. "Don't you see? Everything I've become… every success I've enjoyed…the wealth I've built…it's because of Amici. My entire foundation is a lie and a farce. I'm a fraud."

Max leaned across the table and poked Michael in his chest with a thick index finger. "WRONG! You're a decent, ethical, nice guy who wouldn't hurt a flea, except for that sonofabitch corrupt Arizona Sheriff you stabbed to death last year."

Michael jerked his head up to face Max. "Hey, that was self defense."

"Yes it was. And now that I have your attention... You've taken positive advantage of every opportunity you've encountered in life. You didn't have to be a good student or a good grocery clerk or do well on your law school entrance exams. No one coerced you into supporting your mom. Who's leaned on you for all the pro bono work you've done since law school? You work your ass off for your clients, and you play fair and square in court. Instead of being some half-assed attorney, you're an outstanding one. You never cheat anybody. And you pay my bills on time too. Hell, maybe more people should be sired by the Tony Amici's of the world."

Michael smiled at the thought. "You never cease to amaze me, Max. Guess I was mired in my emotional weeds. You know, I look up to you in a lot of ways."

"I look up to you too, being six inches taller than me. Stop punishing yourself. Stop whining. Just buy me a thick steak for lunch. Problem solved. Now drink up."

10

After a century in operation, The George Washington University Hospital opened a new facility in 2002 on 23rd Street in northwest D.C. Its administration called it a "technologically advanced hospital." But Ruddock knew one other feature of the hospital. Like all such facilities, with hundreds of people milling about, numerous entrances, exits, hallways, closets, offices and other cubbyholes, little could ensure the personal security of patients. Even with all the security guards and cameras in place.

He regarded its edifice from the corner of I Street and 23rd, just south of Washington Circle. Having arrived mid-afternoon from Savannah, bag stashed at a Marriott hotel, he planned a little reconnaissance before the event. Karen Weinstein, *AKA* Destiny, became an inpatient four nights earlier with compound fractures up and down her right leg. Ruddock knew from Karen's call to St. John that the docs knitted her bones together with intramedullary nails, cannulated screws and something called Simplex P Bone Cement. She sported an ankle-to-hip cast. Was she ambulatory? A quick peek at her in the hospital would confirm her location and her mobility status.

Dressed in his navy blazer and tan slacks from the night before and a clean white shirt and undies, Ruddock found Room 227, two doors from the elevator. *Convenient*, he thought. He passed Karen's room and saw her, dressed in blue-and-white patterned hospital garb, struggling on crutches to leave her bedside. That and the fact visiting hours lasted until 10 PM told him everything he needed to know.

This could be tricky. But, as my old Latin teacher used to say, "Aut viam inveniam aut faciam." I will either find a way or make one. Wonder if Tony ever killed someone with his bare hands and eight fingers? Prick probably always had other schmucks do his dirty work. He decided to dine early and plot Karen's expiration.

To avoid the oppressive D.C. summer humidity, Ruddock taxi'd to the Komi Restaurant on 17th Street for Mediterranean cuisine. He'd eaten there once and knew it as a tiny, family-style eatery. One paid $125 and ate whatever the chef served.

As he supped, a plan came to mind. Karen didn't know him, but he knew her from all the video footage he'd shot. He'd present himself as a physical therapist, there to help her take a few steps using her crutches. He'd walk up behind her and plunge a long needle-like object up and through her foramen magnum, the opening in the base of her skull through which her spinal cord passed. He'd scramble her brains, lay over in Alexandria afterwards at the Marriott where he'd checked his bag, and take a morning hop from Reagan National Airport to Chicago O'Hare.

The Komi host seated two bearded Arabic men at a table an elbow's width from his. One lit a cigarette as Ruddock savored the next to last bite of his baklava.

"Hey moron, this is a non-smoking restaurant," Ruddock said.

"Fuck you. I'm in the smoking section," the smoker replied, laughing.

"A smoking section in a restaurant is like a pissing section in a swimming pool. Put it out," Ruddock demanded.

"Who the fuck are...?"

Ruddock reached over and gripped the man's cigarette hand so fast the smoker had no time to react. He squeezed the hand for three seconds in a steel vice-like hold. The smoker squealed with pain and dropped his cigarette. Ruddock let the smoker's hand go and said with menace, "If that isn't enough to convince you smoking is bad for your health, try lighting another." The two Arabs fled the restaurant.

Ruddock casually finished his baklava. He dropped $160 on the table and departed Komi's for a nearby CVS pharmacy. Ruddock moseyed up and down the aisles, searching for the right death implement and found it in the household section—a flathead screwdriver with a seven-inch steel shaft. *Just what the doctor ordered.*

Back at the hospital, his watch read 7:22 PM. He made his move. When a dietary grunt shuffled out of Karen's room with her dinner tray, Ruddock entered.

"Ms. Weinstein, I'm Jim, a physical therapist. How are you?"

"I've been a helluva lot better," she said, pulling her hair into a ponytail.

"I know this is tough. To recover, you have to take a few steps every so often."

"That's what they've told me, and I've been doing it. But I'm tired tonight."

"I know, but we've got to keep you moving. It's for the best. Let's see you walk from your bed to the door and back. That'll do it for now. Okay?"

"Oh, all right," she said, groaning.

With difficulty, Karen swung her legs over the bed's edge and sat up. Ruddock handed Karen her crutches. She stood, a bit wobbly. She took a step, then a second.

"Very good," he said behind her while pulling on a pair of latex-free gloves.

Karen took a third step, a fourth and then her last when the CVS screwdriver punctured her scalp at the base of her skull and slid up and into her brain all the way to the handle. She froze mid-stride, back and shoulders arched, clinging to her crutches. After a few rotations of the handle, Karen fell to the floor, her life fading. Ruddock removed the screwdriver. He rinsed it in the bath and made a beeline to the lobby and out the building. The screwdriver and gloves found a home in a dumpster a mile away.

One more to go and I'm done. If this happens again, maybe I'll off the politician too for good measure.

11

"We'll operate tomorrow morning at seven," Dr. Goretski said. "Ms. Butler's lucky to have a friend like you, Carrie. You've lifted her spirits." They stood eighteen inches apart in the hallway outside Brenda's room, conferring quietly.

"Glad I could be here. Only wish she'd tell me who hurt her, but she won't." Carrie didn't know the culprit's name, but she'd kept Brenda's confidence with everyone except Michael about Brenda's involvement in the blackmail scheme.

"Her vitals look good. We'll see how much we can accomplish tomorrow. Might need additional surgeries, given the extent of damage."

"She knows. Brenda's a strong woman. Will I see you tomorrow?"

"As soon as I'm out of surgery. I'll meet you in the post-op waiting room."

Dr. Goretski turned to leave, and Carrie entered Brenda's room. Her hospital visits with Brenda afforded them time to renew their college friendship. They'd quickly picked up where they left off in college. Now and then, Carrie peppered her with questions about her attacker, but Brenda fended off each round of inquiry. Carrie figured it time to put the questions on the back burner, at least until Brenda recovered.

• • •

Ruddock's flight from Reagan National landed at Chicago O'Hare at noon. *So far so good. One more loose end to clean up, and it'll be back to business as usual.* On the way from the terminal, he heard talk of an enormous traffic jam on the route into the city. Ruddock checked in at the Airport Hilton and parked his bag. After changing into a light gray suit and blue-and-white striped shirt with open collar, he walked to the airport concourse level to catch the Central Transit Authority train to downtown.

As the train sped toward Chicago, Ruddock studied the snarled traffic on the adjacent roadways that he'd managed to avoid. *All those people. Waiting impatiently to get to their destinations. Wonder what they do for a living? . . .Bet I make more than any five of them combined. Of course, they probably don't kill people for a living.*

When Ruddock entered the Nevada State Prison for manslaughter, he counted the number of people he'd murdered. Since his release, he'd put a couple more notches on the grip of his mental handgun. Including Ramona and Karen, the total reached nineteen. Brenda Butler would make twenty. Ruddock decided that'd be a good place to stop counting. At thirty-five, he'd likely kill several more before his career or life ended. He spent the rest of the train ride contemplating Brenda's demise.

Ruddock stepped off the train at the Chicago Station stop at the intersection of Chicago and Milwaukee Avenues. He caught a taxi, east to Northwestern Memorial.

The elevator stopped on the fourth floor, and Ruddock began inspecting the killing ground. The nurses' station lay between the elevator and Room 423. *Not good.* But a staircase beyond Brenda's room led to the first floor lobby and an exit door to the outside at the base of the staircase. *Excellent.*

Ruddock found a white lab coat hanging on a hook. He squeezed into it. Appearing like part of the system, he wandered up and down the hall along Brenda's corridor, observing the scene.

Few entered or exited Room 423, except for a remarkably good looking blond woman. Before entering the room, she'd shaken her head, to allow her long blond hair to fall into place before donning a green cap and mask. *Hmm, not like any hospital worker I've ever seen. A visitor?* He glanced at his watch—2:33 PM. *No visitor likes to hang around for hours. Maybe she's a doc. I'll come back after dinner.*

• • •

"Enough about me already," Brenda said. "Tell me about your love life."

"Not much to tell," Carrie said. "I've had a handful of boyfriends over the years, but it took psychotherapy to crack the shell I'd built to keep them at a distance."

Carrie sat on the pea green lounge chair in the room, recapping how her mother had died during her infancy and her father had raised her alone. He too passed away shortly after she'd graduated college. She told Brenda how her father's accountant sexually molested her as a little girl. It had caused a litany of psychological problems throughout her life in relationships, sleep, her attitude toward those who abused others and more. "I'd even panic when time rolled around for annual pelvic exams. I became alcoholic too. Remember when we met at Neiman's a few years back?"

"Yeah," Brenda said.

"I was embarrassed. You were stunning. . . .I looked like a homeless person."

"You didn't look *that* bad, but I did wonder what was up with you," Brenda said. "Figured it was none of my business."

"Then I met a wonderful guy. Name's Michael Taylor. He's every girl's dream. Six foot tall, handsome but not pretty, athletic build, super smart and really nice. . . .Oh, and he's wealthy. A self-made man. He loves me too." She smiled.

"Why aren't you with him?" Brenda asked.

Carrie's eyes began to water. "Ah well. . .I messed up."

"How?"

Carrie let out a sigh. "I get a rush chasing stories about creeps who hurt people and escape justice. A few times, I went beyond getting the stories and became part of them." Carrie shared a thumbnail sketch of her involvement with a vigilante who murdered pedophiles and her efforts to stop a ring of mobsters who slaughtered Mexican illegals for body parts. "I wound up in the hospital and so did Michael and others who saved my life. Fell off the wagon a few times too. Michael loves me, but he sees me as a disaster magnet. I don't blame him, but I can't curb my obsession."

The swelling around Brenda's right eye had partially subsided. "Girl, in my view, you're a good looking woman, bright as hell and head and shoulders more successful than anyone I know. You're a damn good friend too. Your problems are pretty dinky, compared with lots of folks. Michael would be lucky to have you."

"Thanks for saying that," Carrie said. She swiped a few tears away.

Brenda groaned and shuddered with pain.

"Hold on. I'll get the nurse." Carrie ran to the nurses' station.

• • •

What to eat? No use going all the way out to the Hilton and then traipsing back into town. Hate hotel food anyway, but maybe there's an exception to the rule.

Ruddock departed the hospital at 3:10 PM and strolled a block west to North Michigan Avenue and a few blocks north to the Park Hyatt Hotel. On the train and over another passenger's shoulder, he'd peeked at a newspaper article. It described a restaurant called NoMI's that had won several culinary awards. It had recently been redesigned in line with a casual, but elegant concept. Dishes featured regionally grown ingredients. The restaurant drew patrons, seeking to enjoy the spectacular view of Chicago's *Miracle Mile*, imbibe fine wines and eat world class cuisine.

He entered the Park Hyatt's swank lobby and strode across the pale marble floor to the elevator. On the seventh floor he made early dinner reservations with the restaurant's maitre d' and settled into a chair in the NoMI lounge for a glass of wine.

Got to pace myself. Need to keep a clear head. Ruddock sipped a $215 glass of Opus One Cabernet until his 5:30 PM dinner reservation. A review of the menu had convinced him he'd come to a unique hotel restaurant. Dinner tonight would cost him a half month's rent on his Las Vegas garden apartment. Easily affordable. He started with yellowfin tuna ceviche, followed by New York Strip steak with sides of fingerling potatoes and English peas. Another glass of the cabernet accompanied the meal, which he topped off with a quartet of sorbets and coffee.

At least no one has the brass and bad manners to light a cigarette in here. He mulled over what to do with Brenda, *AKA* Heaven. Of all the talent in the pool, he liked Brenda the best. He'd considered taking her offline, despite Tony's admonition, and developing a relationship with her. He flushed those fantasies from his mind.

Thanks to Representative Jimmy Novotchin, Chair of the House Committee on Ways and Means, her disfigurement meant she could no longer work. The prick had put her in his crosshairs. Jimmy's new charter? Modify the U.S. tax code in ways favorable to business. News reports indicated he'd dived into his assignment.

What a pity. Brenda was indeed "heavenly." Don't want to make her suffer. Something quick. Yeah. Just snap her neck. What a waste of talent.

He finished his meal, paid the bill and then ambled south to the hospital.

7:50 PM. Back on the fourth floor, he recovered the two-sizes-too-small lab coat he'd worn earlier and squirreled away in a closet for re-use. Ruddock observed Room 423 for two minutes as he cruised the floor, no one paying any attention to him, except to smile or nod when he passed.

Enough. Ruddock entered Room 423, closing the door behind him. He saw Brenda lying on her stomach. The room minimally lit by the ambient light from the hallway leaking in around the door jamb. He approached her bed.

Ruddock had barely grasped Brenda's skull when the door swung open. The room illuminated, and the beautiful blond from earlier stood, backlit, in the doorway.

"Who are you?" Carrie asked. His hands, gloved in leather, were wrapped around Brenda's head, and she was grunting in pain.

Ruddock let Brenda's head go and she gasped, "He's trying to kill me."

A loud animal cry escaped Carrie. She bounded across the room in three strides, fists balled. She hit Ruddock twice on his chest before he gathered his wits. He leveled her with a roundhouse to her right temple. On her way to the floor, she struck the left side of her head on the white melamine bedside table. She crumbled.

Ruddock rushed from the room to the stairwell. En route, he bumped into three medical personnel who converged on Room 423, the source of the disturbance.

• • •

At 10 PM eastern time, Michael Taylor received a call from the Chicago PD. Brenda had told them to phone Michael since Carrie had no relatives. They located his contact information on Carrie's cell and informed him about the assault and her status.

The hospital's trauma doctor admitted Carrie for observation. She'd been unconscious for three minutes, having suffered a concussion and large blue bumps and bruises on both sides of her head—one from Ruddock's fist, the other from the table. Dr. Goretski postponed Brenda's surgery to ensure she was medically stable.

After reviewing the hospital's security videos and interviewing hospital personnel and Carrie and Brenda, no one could identify Ruddock. But Carrie and Brenda had a very good idea of who'd paid a visit to Room 423 that night.

12

_____

Max perused the *Wall Street Journal* while Michael, seated next to him in the Boeing 737, reviewed the transcript of a witness deposition he'd taken the day before.

"Market's booming. Dow's up eleven hundred points in a week," Max said. He nudged Michael, pointing to the paper. "Says leading D.C. politicians at last have their heads screwed on straight. They've reversed their anti-business positions, loosened the purse strings and tamped down regulatory zeal. They're letting free enterprise do its thing. My portfolio's going gangbusters. ...Huh, maybe I'll do your next job gratis."

"That'll be the day," Michael said. "Now do you believe Carrie's story? You know? The one you dismissed so easily? Politicians rarely do one-eighties en masse."

In an hour, they'd land at O'Hare and go directly to the hospital. After the Chicago PD call, Michael had called Max and told him to pack for a few days. Then he reserved two first class tickets on a mid-morning flight the next day to Chicago.

"This should *not* have happened to Carrie," Max said. "She stuck her nose in a place it didn't belong. Like usual. For future reference, you might tell her it's inadvisable to pick a fight with a muscle bound man a half foot taller who outweighs her by a hundred pounds or more."

Michael shook his head and pinched the bridge of his nose. "The toothpaste is out of the tube. Let's focus on protecting her. Maybe the cops can identify the guy."

"Wishful thinking."

Michael glared at him.

"Okay, consider her protected." He raised his palms in a peaceful gesture.

They entered Carrie's hospital room as she swallowed the remaining apple juice from her lunch tray. "Hey, what are you doing here?" Michael chided her lovingly. He stepped to her bed and gave her a hug.

"I didn't know they called you," Carrie said. "I didn't want to involve…"

"Stop. We're here. And we're going to take care of you," he said.

"Hi Max."

"Hi yourself. Nice color those bruises. Work well with your hospital gown."

Carrie responded with a half smile. "All I did was visit my old college friend, and this guy tried to kill her. If I'd shown up a few seconds later, she'd be dead."

"If that asshole had hit you with a bit more force, *you'd* be dead," Max stated.

"Enough," Michael said. "We stopped by the nurses' station. They're going to release you early tomorrow. Here's what's going to happen. First, we'll check with the police to see if they've learned anything. In the morning, we'll take you home, and Max will spend a couple of days with you to ensure you're out of danger. Meanwhile, let the docs take care of your friend. There's nothing more you can do."

"But Michael…"

"No buts. You've done enough," he said.

Max tapped him on the shoulder. "Why don't you two spend the afternoon together? I'll go talk with my old buddy with the Chicago PD and see what they've got. That doesn't require two of us. Mind if I leave my suitcase with you?"

"Sure. Thanks Max. See you at the Park Hyatt at six. Dinner's on me."

"It always is," Max said, and he left.

• • •

Max taxi'd to Lieutenant Jimmy Jablonski's 1940's era precinct building and asked the Desk Sergeant to call him. "Tell him Max Foerce needs to see him."

Max took a seat on a scarred, cranberry red plastic chair in the precinct lobby. He sat next to a young Hispanic woman who cradled a sleeping infant in her arms while trying to corral two toddlers who played tag in the small waiting area.

Twenty minutes later, a husky man with heavy shoulders, a ruddy complexion and red close-cropped hair appeared at the top of the staircase. He hobbled down to the tiny lobby, wearing a glen plaid polyester suit with a yellow shirt and a tie that didn't go. His left foot bound in a cast, right foot shod with a black shoe, thick sole.

"Maximum Force! What brings you to the windy city, you old S.O.B.? And dressed like a high-priced gigolo too!"

"And you're dressed like," Max winced, "never mind."

They laughed and gave each other a bear hug. Decades ago, they'd worked together to bust up a drug ring, operating on Chicago's South side. The gun battle that ensued ended with three bad guys dead from service revolvers belonging to Jimmy and Max. After a subsequent investigation cleared them, Jimmy received a promotion.

"What's with the foot?" Max asked.

"Chased a goddamn gang banger six blocks. Caught up with the little prick as he jumped into his ride. The fuckers ran over my foot."

"Ouch." Max grimaced while chuckling at Jimmy's story.

"Broke a few bones, but the doc says I'll be okay. I'm getting too old for this."

They settled into a meeting room the size of a small walk-in closet, and Max gave Jimmy a rundown on events at the hospital. When he finished, Jimmy picked up a phone and dialed a number. "Hey Milo, this is Jablonski. . . . Yeah, hehehe, I know what you mean. That IAD guy's a piece of work. Listen. I heard Hector Rodriguez pulled duty on an assault and battery, possibly attempted murder over at Northwestern Memorial last night. Put him on."

A half hour later, Jimmy hung up. He eyed Max, shrugged his shoulders and said, "Dead end."

"They often are," Max replied. "Just trying to figure out what kind of risk my client's girlfriend faces since she foiled the attempted murder."

"My guess? Little to no risk. But I'd tell her to stay clear of the prostitute."

"Huh. . .you don't know Carrie Linden."

"I read her articles. See her on TV too."

• • •

Michael drank a virgin Arnold Palmer at the NoMI bar while Max sipped a glass of Duckhorn Merlot. "There won't be further investigation," Max said. "They only have fuzzy pictures of a big guy leaving the premises. No fancy CSI evidence. And Carrie's friend won't give the cops any leads on who almost cremated her in the first place. I'm sure she knows the perp's name, rank and serial number."

"Too bad. We'll get Carrie home tomorrow, but I've got to head back to D.C. afterwards. Court duty the next day. You can stay, right?"

"I'll stick around. Make sure she's okay. My take is Carrie surprised the doer. She was a wild card in his equation. He probably doesn't even know who she is, so stop worrying. She's got nothing to fret about, unless she pursues it."

"She promised she wouldn't."

"Yeah?" Max raised an eyebrow. "We'll see. Hey, they're serving a Yorkshire pork porterhouse down the hall. Never had one of those."

13

"Job done?" Tony spoke into one of his disposable phones behind his metal desk at EZ-Bonds, looking up expectantly at the white asbestos popcorn ceiling.

"Two down, one to go." Ruddock didn't dare tell Tony about the mishap in Chicago. "I'm video recording a few new clients in D.C. first. We have seven new ones. We're collecting like clockwork and everyone's performing as directed. I'll resolve our final problem in a few days."

"Time could be our enemy if that *final problem* talks. I want that problem fixed. Understand?"

"Understood boss," Ruddock said. "The problem's had opportunity but has remained quiet. Rest assured, I'll take care of it."

Ruddock disconnected. *Jesus he makes me squirm. Got to finish up with the videos, then back to Chi-town. Damn, why did that ass Novotchin have to do a number on Brenda?*

He dialed St. John.

"Whaz up?" she answered as she perused the rows of clothing in a men's haberdashery with her coed lover.

"Any news from Chicago?"

"Just waiting for medical claims, assuming she gets a chance to file any with me. Remember? We agreed to split medical bills, and these will be huge. I don't want to pay squat."

"Have you heard anything about visitors to her room?"

"What the fuck are you talking about? You better fix that situation soon."

"I'll need a couple more days. What's happening with recruiting?"

"Like I figured, I've mostly had rejections but one acceptance. The new one has skills as a dominatrix. That certainly adds variety. I've got two other strong leads."

"Stay on it." He hung up. *She'd better get a move on. We've taken Tony's expense money, and we need to produce something. He'll expect results.*

• • •

Toward the end of her second day out of the hospital, Max escorted Carrie to her primary care physician for a check-up. Carrie's black and blue bruises had begun to yellow. While at the hospital, she'd had an x-ray and an MRI, both of which registered normal. She passed her doctor's clinical evaluation, which indicated no noticeable after effects from the concussion, except aches and pains from bruising.

Outside the doctor's office, Carrie said, "Max, you've been a peach these last couple of days. I realize babysitting me is not uppermost on your wish list of assignments. But I want you to know I appreciate it, and I'll pay for your time."

"No charge, Carrie. …I misjudged you. I thought you were on one of your wild crusades when you were simply being present for a friend. I apologize."

Warm blankets of summer air repeatedly wrapped them and then dissolved as they walked to Carrie's Mini-Cooper. She wore a simple, pink cotton dress from Talbots with matching pumps. Max sported a tan-and-white striped seersucker suit with an open collar white button down shirt and brown alligator loafers.

"It's after five, and we're dressed to go out," Max said. "Dinner's on me."

They headed to Roditys in Greektown where they'd once dined. On that occasion, Max ate while answering Carrie's questions about the black market for human body parts. Carrie's appetite had vanished as she listened to Max's answers.

Over two gyros platters with water for Carrie and two Mythos beers for Max, she asked, "You think there's a chance for Michael and me?"

Max swallowed his bite and studied her face for three seconds. "I'll tell you what I know and what I think." He took another bite before continuing to buy time to avoid stepping on any emotional land mines with Carrie.

Finally, he took a deep breath, looked into Carrie's eyes and said, "Michael loves you. Since you guys split last year, there's been no one else. Guy like Michael…he could have any number of women. He's not even looking."

Max took a swig of beer and a bite of pita bread, layered with tzatziki sauce. "I also know he aches inside when you get close to life's flames. He can't bear you getting hurt or worse. Michael can't be with you twenty-four-seven to protect you, so he gravitates to the other extreme—avoiding you altogether. Same applies to your drinking." He looked down at his plate to fork some meat and onion.

Carrie straightened her back. "I've been sober for almost a year. I've got it under control, I've..."

"Yeah?" He looked up. "Well, pardon the interruption sweetie, but Michael's the former son of a chronic alcoholic who went through sober patches and always returned to the bottle. You have to understand. That's his frame of reference.

"I'm no psychologist, but I think you guys need to deal with two issues." He paused to take a tug from his bottle of Mythos. "First, you've got to stay sober. Michael intellectually understands alcoholism is a disease, but he quite naturally focuses on the negative behavioral aspects of the illness. You know what I mean. I'm not out to embarrass you, but only you can control that problem. Enough said."

"I know," Carrie said and nodded with her eyes closed. "I really do have it under control though."

"Second, Michael needs to deal with the fact that you're a justice junkie. I get you. I'm one too, and I don't see you changing one iota. It bothers me for your safety because you're not schooled in the art of self-defense. But, in the end, it's your call. Michael has to choose whether he can live with your obsessions."

"Gee, Max, you sound like a shrink." She smiled.

"I was an FBI profiler. Remember? You asked. I answered. If you guys can resolve those items, I think you've got a shot at a wonderful life together."

"One of the things I like about you, Max, is you're always straightforward. Direct. There's no holding back with you. No room to misinterpret."

"That's been one of my biggest failings with women over the years. They never liked my direct style. They also didn't like the danger in my line of work and my travel-at-the-drop-of-a-hat schedule. Guess it's different with a female friend."

They finished their meals in silence, walked part way back to her brownstone apartment and then flagged a taxi to ride the rest of the way. Before turning in for the night, Carrie asked, "Max, how does somebody create a prostitution ring to go after politicians?"

He stared at her with furrowed brow. "You know, there are millions of questions in this life you could inquire about. Seeking an answer to that kind of question is precisely what puts you in harms way. See you in the morning." He stepped into Carrie's guest bedroom, turned and gave her a curt nod before closing the door behind him.

Carrie turned on her heels and disappeared into her master suite.

14

Carrie slept erratically. She kept thinking, *If only I understood more about running a prostitution ring. That'd be a first step toward learning who tortured Brenda. I can see the headline. Busted: U.S. Congressman for Whoring, Imprisonment and Torture.* She giggled to herself. *Yeah. Put the bastard in jail where he belongs.*

The moment Max left for O'Hare, Carrie fired up her laptop and surfed the internet for "prostitution." After three hours, she'd failed to gain any insights. *Who've I met that knows all about the prostitution business?* She padded from her desk to the kitchen to fix a ham sandwich and grab an Orangina. Carrie gazed out her window at passersby. Their faces were downcast from the suffocating heat. Suddenly, *That's it!*

She'd last experienced severe heat in Arizona with Michael, Max and the FBI when they broke up a black market human body parts operation. Through the FBI, she learned about a sinister figure who they said ran the operation. But they never nailed him—Tony Amici. He supposedly controlled most types of prostitution in Las Vegas.

Who better to ask about organized prostitution than a master pimp? As a journalist, I'll guarantee his anonymity. He doesn't know me. I'll meet him in broad daylight. I might want to bring a friend along though. . . . Can't tell Michael, and certainly not Max. They'd have a cow.

Carrie stood up from her desk chair, stretched and headed back to the kitchen. As she bit into a chocolate chip cookie, a plan began to form. *I'll sleep on it. If it still seems like a good idea in the morning. . .*

• • •

On the third ring, Melvin Grimes lifted the receiver from his yellow kitchen wall phone and put it to his ear while he slurped his black morning coffee. "Hullo?"

"Melvin, this is Carrie, how are you?"

"Been good."

Carrie paused. *Never a very talkative fellow.* Carrie considered Melvin part surrogate father and part friend. Melvin was a man's man. The seventy-year-old, retired grain mill worker would challenge any man half his age in a fitness contest. Topping six foot two and carrying two hundred twenty muscular pounds, he maintained his fitness with rigorous, daily exercises he'd learned in the Marine Corps. His wife had passed away more than a decade ago, but his children and grandchildren lived in Marion, Iowa. Melvin owned a ten acre non-working farm outside Marion.

Carrie thought about the constant sparkle in Melvin's sky blue eyes, his full head of white hair and deeply weathered face. She also recalled the man had rendered vigilante justice, executing more than twenty pedophiles who'd slipped through the justice system due to legal technicalities, despite their horrific and provable crimes against children. Actually, he'd killed over forty. Carrie only knew about half of them.

They'd met when Carrie identified a countrywide pattern of executions of pedophiles, all committed the same way—blunt force trauma to the head. No one had believed Carrie's vigilante theory. Maybe the authorities were happy to have someone cleaning the streets. She'd identified Melvin and met him. Their values aligned about what should be done to pedophiles that didn't get punished. Melvin had also saved her life a year ago when a man attacked her in her apartment. For his heroism, he'd been gutshot. The crises they'd shared forged an unbreakable bond between them.

"Cat got yer tongue?" he asked.

"Sorry. Just thinking."

"How's Michael?"

Carrie summed up the status of her relationship with Michael.

"He'll come 'round...'ventually."

She told Melvin about Brenda and the scheme to corrupt U.S. politicians.

"Don't that beat all. I tell ya, I'm not surprised them jackals are fallin' fer it."

"Yup. But we don't know *what* they're being forced to do."

"Screw the little guy is *what*," he said. "Maybe more 'n usual be my guess."

She paused and looked out her brownstone window at a passerby.

"What ya thinkin' 'bout doin'?"

"For openers, find out more about organized prostitution."

Melvin downed the rest of his coffee. "Guess ya didn't learn nothin' from our last caper. Or maybe ya did but can't help yerself."

Carrie ignored the dig. "Here's what I thought I'd do." She explained her idea of interviewing Tony Amici for background on prostitution.

"What makes ya think he's gonna talk?" Melvin knew Amici's history too.

"I won't ask him to admit he's a criminal. I'll pay him a surprise visit. Ask him general questions. Treat him like a source. You know, First Amendment and all that."

Melvin didn't say anything for ten seconds. "Lil' girl, yer nuts."

"I think it'll work."

"Why're ya callin' me, as if I didn't know?"

"Want to ride along?" Carrie clenched her jaw, anticipating his response.

Melvin sighed and paused. "Well, I ain't gittin' any younger, and I ain't doin' nothin' productive. What the hey. When ya wanna go?"

15

At 6 PM Pacific Standard Time, 9 AM CST or China Standard Time, Tony dialed the number in Shanghai or, as natives called it, Zhong Guo. The man with the Chinese accent answered. "Report."

"Everything's per plan," Tony said. "We have participation from forty-nine, and we're on schedule to secure the remaining seven. Should have them in a few weeks. All are performing as directed, and it's having the desired effect."

"The market results support what you say and then some."

"It's time for my progress payment," Tony said.

"You will receive the agreed upon sum in the usual manner next week."

"Thank you. Give me advance warning when you want me to pull the rug out from under this pro-business agenda in D.C. I need time to bail from the market."

"Hold your tongue! Are you not a professional?"

"I apologize," Tony said, properly chastised.

"You will be told when. In the meantime, have you organized phase two?"

"I'm meeting with the contractor tonight. I'll require the funds for phase two."

"You will receive them next week, separately from your progress payment. Do not, I repeat, do not launch phase two until directed. Am I clear?"

"Crystal clear," Tony replied.

The line went dead in Shanghai.

Oops, I got carried away. Uncharacteristic. There's just so much money to be made, not to mention the million I'll get in my Mail Boxes Etc. bin next week. Chump change, I'm sure, compared with what they'll rake in from the stock market.

Two years earlier, representatives from a Chinese underworld gang had visited Tony in Las Vegas. They served up a proposition he couldn't resist. In return for his services to blackmail politicians for their sexual peccadilloes, the Chinese would pay him a million per quarter during the course of the operation, plus any extraordinary expenses. They'd also pop for the costs to retain special services for phase two of the operation. When he asked how they knew St. John, they claimed someone from their embassy had recommended her very highly. Apparently, the source was well-informed. St. John had not disappointed. His employers never shared their objectives, but their scheme was obvious. Even if they had other ulterior motives, Tony didn't care so long as he got paid.

Tony knew that, however much he'd earn, the group in Shanghai, if it was only Shanghai, would reel in vast sums from the stock market. *Best to be happy with what I have, hehehe. Now I need to skim a little from the mechanic's fee. That will require some cunning.*

· · ·

"So you see, your assignment is quite straightforward and short in duration," Tony said. After dinner, they conferred over Cohiba Espléndidos Cuban cigars and a fifty-year-old port from Portugal's Douro Valley—Tony's preferred after dinner drink.

A fifty-four-year-old man sat across from Tony in the private back room of a rumored-to-be mob-run Italian restaurant. The lighting in the room came more from the candles on the table than the wall sconces. Waiters had cleared and de-crumbed the table and disappeared into the kitchen, leaving the two men alone.

The mechanic took a drag from his 6.9-inch cigar. He blew rings toward the ceiling as he considered the assignment. He wore white attire from head to white, ostrich-booted toe. The fingers of his left hand caressed the scar that ran over the top of his bald head from one ear to the other. The scar gleamed in the candle light.

It had become a frequent habit—touching his ridged scar that pulsated under his fingertips. Decades earlier, field surgeons inserted a steel plate in his head after a mission in Kosovo when he'd been hit twice on his skull with a hammer. It felt soothing to touch the edges along the scar line. Feeling it always reminded him of the dangers of his profession. He also noticed this habit struck fear in those who watched him fondle his scar.

A large gold signet ring with the shape of a swastika engraved on its face graced his right ring finger. While holding the Cohiba between his index and middle fingers, he used his thumb to roll the ring around his fourth finger. Another habit.

The mechanic paused to take a sip of port. "It is definitely a short project, but if it was so straightforward, you would not be talking to me."

"So…we're negotiating?" Tony asked rhetorically.

The mechanic watched as Tony gave him *the look*. He stared right back into Tony's eyes, unflinching and amused that Tony would attempt to intimidate him.

"You want me to perform public assassinations of twelve top executives, each from a different leading corporation, spanning four industries and four metro areas. You will select every target, and you want this completed over the course of two weeks, which you select. Am I correct?"

"That's right," Tony said. "The twelve targets are evenly spread across New York, New Jersey, Houston and Silicon Valley. You'll have geographic proximity and advance notice of the targets. And the executions must absolutely be very public. ...Oh, and none of your operatives can know of my involvement. In fact, if you want, terminate them too when this is over and keep the entire fee for yourself. HEHEHE."

"There is honor in my profession. You are speaking of my colleagues. What you have suggested would be dishonorable. Perhaps you do not have the capacity to grasp that fact," the mechanic said in a harsh tone.

Tony's face turned red. His mouth opened and closed but no words came forth. The mechanic knew Tony was unaccustomed to receiving a rebuke. *Maybe I'll collect my fee and rid the planet of this dego prick.*

"Here is how this will work," the mechanic said. "I will secure three top-flight snipers. I will be a fourth. I will assign each of us three targets. Since you will choose the weeks, we will choose the days of the week. We will hit eight early the first week and the remaining four during week two."

"Why that schedule?" Tony demanded.

"We will complete seventy-five percent of the hits early that initial week when we have the element of surprise working for us. Afterwards, every top executive of any major corporation will receive a significant amount of protection, making them difficult targets. Then, after several days of inactivity, their guardians will get lax, and we will take out the rest. We will find them. And we will assassinate them all."

"Why use snipers? How about finding out where they're eating lunch and toss a grenade on their plates? HEHEHE."

The bald mechanic gave Tony a condescending look. "You are paying for professional, coordinated hits that strike terror among a defined population. We are professionals, and we do not wish to be caught. We will not engage in puerile tactics that endanger the lives of countless innocents in the area. We will take the shots from, say, five hundred meters or more."

Tony fidgeted with his cigar. "I'll give you a million-eight. Half up front and the remainder upon completion—a hundred fifty grand a head. Generous I think."

"No. You will give me four million, three quarters in advance and one quarter after. I will need the target list and their work and home addresses with the first payment. We will handle all our expenses."

Tony sat on the edge of his seat, red-faced. "This is extortion," he said between clenched teeth.

"No. It is a fair price, given the circumstances. If you believe it is too much, give the contract to another." He offered Tony a half-smile and looked him squarely in the eye, knowing Tony had few if any other options.

Ten seconds passed. "Done," Tony said. "You'll receive three million and the list next week. But when I say 'go,' you'd better be ready to pull the trigger."

"I have never failed a client."

• • •

The mechanic disappeared through the restaurant's back door, leaving Tony sitting with his half-smoked Cohiba and a freshly poured glass of port.

Hehehe. Nameless sonofabitch. If that bald prick only knew the Chinks are paying five million for the job. . . .Hmm, maybe I'll put a contract on his Nazi ass and pocket his final payment. . . . Something to consider.

16

The morning Brenda underwent surgery, Carrie stayed home, awaiting a call from Dr. Goretski. While the hours passed, Carrie pondered how to approach Amici. *I'll treat him like I would any other source. Tell him I'm researching organized prostitution. If he asks what that has to do with him, I'll say, "nothing." Being in the bail bonds business, he probably comes across a lot of unsavory characters. That'd give him inside knowledge. And, among other things, Vegas is known for prostitution. I'll ask a bunch of what-if type questions so he doesn't feel boxed in or exposed. Maybe he can shed light on how to corrupt a politician.*

She called Melvin and told him her plan.

"I got one question fer ya," he said. "How're ya gonna explain why ya looked *him* up, 'stead of someone in Chicago? Ya got pimps operatin' in Chicago too."

"Oh, uh, yeah, I see your point. Good question."

A second call came on Carrie's line. "Melvin, I've gotta go. I think someone from the hospital's calling. I'll get back to you." She touched the flash key. "Hello?"

"This is Dr. Goretski."

"How'd it go?"

"Quite well. Ms. Butler's in recovery, but we'll need to wait a few days to see how the grafts have taken. She may need some touch up plastic surgery down the road, but I think we've accomplished what we needed to do at this time."

Carrie blew out a long stream of air. "Great news. Does she need anything?"

"Rest and recovery at the moment. No excitement, if you get my meaning."

"Is she still under police protection?" Carrie asked.

"The cops are stationed outside her door, twenty-four-seven. It'd be foolhardy for anyone to make another attempt on her life while she's here."

"Can I call her?"

"Try tomorrow morning, but make it short. I have to go."

Carrie hung up, wondering how long Brenda would receive police protection. *Probably not long if she doesn't cough up any info about her attacker. Wonder who's paying her hospital tab. I never asked if she had insurance.*

Carrie wandered into her bathroom and looked at her face in a magnified makeup mirror. Her bruises had begun to disappear, but they remained ugly reminders of the monsters that existed in society and their callous disregard for human life. She gave her hair a good brushing and decided to order dinner in.

Forty-five minutes later, a deep dish pepperoni pizza arrived. Halfway through, Carrie had a brainstorm. *I'll tell Amici I'm doing a nationwide story about bail bondsmen. I'm shooting for a dozen interviews across the U.S. I'll drop a few names of other bondsmen. Once we're talking, I'll steer the conversation to prostitution.*

Pleased with her solution to Melvin's insightful question, she showered, brushed her teeth and changed into yellow cotton pajamas. After downing a cup of warm milk, she rolled into bed for the night with a smile on her face.

Carrie called Brenda the next morning. Despite Brenda's post-surgery discomfort, she sounded okay. "I'll call you each day until you leave the hospital."

"Thanks, Carrie. I owe you big time."

"You gonna tell me or the cops who tortured you?"

"No."

"You know, they won't protect you if you refuse to give them a lead."

"I'll be fine if I don't rat them out. Spoke with the dyke who recruited me. Said to email her copies of my hospital receipts. She's gonna reimburse me."

On a blank sheet of paper, Carrie scribbled, *Madam to pay med costs.* "You're taking a big chance. You oughta let the authorities take these creeps down."

"Easy for you to say. Maybe the cops could, maybe not. If my, uh, associates didn't snuff me, I might face jail time. Politicians and their entourage know how to paint people like me as vermin…unreliable leeches out to make a buck."

"Your choice. I'm headed out of town in a few days. You should be home when I return. Can I visit?"

"I hope you will."

When she signed off, Carrie sat for a moment, thinking of her friend's future. *How am I going to help her get a real job? Have to think about that later.* She called Melvin and brought him up to speed on her strategy for meeting with Amici.

"Sounds jes' like what ya did with that body parts middleman in Albuquerque months back. Ya 'member what happened to us when we got home?"

"I know. That hoodlum Bill Barrett attacked us. Beat me up and shot you in the stomach. But this is different. Amici runs stuff in Las Vegas and the southwest. I'm checking out something going on with D.C. politicians."

Several seconds slipped by. Melvin remained silent.

"Melvin? You there?"

"Jes' thinkin'. …I'll need to pick somethin' up when we git to Las Vegas, and I'm not lettin' ya outa my sight for a while after we git back."

"Fine, but believe me, this is *really* different."

17

Stroking the scar on his bald head, the mechanic gazed at the serene Gulf of Mexico. He lounged on the terrace of his penthouse condo in Clearwater, Florida. This morning, he sat on one of his padded rattan chairs, drinking a strong thick cup of black Columbian coffee beneath the undulating breeze from an outdoor ceiling fan.

Over the years, he'd acquired four residences—the one he presently inhabited, an estate in the fabled movie colony of Palm Springs, California, a villa in the heart of the Costa del Sol in Marbella, Spain. The fourth came through a barter arrangement. In return for snuffing a top casino executive in Kuala Lumpur whom the owners caught skimming the take, he'd received a new and unusually spacious three-bedroom, top floor condo in Singapore, halfway between the airport and downtown.

This morning, a small armada of sailboats dotted the waters of the Gulf close to his building. He imagined a day when he had nothing better to do than sail on the Gulf with a handful of friends, maybe a wife, without looking over his shoulder, worrying someone had been commissioned to cap his ass. *Friends. Now that's something I'd have to develop. A wife? Might be a stretch. Might have to settle elsewhere too.* Though he believed his whereabouts were unknown to others, those in his profession could never know for sure until a bullet found their skulls.

His Tommy Bahama white-on-white floral shirt flapped from the fan's comforting air stream. He pulled an 18K gold Visconti fountain pen from his pocket. From memory, he jotted three phone numbers on a white legal pad. The numbers tied to three of the best snipers he'd ever worked with. He also selected them because each made their home base near one of the target metropolitan areas—convenient. Amici had faxed tactical information about the executive targets to him in care of a FedEx office 25 miles away. The mechanic simply needed to pull his team together.

He'd performed a previous job for Amici—the assassination of one of Tony's henchmen whom he tracked to Uruguay. Turned out the man had morphed into an honest citizen and good neighbor. But instead of being a mediocre thug, the target was in fact a highly skilled combatant who not only killed the mechanic's partner but got the drop on him too. They'd worked out a compromise in which both could survive. If the target killed the mechanic, Tony would have sent another assassin. A photograph of the severed head of his partner with similar hair color, battered beyond recognition, a severed penis in its mouth and the target's diamond stud in one ear gave Tony adequate proof the mechanic had accomplished his mission. The target agreed to stay in Uruguay, and the mechanic promised never to pursue him again. A treaty of sorts.

The mechanic used a throwaway phone to dial the first number. A woman with a husky middle eastern accent answered on the second ring. "Speak," she said.

"Are you available in the next one to two months?" the mechanic asked.

"Depends."

"Fair enough." He spoke in code she readily understood. "You will fix three units, two early in week one and one in week two, all in your area. The fixes will be done remotely but publicly. I will provide unit info shortly. You will decide the order and locations. They *must* be public. You will handle tools and expenses as usual."

"Type of units?"

He smiled. Of the three, this former Israeli commando was the finest shooter. Reliable, deadly and business-oriented. Like the others, an avowed solo operator. "Getting to that." He described the "units" as "key but not political."

"Compensation?"

"One hundred fifty per, with half up front and the rest at the back end."

"What's your cut?" she asked with a tinge of sarcasm.

"Not your concern. Either accept or decline, but I require an answer now."

Seven seconds passed. "I'm in."

He smiled knowingly. "You will receive details and your front-end fee in three days in the usual way. You will then have five to six days to be ready at any moment, likely one to two months out. Any other questions?"

"Ten-four," she said and disconnected.

The next two calls went similarly—a black former U.S. Navy Seal and a Cuban ex-Army Ranger. Despite his enormous, muscular bulk, the black Seal never complained, never challenged. He just accepted assignments and performed brilliantly. By contrast, the little Cuban whined he had a family to feed, a mortgage to pay and a mistress to maintain. He argued unsuccessfully for a fee enhancement.

This will be the easiest four hundred fifty K they will ever make. They'd get a rush from the hunt, lining up a target in their crosshairs and the kill. There'd be three back-to-back per shooter—a sniper's orgasm. They'd view it as honing their skills, which went unused for long periods, despite occasional duty in various hell holes.

Their locations aligned perfectly with the job specs. The Israeli lived somewhere in the San Francisco Bay Area with her girl friend and lover. She would hit three CEOs of leading hi-tech firms in California's Silicon Valley—a short drive south of San Francisco. The former Seal would take out three New York financial execs. He lived a monastic life in a five story walk-up in the West Village. Rumor was he'd accumulated a large cache of weapons and explosives, booby trapping windows and doors—just in case an uninvited guest showed up. The mechanic didn't believe the rumors. The Cuban and his wife and five kids resided in a small housing development in Kingston, New Jersey, just north of Princeton. He made no secret of his residence, hiding in plain sight as an average family man. Three New Jersey pharmaceutical leaders would get caught in his crosshairs.

The mechanic would put down three oil company tycoons in Houston. He'd grown up in Pasadena, a small suburb on the southeast corner of Houston. Having worked south of the city in an oil field for two years after graduating high school, the mechanic was quite familiar with the Houston area and the places frequented by those with wealth. The U.S. Marine Corps had been his ticket out of town and into his thirty-plus year deadly profession.

Apparently, Tony is targeting specific industry sectors to simultaneously hurt them and probably help himself and others financially. But how? The stock market? Well it certainly justifies the mark-up on the job—two and two-thirds mil for me and the rest spread across the team. Hey, I could retire after this.

Though highly competent, he wondered whether his shooters even knew the origin of the term "sniper." When the British occupied India in the 19th century, "snipers" referred to those who hunted game birds, called snipes. Skilled marksmen became highly sought after, beginning in the U.S. Civil War and every conflict since.

The mechanic knew each sniper would use his or her own signature weapon. A reliable and familiar tool provided a sense of confidence and comfort—a long rifle, not a handgun, to make the hits public and enable the shooter to escape.

The Israeli relied on a bolt-action Swedish PSG-90 rifle that normally took a 7.62x51mm round. She'd use a 4.81mm tungsten carbide round instead. It would exit the barrel at 4,400 feet per second. While less accurate than the 7.62mm round, it was twice as fast over a distance of 1,000 meters—an acceptable tradeoff. She'd be closer.

A German Mauser 86 SR was the former Navy Seal's preferred weapon, but he'd use 7.62mm rounds. The Cuban would opt for a U.S. made Tango-51 with a light 2.25 pound trigger pull. By reputation, the rifle exceeded accuracy guarantees.

All used the pricey Zeiss Diavari V 6-24x56 T scope. The optical quality and reliability were unbeaten. Importantly, it enabled very precise focusing at every range.

While the mechanic planned to use his Zeiss scope too, he'd recently acquired a new French FR-F2. Its effective range was limited to 800 meters, but he knew he'd be closer to his targets. He liked the feel of the French rifle.

Every shooter would use a rifle never before in service. Except for the scopes, which they'd keep, the rifles would end up disassembled with the pieces scattered after completing the assignment.

The mechanic leaned his head back and let the ceiling fan's air stream caress his face and neck. *Feels good. Life is good. I will confirm the three million dollar deposit in my Cayman Island account later today, and we will be launched.* He picked up his Bushnell binoculars with laser rangefinding capability and studied the group of sailboats, moving in synchrony north and west of Clearwater. At the push of a button, his binocs could register the distance of an object up to 1,600 meters. During the calls to his team, the armada had moved out of range.

None of his snipers knew one another, and he'd keep it that way. *They are the spokes; I am the hub. Good way to maintain control.*

18

St. John located the tiny diner in Romney, West Virginia—one block north of the main drag and what, for more than a half century, had been the only traffic light in town. She wore a single breasted, charcoal pin-striped suit with a dove gray buttoned blouse, black leather string tie and black flats. *I'm overdressed for this hamlet.*

She sat at the back, facing the front of Jimmy's—an eleven table greasy spoon with another seven stools at the bar. St. John rested her hand on the tabletop and instantly removed it from the sticky surface. Among the condiments on the table, she spied a jar of maple syrup with streams of its contents coating the outside. Sunlight cut through the front window, illuminating a cloud of fine dust particles filling the air chamber inside the diner. *Fuck! This is what it's become. Hanging out in a shithole, waiting to interview some hillbilly whore. This better be damn well worth the drive.*

After weeks of dogged recruiting, St. John had fully tapped her known sources for exclusive call girls. The seasoned dominatrix from Richmond, Virginia had eagerly signed on for a fee and the promise of a far more upscale clientele. St. John also landed a feisty, beautiful redhead from Princeton, New Jersey, also for a fee. The latter had graduated Princeton University, pleasing her well-to-do parents, but stayed in town afterwards to service several local barristers who'd taken a shine to her. Though thin as a rail, her college girl persona and attire appealed to a certain market segment.

Unfortunately, St. John's rejections outnumbered the acceptances. One of the pros in her stable recommended her cousin in Romney. The girl had graduated high school a month earlier, eager to earn money doing what she'd learned in her extracurricular activities. She presently charged $50 for a lay and $15 for BJs—big pocket change for high school boys and even a stretch for some of the male faculty.

At 12:27 PM, St. John considered heading back to D.C. The girl was late for their noon appointment. Seconds ticked by and a beautiful brunette entered the diner. She had an hourglass figure with shoulder length, wavy dark brown hair. The few customers in the diner shot glances her way, admiring her body, which she'd dressed in a revealing red halter top, short jean cutoffs and platform Croc shoes. She flounced to the back of the restaurant. St. John thought, *Holy shit, the local poke has arrived.*

"Hi, I'm Ginger," the girl said seductively, extending her hand to St. John.

"No. You're late," St. John said, not taking the offered hand. "Sit down."

"Sorry, I had a customer. He took longer than I 'spected."

"Really? Was it worth it?" St. John asked in a condescending tone.

"Oh, he's a reg'lar. I got a deal goin' where I give ten BJs for the price of nine. Fifteen bucks each. This was his tenth, so it was a freebie." She giggled. "Guess he wanted it to last." With her pinky nail, she scraped at the corner of her mouth.

"How enterprising." As the girl babbled away, St. John scrutinized the country bumpkin in front of her, trying to imagine how she could possibly prepare this tramp to fulfill the fantasies of a few high ranking politicians. *She's got the body, but she has zero class. There's no way I can transform this lump.*

Ginger rambled on, "I do whatever my customers want. Full service, ya know? I can do a few guys at once or a line of 'em at like bachelor parties."

She belongs on the Beverly Hillbillies—the x-rated fuck version.

"I'll take it in my butt if they want. I got this one dude..."

"STOP," St. John said. "I don't want to hear another fucking word from you. Listen to me for the next ten minutes. I'll then ask you a simple yes or no question, and we're done."

"Okay, but I was..." Ginger continued.

"You must have a hearing problem. Or maybe you didn't learn English out here in hicksville. Shut the fuck up, or I'm gone."

Ginger opened and closed her mouth a few times without making a noise. Finally, she shut it and put a pout on her face, glaring at St. John.

"I drove out here to offer you the opportunity of *your* life. In my business, you don't earn fifteen dollars a blow job. You make three grand for a couple hours doing whatever the client wants. You'd have two or three clients a week. Do the math...if you can."

Ginger's pout vanished. She sat upright, eyes wide, and leaned toward St. John, appearing to lap up every syllable her prospective madam uttered.

"I'm talking wealthy male and, possibly, female clients whom you'd service at top hotels, like the Ritz Carlton or Four Seasons. You'd live in D.C., work exclusively for me, dress well, live in a nice apartment and eat at fine restaurants. It's a life of luxury, but absolute discretion is required."

A quizzical look formed on Ginger's face.

"*Discretion* means you won't tell anyone anything about what you do or whom you do it with. You violate this rule and you die. Understand? You'll be killed. …Don't speak. Nod your head if you understand what I just said."

Ginger nodded slowly, mouth agape.

"But we've got a problem," St. John said. *Ugh, where do I even begin?* "I'll give it to you straight. You're good looking. And I'm sure you've traded on your looks. But you're just the local fuck hole in this dump of a town. Ten years from now in this berg, you'll be an aging hag who'll be turning two-for-one tricks. You completely lack style and class. None of our clients will be interested in your uneducated, unsophisticated and inarticulate rube bullshit. Nod if you follow me."

Tears welled in Ginger's eyes, but she nodded her head.

"So here's the deal. I haven't the time to reenact *Pygmalion* with you."

Ginger tilted her head and squinted.

"Never heard of *My Fair Lady*? Henry Higgins? Eliza Doolittle? …Never mind. I don't have time and you haven't the right stuff to change in any material way. I'll promote you as a country hick—Ellie May Clampett from the *Beverly Hillbillies*."

That produced a big smile and nods of recognition from Ginger.

"You'll be simple and innocent like Ellie May. In fact, from now on your name is Ellie May, and *don't* you forget it. You'll be Ellie May from the sticks who's come to the big city, amazed at every sight and experience. Whatever you do with your clients, you'll do it like a pro with enthusiasm, but you'll pretend it's your first time, every time. You'll act, in a word, *astonished*. You'll wear what I tell you to wear, go where I tell you to go and do what your clients tell you to do. Nod if you understand."

Ginger sat on the edge of her wooden chair in Jimmy's, nodding excitedly.

"I'll cover any medical expenses you incur, including a full physical exam before you start. One final reminder…you tell *anyone* about what you do or who you're doing it with and you're dead. D…E…A…D. …Want in? Yes or no."

• • •

On the two-hour drive back to D.C. in her Mercedes C-Class convertible with the top down, St. John's cell phone rang. "Whaz up?"

"It's me. What's the status of your recruiting efforts."

"I'm glad you called, shit bird. When are you going to take care of the problem in Chicago? The medical bills are gonna start rollin' in, and I don't want to pay them."

Ruddock despised every interaction with St. John. "That matter will be resolved in a matter of days. Ignore the bills. Now answer my question."

"I've filled three of four slots. Just landed number three. It hasn't been easy, and it's cost me seventeen grand so far for two signing bonuses, moving expenses, fuck-me wardrobes and physical exams."

At this rate, Ms. Butch will spend around $20K of the fifty Tony gave me. I can pocket the rest. Faber est suae quisque fortunae. Every man makes his own fortune.

"You're doing a great job. Full reimbursement will be in your post box in three days." At Ruddock's request and like Tony, St. John had set up an account with a local Mail Boxes Etc. and had given him a key for such deposits. She'd also set up fictitious and unique email accounts for limited correspondence with each girl, like Brenda Butler. The email addresses could only be traced to internet cafés around D.C.

"How long will it take to fill the fourth position?" Ruddock asked.

"Beats the shit out of me. Luckily we haven't hooked all fifty-six pols yet. I've got a few girls whining because they're pulling extra tricks. Of course, they don't complain about collecting additional fees."

"Keep at it. I'll be in touch."

"Just get me my fucking expense money, shit bird."

Ruddock disconnected and began planning his upcoming meeting with Tony.

19

The sixth day after Brenda's surgery, Carrie made her daily call to the hospital.

"I'm feeling much better," Brenda said, "but I haven't been able to check out what they did to my back yet. I dread seeing the results."

"I understand," Carrie said. "What's important though is you're alive and getting well. Have they told you when you can go home?"

"Couple of days. My neighbor swung by yesterday and said she'll help me get resettled. You know, clean my condo, buy groceries, pick up prescriptions and so forth. Susan Atwater's a stay-at-home wife. Lucky for me, she's got the time. I'll have in-home care for a few weeks so someone can change my dressings and check me over. Susan will ferry me back and forth to the doc over the next month or two."

"That's terrific," Carrie replied, but she heard anxiety in Brenda's voice.

Brenda began to cry softly. "I don't know what I'm going to do."

"Sweetie, we'll figure that out together. You've got a college degree and you're smart and good looking. There are tons of opportunities out there for you."

"Right. Just not what I've been doing for fifteen years."

"Correct. But you knew *that* had to end at some point. Right? You're going to have to work like the rest of us poor slobs. And you know what? It'll be safer. Maybe you'll meet someone special. Settle down. Who knows?"

"Yeah, sure."

"And I think it'd do you good to see a therapist. There's a Dr. Leo Bernstein who brought me back from the brink. I'll be glad to make intros. You oughta try one or two sessions. See if it helps."

"Just what I need," Brenda said, "a shrink telling me I belong in a looney bin."

"That's not how it works. Believe me. He's very good at what he does. ...By the way, have you talked with that lesbo madam?"

"Yeah. A second time since I've been in the hospital. Once again, she told me to email my hospital bills when I get them, and she'll reimburse me. ...Oh, and she reminded me to keep my mouth shut if I knew what was good for me."

Carrie looked out her brownstone apartment window at kids playing kick-ball in the street below, wondering what she could do to get Brenda to open up and how she could protect her if she did. "Look. I'm leaving town tomorrow for a couple of days. When I return, we'll sit down and talk about the future."

After hanging up, Carrie phoned Melvin. They agreed to meet the next day to catch a late afternoon nonstop United flight to Las Vegas. Melvin would depart from his farm in Marion, Iowa early and make the four-and-a-half hour drive to Carrie's home. He'd leave his aging Chevy Tahoe with over a half million miles parked next to Carrie's building, and they'd cab it to O'Hare. Traveling together would give them time to reconnect in person and to plan their approach to Tony Amici.

• • •

"Whatcha tell Michael and Max 'bout our lil' trip?" Melvin asked as they waited to board their flight.

"Nothing. It's really none of their business." She stared at the big man seated next to her, dressed in a long sleeve, faded red and black plaid shirt, khaki chinos and scuffed brown work boots. From a certain perspective, Melvin looked like a tough-as-nails back woodsman from the movie *Deliverance*. From another, he merely resembled a humble farmer. Carrie knew he was a combination, and that made Melvin a very dangerous man.

"Didn't ya say they came to Chicago when ya got hurt a few weeks back?"

"Sure. That was very kind of them, but what's your point?"

Shaking his head, Melvin made a tch, tch, tch sound, flicking his tongue against the back of his front upper teeth. "If ya was my kid, I'd turn ya o'er my knee. Ya can't lean on good folks fer help and keep 'em outa the picture on what yer doin' with yer life."

Carrie looked into Melvin's craggy face and his bunched eyebrows. "I appreciate all they've done for me, but I don't like them throwing up roadblocks to my projects. And they'd drop a mountain in front of me for what I'm about to do."

"With good reason." He carried his Marine duffel bag to the line for boarding.

Carrie pursed her lips and fixed an annoyed look on her face. "You said you wanted to come along. If you're coming, I don't want to discuss this further. If you'd rather not, I'll get a refund for your ticket."

Melvin chuckled at Carrie's pluck. "Oh, I'm comin' all right. Somebody has to. You gotta be protected from yerself."

They spent the four-hour flight to Vegas in silence. Melvin grabbed some needed shut-eye, while Carrie pulled out her iPad and began reading the latest Lee Child novel about another of Jack Reacher's adventures.

On the way to the Hertz rental center at the airport, Carrie said, "I've booked rooms for us at Embassy Suites for two nights. Tomorrow, we can drive by EZ-Bonds and plan our approach to Amici. If we can't see him tomorrow, we'll catch him the next day before we fly out."

"How ya know he'll be there?" Melvin asked.

"When we broke up that body parts ring, the FBI said he reliably sits in his shop six days a week. He'll be there."

Once in the rental car, Melvin said, "Okey-dokey. Let's git some din din, and I wanna stop by Home Depot 'fore I go to bed." During his vigilante days, Melvin became a loyal Home Depot customer. The store carried a vast array of hand tools Melvin used to dispatch child predators who escaped punishment by the legal system.

Melvin seldom ate steak. He loved it but couldn't afford the indulgence with any regularity. In part because she knew Melvin would enjoy it and due to the minor quarrel they'd had at the outset of the trip, Carrie treated Melvin to a sumptuous steak dinner with a handful of sides at Smith & Wolensky's on the Vegas strip.

Over coffee, Melvin asked, "So how're we gonna play this thing t'morrow?"

"He doesn't know us. I'll give him the cover that I'm working on a story about bail bondsmen. That I'm interviewing leading bondsmen in key U.S. cities."

"Who'm I s'posed to be?"

"Oh yeah. I hadn't thought about that. ...Uh, I'll say you're my uncle who's escorting me around the country. That's partly true."

"Yup, the part 'bout me bein' an escort. Well, let's git o'er to Home Depot. I got somethin' I need for t'morrow so's I can be an *armed* escort."

They drove east from the strip to a Home Depot store on South Lamb Road. Once in the big box store, Melvin took off with big strides, making a beeline to the tools department. Carrie barely kept pace. But she knew what he was after—a weapon.

He paraded up and down the short aisles filled with tools until his eyes settled on a 21-inch long Estwing forged steel pry bar, a tad under two pounds. He held it in one hand, gauging its heft. From experience, Melvin knew he could conceal this tool up his long shirtsleeve. It'd slide down his arm and into his large, calloused hand in a second if needed, and he well knew how to wield it for maximum impact.

"Perfecto. But it's kinda pricey."

"Melvin, if I can treat you to an S&W steak, I can certainly afford fifteen bucks if you feel you have to have this pry bar."

"Lil' girl, we *need* it. You got no idea what we're walkin' into t'morrow."

"Let's try to avoid any violence. We didn't come here for that."

"I'll bet ya a McDonald's burger you'll be happy we bought this tonight."

After the Home Depot purchase they checked into Embassy Suites for the night. Before getting into bed at 11 PM, Carrie called Michael.

"Hey you," he said. "I've missed you. You're up awfully late."

"Oh, sorry, I forgot the time. Jeez, it's two in the morning your time."

"No problem. You feeling okay? No after effects from the concussions?"

"I'm good."

"I was thinking of flying to Chicago tomorrow to spend the day with you."

"Uh, no, uh, that wouldn't work. I'm pretty tied up."

"You've got to eat. We could have dinner," Michael said.

"No, uh, that's not possible." Carrie began to perspire. *I shouldn't have called him. Gotta change the subject.*

"What's wrong? I get a feeling you're hiding something."

"Well, if you must know, I'm out of town on business." *Oh god I'm on a slippery slope.*

"Okay, you sounded a bit...evasive. Where are you?"

"I...uh...I'm in...uh...Las Vegas."

"That sounds like pleasure, not work," Michael said in jest.

"Oh, I'm working all right." *How do I get out of this?*

"What are you working on?"

"I'm interviewing someone for a story. But let's not talk about it."

"Who?"

She paused several seconds and then blurted out, "Tony Amici."

"WHAT!"

"I've got to go now. I'll call in a few days." She terminated the call, turned off her cell and flopped down on her queen size bed. Carrie pulled a pillow over her head and hugged it. *Damn, what a dope I am. Why'd I call him? ...Now I'm in trouble.*

20

Max reached for his bedside phone when the marimba ringtone sounded. He glanced at the Big Ben clock on his nightstand—2:53 AM. "This had better be damn good," he muttered. He barked into the phone, "Speak and make it worth my time."

"It's Michael. Sorry to call at this hour. Something's come up."

Max cleared his throat and grumbled, "Must be a pretty damn important something." Dressed in a white cotton wife beater and silk paisley boxers, he flipped on a lamp and rolled to a seated position on the side of his bed. He rubbed the sleep from his eyes, worked his jaw muscles and tried to get his brain in gear.

"Carrie's in Las Vegas, and she's going to meet with Tony Amici."

"What? Run that by me again."

Michael told him the little he knew from his brief conversation with Carrie. "She was evasive but, after a few simple questions, she coughed up where she was and what she was doing there. Clearly, she didn't want me to know. Now her cell is off."

Max pushed his thick white hair off his face. "Ah Michael, this girl's a danger junkie. She knows all about Amici. The three of us sat in the same room in Phoenix when the FBI briefed us on the prick. He probably ordered Bill Barrett to attack her in her apartment last year. And she chances a sit down with that devil? This is the height of stupidity or naïveté...probably both."

"I don't know what to do," Michael said.

"NOTHING! That's what you do. Nothing. Did you tell her you believe Amici is your biological father?"

"No."

"Well...she's on her own. Knowing full well who this cretin is, she sneaked off to Vegas to meet him. There's an old saying, 'you can't cure stupid.' There are some people you just can't help. Carrie's one. And you'd better get used to that fact."

"I love her, Max."

"I've got two pieces of advice for you. First, take an Ambien and go to bed. Second, get over Carrie. She's a walking time bomb."

"I...I..."

"Michael? I'm hanging up now. Go to bed, and we'll talk later this morning." Max disconnected. He scratched his sculpted chest and scanned his bedroom as if searching for a clue for what he should do next. *Shit. Now I can't sleep. Maybe I'll go to 24Hour Fitness. Get an early workout. Michael better get his head screwed on straight. Such a bright, effective guy, but this broad's got him completed addled.*

• • •

Ruddock finished shaving in his Las Vegas garden apartment and began dressing for his meeting with Tony. He pulled on a white polo shirt with olive Dockers, white socks and black loafers, and snapped the clasp of his Rolex on his wrist. *I'm going to squeeze more cash out of the bastard. But how? ...Ah! I'll focus on my success...that's how. Then I'll tell him I'm short on recruiting expenses.*

An hour later, he sat across Tony in his EZ-Bonds office. "Everything's progressing well. We've replaced three girls, and we've nearly landed a fourth. A few more pols are in the fold. I'll get them working for us shortly."

Tony sat still, listening to Ruddock's report while admiring his eight-finger manicure. "Did you extinguish our problem in Chicago?"

Ruddock squirmed in his chair, imperceptibly he hoped. "I'll finish that in a couple of days when she leaves the hospital. She hasn't spoken or we'd know it by now. She's under twenty-four hour police protection at the hospital. St. John's been in contact with her about paying her medical expenses. Everything's under control."

He searched Tony's face for reaction. Tony sat Sphinx-like, expressionless. "Hmm, sounds like things are going as planned, despite a few hiccups."

"Yessir. They are indeed. And I've brought you the take so far from this month." He handed Tony a briefcase filled with $175K in cash.

Tony frowned. "I've told you before. Don't bring money like this into my office. Leave it in the post box." Tony hurriedly squirreled the money into the floor safe beneath his filing cabinet.

"Sorry boss. I had it with me, and I'm about to leave town. I thought..."

"You thought wrong." Tony cut him off—an angry expression on his face. Once reseated in his executive black leather chair, Tony adjusted his silk floral tie and straightened the creases in his gray herringbone slacks. "What else do you have?"

Damn! I shouldn't have brought the take. I thought he'd be excited receiving so much so early in the month. What do I say now?

"Uh…from all indications, the politicians we've hooked have behaved precisely in line with our demands. Not one has complained. They regularly pay their fees, and there's no evidence any have gone to the authorities."

"Good, good, good. I like that," Tony said. "Good work, Jim."

"There's one small thing." Ruddock tensed.

"What?" Tony arched an eyebrow.

"We've run through the fifty large you gave me for recruitment to land the first three girls." *God, this is risky. I hope he doesn't ask for an accounting.*

Tony peered over his reading glasses, and Ruddock looked straight into Tony's eyes. Ten seconds passed. *Silentium est auream. Silence is golden. Wait for a reaction.*

Finally, Tony broke eye contact and walked to his floor safe. "You could have saved me an extra trip to my safe. Will another twenty grand be enough?"

"Yessir. I'll return any surplus…Oh, and I'll deposit it in your post box."

The meeting ended and Ruddock started to leave the office on his way to McCarran International Airport. He pulled open the front door to EZ-Bonds, and a good looking blond woman walked in, followed by a tall, aging rough-hewn fellow.

Carrie looked up at Ruddock and said, "Excuse me." When she and her companion stepped to the reception counter, Ruddock bolted from the premises.

Holy shit! What's she doing here? And who's the goon with her? For three minutes, he waited across the street, seated in his Cadillac with the engine and the AC running, heart beating faster than normal. *Must not have recognized me. If she had, they would've run right back out. Damn, that was close.*

Ruddock took a deep breath and exhaled, trying to center himself before driving to the airport. He inspected the contents of the brown sandwich bag Tony had given him. Ruddock's eyes crinkled at the sight of four bound stacks of five grand in hundred dollar bills. The corners of his mouth turned up. "Huh, you clever dude," he muttered. *That was an easy twenty large. Tony's pretty smart—up to a point.*

• • •

"Hi, my name's Carrie Linden, and this is my uncle Melvin. Is Mr. Amici in?"

A chubby middle-aged Hispanic receptionist in a tight polyester lime green dress eyed the two unusual visitors and replied, "Wait here. I'll go see."

21

"I'm going to Vegas," Michael said as he packed his suitcase.

Max sipped coffee with a touch of cream from a large mug Michael handed him when he entered Michael's condo. "What do you hope to accomplish?"

"For one thing, I'll confront Amici with these." Michael held up the stacks of letters Tony had written to Jeannie. "I'm grateful for the support he gave us, but I want him out of my life. I want him to stay away from Carrie too."

"Newsflash Michael. He's not *in* your life. But by meeting him, you'll invite him in. Carrie's actively engaging Amici in hers. She's deliberately asking for trouble, although I'm sure she doesn't see it that way. And who knows whether the FBI has surveillance going. It wouldn't be the first or even the second time. You don't want to get caught on video with Amici no matter how innocent your purpose being there."

Michael stopped packing. He sat on the edge of his bed, bent over and put his face in his hands. "My gut's in a knot. I want to protect her. Pull her out of there."

Max said, "Ah Michael. You're a hard-nosed attorney, but this girl has you all tangled up in your underwear. Trust me. There's nothing you can do. Based on my experience with the likes of Amici, nothing bad will happen to her while she's in Las Vegas. If I'm wrong, it'd be done before you even landed out there. Wait 'till she gets home. Then have a serious conversation with her—a talk that will end her reckless behavior or your relationship. You've got to bring this to a head."

With shoulders slumped, Michael said, "I know. I'm acting like a dope with a high school crush on a girl who won't listen to reason."

He clapped Michael on the back. "You have clients depending on you son. Get dressed and go to work. Call me later." With that admonition, Max saw himself out.

• • •

"Mr. Amici will see you now," the receptionist said. She extended an arm, flesh sagging heavily under her tricep. She pointed in the direction of Tony's office—five steps behind the reception desk.

Carrie, followed by Melvin, took the cue and stepped to Tony's open doorway.

"Come in. I don't believe we've ever met, though I've read your column, Ms. Linden." He gave her the large, winsome smile he reserved for Sundays and legitimate public events. *Why's she here, and who's the heavy she's brought along?*

Carrie offered Tony her hand. "Please call me Carrie. This is my Uncle Melvin who's traveling with me. I hope we're not intruding, but I'd appreciate a few minutes of your time for an article I'm writing."

Melvin didn't extend his hand.

Tony sized her up. *A pretty Midwestern girl. Yellow shirtwaist dress with a checked pattern. Little makeup. Understated. That's it. Understated. Shapely too. No wonder Michael likes her.* Tony remembered learning the two were lovers when they interfered with his illegal human body parts business. *She'd make a welcome addition to my little enterprise too. We need one more girl.* Then he gave Melvin the once over. *This can't be her uncle. Right age, but no family resemblance. Dressed like a mountain man. Guy's a brute.*

A few seconds passed. "Uh, please have a seat." They took the two metal chairs with orange plastic-coated backs and seats in front of Tony's desk. Tony adjusted his gray herringbone suit and shot his French cuffs. He sat in his executive chair, elbows on his desk, palms together under his chin with eight fingers in a steeple. "How may I be of service? Need a bond? HEHEHE."

Carrie related her cover of writing a story about the bail bonds business. She explained her plan to interview leading bondsmen around the country and dropped names of a few whom she planned to meet in San Francisco and LA while out west. On the surface, it sounded legit, and Carrie seemed sincere.

Bullshit! What's she really after? Only one way to find out.

Tony made a show of looking at his solid gold Cartier. "It's eleven. I'll give you forty minutes, but then I have to leave for lunch with the Mayor. He's launching another charity drive, and he wants me to organize it. Charity work does have its rewards, you know?" That said, Tony pointed up as if heaven awaited his arrival.

Carrie's mouth dropped open as if she couldn't believe what he'd just said. But she quickly switched into professional mode and began peppering Tony with prepared questions about the bail bonds business.

Melvin sat erect, like a Marine drill sergeant, to Carrie's right throughout the interview, staring directly at Tony. His right arm hung straight down next to his chair, holding the pry bar up his shirt sleeve.

Fifteen minutes into the Q&A, Carrie asked, "I guess you've encountered people who run prostitution rings. Right?" Carrie moved a bit in her chair.

"Of course." His eyes narrowed. *Finally, she's getting to the heart of why she's here with this goon.*

"I mean very high class prostitutes. Girls with education and good looks."

"Yes. Like most industries, prostitution is tiered. Different strokes for different folks. Not every segment caters solely to street traffic...if you know what I mean." His mouth smiled, but his eyes didn't.

"I understand." Carrie paused as if framing her next question. "Suppose I wanted to start a high class prostitution ring, what..."

"Where is this going, Ms. Linden?" He arched his left eyebrow.

"I didn't finish my question. Suppose I wanted to do that for the purpose of blackmailing U.S. Representatives and Senators..."

"Stop right there." An alarm went off in Tony's head. *Where the hell is she going with this? Who sent her? ...Stay cool. Send her packing with her guard dog.* He cleared his throat and leaned forward. "As part of my bail bonds business, I've met many people who run prostitutes. I can only speculate as to the source of their, uh, talent and how they acquire clientele. I have no knowledge of the ins and outs of their businesses, and I certainly have no insights into blackmailing politicians." His eight fingers, now in his fists, rested on his desk. Tony gave his visitors *the look*. Carrie averted her eyes, but Melvin glared back.

She took a deep breath and continued, "Come now, Mr. Amici, the FBI says you run every tier of the prostitution industry in Vegas. I'm asking how you'd use that type of business to blackmail national politicians and for what purpose."

Tony leaned back in his chair, feeling Carrie's deep probe. He scrutinized her for a few seconds and made a decision. Pushing a concealed button under his desk, he said, "If you believe what you claim the FBI says to be true about me, then you must also believe I could be involved in other criminal activities, some of which could be life threatening to others."

Carrie stammered and said, "Yes, uh, uh, I believe that could be true."

Two enormous thugs from an adjacent office materialized in Tony's doorway. Their presence obvious from heavy breathing and an overpowering stench of garlic.

With great menace, Tony replied, "Then you must be a very brave or a very stupid girl coming to see a man whom you believe could arrange grave bodily harm or worse to you and your, uh, uncle here."

Before Carrie could respond, Melvin spoke up, "Time to git." He shoved his big left hand under Carrie's arm and lifted her from her chair as he stood.

They turned toward the men in the doorway and glanced back at Tony when he said, "A piece of advice…I don't know who'd try to run a scam such as you've described. But I know one thing. If you investigate them, they'll likely kill you."

The two hulks in the doorway didn't budge. Melvin let the pry bar slip down his sleeve, catching the end in his big calloused right hand. He raised it until it came to rest on his shoulder. "'Scuse us boys," he said. When they didn't move, Melvin repeated his statement, "I said 'scuse us. Ya speak English, right?"

"Whatcha think you're gonna do with that, old man?" One of them asked.

"Ya don't wanna find out." Melvin replied harshly, staring them both down.

Tony signaled his men to let them pass. They backed out of the doorway, and Melvin pulled Carrie through it. He pushed her ahead of him, and he walked backwards to EZ-Bonds' storefront door. The receptionist stood, watching, hands on her mammoth hips. The two thugs slowly followed Melvin to the door. "Nice meetin' y'all. We won't be back," Melvin said with a smile as they stepped onto the sidewalk.

Tony watched as the front door closed behind them. Then he picked up a cell phone, slammed the door to his office and called Ruddock.

"You know a woman named Carrie Linden?"

"No."

"She walked in when you left. Good looking blond. Mid-thirties. Lives in Chicago. Very well known reporter. Showed up with a tall, tough guy."

"Didn't notice them."

"She inquired about using a prostitution ring to blackmail members of Congress. Any idea why she'd ask *me* about that?"

"Not a clue."

"Pay her a visit at home. Convince her she needs to focus on other stories. And for chrissake put an end to the problem in Chicago. I don't want any further visits from this woman. Understand?"

"It'll be done, boss."

• • •

Carrie trembled all the way to the car and throughout their drive to Embassy Suites. "Them boys woulda eaten you alive," Melvin said. "Happy we stopped by Home Depot? …Ya oughta stop nosin' 'round. Man threatened to kill us."

"He said *whoever's* running that type of business…"

"C'mon Carrie. Who'd ya think he was talkin' 'bout? Ever hear of talkin' in the third person 'bout yerself? That's what he was doin'. This is one evil fella. Don't know 'bout you, but I'm too young and pretty to die."

Carrie laughed. "That's quite a literary assessment." She put her hand on Melvin's arm. "Thank you so much for coming with me, my friend. But, we've got to do something..."

"Yup. Yer right. We gotta git back home. We gotta mind our own beeswax. And we gotta keep our eyes peeled so's we keep our butts healthy and above ground. Right now, ya owe me a McDonald's burger."

22

"Join us," Bull bellowed when Representative Dale Bennett stuck his head in the Senator's office. Bullman and Senator Mary Grendel sat across from each other on opposing down-filled couches, jackets off and drinks in hand.

Bull stood and walked to his office bar. Already on his second double shot of Jack Daniels, he blurted, "What's your poison tonight, Dale?"

"Whiskey. Neat." Dale dropped into a wingback chair next to the couches and gratefully accepted a glass of Crown Royal from the Senator. "What a fucking day."

"To fewer fucking days," Bull toasted. Everyone raised their glasses and took a drink. "We've known one another for decades," Bull began. "Been on the same side of a lot of battles in both Houses. Had each other's backs on multiple occasions."

"Campaigned together too," Dale added.

"Bull, it's past seven," Mary said, "and I've had a very long day. Get to the point so we can go home." She downed the rest of her scotch in one gulp and headed to the bar for another Dewars and soda.

"Yeah. I agree," Dale said.

Bull lifted a stack of news clippings from the seat cushion next to him, each with a bold headline. For emphasis, he dropped them, one at a time, on his coffee table as he read the headlines aloud. "*Washington Post* writes **Congressional Leaders Flip Flop en Masse**. *New York Times* reports **Congress Lets Business Run Amock**. *Time Magazine's* front cover features a group shot of twenty of our colleagues, suit coats on backwards. The caption reads, **Turncoats**," Bull continued. "These are just today's."

"We've seen these, Bull." Mary said. "You've been painted red too."

"Yes I have. As have you. You're my closest colleagues in the capitol. I've asked you here because I see a pattern in this mess, and we need to resolve it."

"Resolve what?" Dale asked. He wiggled uncomfortably in his wingback chair. "Are you accusing me of something? ...Out with it."

"Listen," Bull said. "I know how challenging it is to hold public office, particularly senior positions. People constantly lean on us for one outcome or another. We're tempted too. Lobbyists and others dangle things in front of us in their attempt to curry favor. They take advantage of our human weaknesses for their own self interests. They violate the law and try to pull us into their corrupt webs."

Mary gently set her empty glass on the coffee table. Her eyes darted from Bull to Dale and back. "What does that have to do with the three of us?"

"We're colleagues," Bull said. "Actually far more than colleagues. We're trusted friends. That is...I think of you that way. We know things about one another that could be used to recall us from office, but we've kept them buried. Deep. Same's true for other members of our party who've been labeled 'Turncoats' and worse."

Dale shucked his suit jacket. He mopped his brow with a hanky and took a gulp of whiskey. "I don't know what you're suggesting, Bull, but I don't like where this discussion's going."

"Me either," Mary said. But neither made a move to leave.

Bull took a pull from his glass. "My staff's gone. No one's recording what we say. It's very difficult for me to have this conversation with you. However, I believe the three of us and several others in our party have been compromised."

"What?" Mary challenged. She began fidgeting with her hands.

"Preposterous!" Dale exclaimed and then looked down at the floor.

The warm, intoxicating effect of the Kentucky bourbon worked on Bull's system. *Who do these assholes think they're talking to? They're as dirty as me. I don't know what they've done or what they've taken, but they've been corrupted.*

"Is it so incredible?" Bull asked. "I'm telling you, off the record, that forty or more Senators and Representatives are in somebody's pocket. I don't have specifics on anyone, nor do I seek or intend to give details. All we need is to examine our own behavior and that of our colleagues over the past several months."

"I don't know what to say..." Mary started.

"Bull, you're headed into a danger zone with this talk," Dale said.

"Yeah? If what I said was untrue, both of you would have stormed out of here by now. I'm not asking anyone for a confession, nor am I offering one. But recently, we have actively and consistently worked against every principle we stand for."

Dale laughed nervously. "Yeah? And my portfolio has shot up as a result. In one month alone the Dow's risen thirty-three percent. All the indices are skyrocketing. And when the tide for U.S. equities rises, it lifts all boats globally."

"That's right," Mary said. "The DAX and the Hang Seng are advancing aggressively. Leading analysts around the world forecast a bull market for the next year or two. Maybe what we and our colleagues have done is fueling success."

"Some on the other side like Davis and Ellis would agree with Mary's conclusion," Dale said, "even though they'll use it against us come election season."

Bull leaned forward and pointed to the news clippings. "So you're saying the means justify the ends? Think about the positions we've fought for over the years. They've centered on creating balance and protecting innocent people and the environment. And, yes, sometimes at the expense of short-term business success."

He waved his arms. "We've abandoned it all. We've capitulated. All because we've succumbed to whatever temptation was set before us...not due to a new-found rationale or philosophy. ...I know. I've talked with all those who've been castigated by the press. So please spare me your bullshit rationalizations. How high do you think the market will go? If it collapses, how badly do you think people will get hurt?"

Mary stood at the bar, filling her glass again and gazing out the window at the lighted Capitol Reflection Pool. She coughed, clearing her throat and said, "I'm not saying I agree with your thesis, Bull, but suppose you're right. What if these elected officials have been compromised? That could lead to a wave of criminal convictions."

"Yeah," Dale spoke up. "Suppose those who corrupted them have concrete evidence against them. What if they've been threatened? You know, if they go to the authorities, they'll be outed and finished politically." His face reddened.

Bull smiled and scratched the stubble on his chin. "Yeah. Suppose all of that. We revel in the power of our positions, but we love this country—I hope. Don't you think we owe it to our country and those we represent to do something about this?"

"I'd lose my...I mean...I can't tell...uh..." Mary's hands visibly trembled. A tear rolled down her cheek. She sighed as if defeated.

"Me too," Bull said in an attempt to self-disclose in a circuitous way.

"I've heard nothing about any investigation," Dale said. "We should let things play out a bit before we take any action. I know some members we're talking about have begun acting strangely. Jimmy Novotchin has almost gone mute. That's totally uncharacteristic. He's begun drinking far more as if that were possible. But we could open *Pandora's Box*. We don't know the extent of the problem—if there even is one."

Mary said, "Besides the fact that Novotchin's a pig and a womanizer, Dale, you're advocating the old put your head in the sand strategy. You think this will all blow over? Who cares who gets hurt? Well I don't think this is going away anytime soon. I believe the problem we're discussing exists and has such dire consequences for our colleagues that, until they leave office, their votes are bought and paid for."

"I agree," Bull said. "I wanted to raise this issue with the two of you because I value your counsel. Maybe we could put our heads together and develop a solution."

"Solution to what?" Dale asked. "We're speculating about something that may be completely false. I don't want any further part of this. Maybe people are simply voting their consciences. I'd like to give everyone the benefit of the doubt."

"HA!" Bull chortled. "I doubt any of us will benefit in the long run, Dale."

"Dale, if you don't want to talk about it," Mary said, "please promise not to breathe a word of this conversation to anyone. And I mean ANYONE."

Dale set his glass on the coffee table and stood. He weaved a bit from the alcohol and walked to the door. "This meeting never took place." He turned and left.

Bull and Mary looked at each other. "Dinner?" Bull asked. They picked up their jackets and briefcases and headed to the Capitol Grille.

• • •

Over burgers at McDonald's in Las Vegas, Carrie said, "I've got an idea."

"Let's first git outa town t'morrow," Melvin said.

"I've built a list of U.S. Representatives and Senators who've been identified as acting against their long held principles. I intend to interview as many as I can. Maybe someone will slip up and this enormous ball of yarn will begin to unravel."

"Jes' make sure it's a big ball a yarn and not a boulder rollin' yer way."

23

Ruddock now had two reasons to visit Chicago. He'd planned to end Brenda's life a few days hence at his convenience, and he needed to move with speed because of the blond reporter's inquiries. Brenda had to go and Carrie would get a hard lesson. Delaying Tony's order wasn't an option.

While waiting for his mid-day flight from McCarran International to O'Hare, he called Northwestern Memorial to check on Brenda's status. *What luck! They sent her home. That makes things so much easier.* He phoned St. John.

"Whaz up?" St. John answered.

"It's me. I need Heaven's home address. She's out of the hospital." He copied Brenda's address onto the back of his boarding pass.

"Make sure you get it done already. The bills are piling up, and they're gonna be huge."

"I'm on it. Like I told you, ignore the bills. How's recruiting coming?"

"Hey shit bird, I'm all over it," St. John said. "Do *your* job, and I'll do mine. Stop fucking bugging me about it. And where's my sixteen grand?" Her voice dripped with antagonism.

"Maybe you should get your hearing or memory checked. I said you'd be paid in three days. Look for it the day after tomorrow, which will be as promised. And stop giving me attitude, or you might join Heaven and the others." He cut the connection. *What a god damn bitch! I don't treat her with disrespect. Maybe when we've met our quota, I'll find someone else to run the talent and say bye-bye to Ms. Butch. Send her to Butch hell. Maybe the devil will force her to have sex with men for eternity. HA!*

That evening, Ruddock dropped his carry-on at the Chicago Airport Hilton and boarded the train to downtown. In town, he taxi'd to the intersection nearest Brenda's building. Nestled between two taller edifices on a residential street, the scrolled concrete details on the brick façade of Brenda's eight-story complex resembled early 20th century construction. It appeared well-maintained and had a locked and alarmed wrought iron and glass entry door. No doorman. Large sash windows from each apartment overlooked the street below. A few were open this hot summer night.

Security was minimal. A resident departing the building politely held the door open for Ruddock to enter. *Idiot.* A quick peek at the ganged up mailboxes in the lobby confirmed Brenda's fourth floor residence, apartment 52—really the sixth floor if you counted the lobby as a floor. Checking the mailbox array, he could see that each floor consisted of four apartments. The stairwell rose in the middle of the building from the lobby to the top floor. A small elevator backed to the staircase. *No internal security cameras. Staircase deserted. So far, so good.*

Ruddock took the stairs two at a time to the first floor apartments. He noted the layout. Apartments 11 and 14 were situated at the front of the building with the other two, 12 and 13, at the back. The back apartments surely had windows, which likely faced an alley behind the building. That gave him an idea.

He continued slowly up the stairs. Faint sounds echoed from several apartments. Being the dinner hour, residents were either eating in or dining out. Approaching Brenda's floor, the door to apartment 52 opened. A young white woman, with frizzy hair and dressed in a lavender tee and blue jeans, stepped through the door. She said, "Okay sweetie, I'll be back a little later to do the dishes and check on you."

"You're a godsend, Susan. I can't thank you enough," Brenda replied.

He watched as she closed Brenda's door and returned to apartment 51, at the front of the building. A family of four left apartment 53, adjacent to Brenda's unit. Ruddock continued his ascent to the next floor, pretending he was on his way to an upper level apartment while the unit 53 kids trundled down the stairs with their parents in tow. *Perfect for what I've got in mind.*

Returning to Brenda's floor, Ruddock pulled on leather gloves and gently knocked on her front door.

Fifteen seconds later, he heard, "Who's there?"

That's my girl Heaven. "My name's Jim. I'm sorry to disturb you, Ms. Butler. A woman named St. John sent me to deliver money for your medical bills," he said.

Five seconds passed. "Thanks. Please slip the envelope under the door."

"I can't. It's not a check. It's a large amount of cash. St. John requires a signature release for the cash. It'll just take a second, and I'll be out of your hair."

The door opened three inches—the full distance the door chain allowed. "Please hand me the cash and what you want me to sign through the opening."

Ruddock glanced around the hallway. *Deserted.* He slammed the gloved palm of his hand against the door, next to the chain. The screws that fastened the chain lock ripped from the door frame, and the portal to Brenda's home opened with a bang.

She quickly backed up and began whimpering as Ruddock shut the door behind him. He rushed Brenda, grabbing her roughly by her throat and hair. She tugged at his thick wrist with both hands, trying to wrest his hand from her neck.

Brenda couldn't scream. She croaked out a "please," which Ruddock ignored.

He dragged her behind him like a Raggedy Ann doll to the back of her apartment. "Nice of you to open your window this evening." Ruddock released her neck and used his free hand to grab the back waistband of her sweatpants. Then he hurled her through her open bedroom window like a sack of potatoes. He watched as her arms and legs flailed a few seconds until she landed, head first, on the alley pavement. *Hmm, no longer dramatis personae, part of the cast.*

Ruddock left Brenda's apartment and jogged down the stairs, removing his gloves once outside the building. From entry to exit, it had taken less than four minutes. Five blocks later, he found a busy intersection and took a taxi to the nearest train station for a ride back to O'Hare.

That went easier than expected. Good thing the fire escape didn't block her window. Woulda had to go to Plan B. Wonder if that reporter's home yet. Pay her a visit tomorrow. Shame to mess up a pretty face. . . . Then it's back to business as usual.

He dialed Tony who was closing EZ-Bonds for the night. "I've resolved the problem we spoke of. Tomorrow I'll check in with the pest you called me about earlier today. Found the address in the phone book here."

"Pest. HEHEHE. I like that term. That *pest* may not be there yet," Tony said.

"I'll keep tabs and deliver the message ASAP." He hung up.

Ruddock called St. John. "Delete the email address you used with Heaven."

"Thank the lord. Hey, you've gotta get to D.C. We just hooked the top Senator on the Armed Services Committee. You've got a primo opportunity to get film footage of this cretin with our new dominatrix. He doesn't care where he does his filthy business. I've set it up at the Key Bridge Marriott for eight tomorrow night. That'll save on hotel expenses. Be there or be square." She disconnected.

Can't pass that up. I'll tell Tony the reporter wasn't home. Meantime I'm on the job. Guess I'll be eating at the Hilton tonight. Damn, I hate hotel food.

24

Halfway through their entrées, Bull asked their Capitol Grille waiter for a second bottle of Chateauneuf-du-Pape. Mary Grendel sat across from him in an out of the way booth that provided a modicum of privacy.

"I've always liked this place," Bull said. "Mostly for the food, but the wait staff know how to keep their distance. Gives people a chance to talk." He wanted to talk. Badly. Get the dark secret off his chest—well, the part about sex and blackmail, but not the part about killing Dakota. No. That had to stay buried. He'd take that nugget to his grave. *Am I sober enough for this conversation? To say the right things? Avoid the really dark stuff? ...Sure, I'm okay. Like that prick marriage counselor told Melissa and me, "I'm okay; you're okay." Well, I'm fucking okay.*

No way could he share his sexual antics with his wife. Melissa even disliked traditional sex. She had no comprehension of the types of bedroom activities he found enjoyable. She'd go running to her eighty-nine year old father who'd never been fond of him. The old prick would relay the story to his cronies in all three of the country clubs he frequented. It'd be like playing telephone. His story would become more embellished with every telling. The word would be out. The FBI, local law enforcement and the Senate Ethics Committee would come after him.

"So where do we start, Bull?" After a few cocktails in Bull's office, a double scotch on the rocks while perusing the menu and, now, on her second glass of wine, Grendel slurred her speech. Her head lolled on her shoulders like a bobble-head doll, and her normally unkempt hair now looked like the do for *Bride of Frankenstein.*

Can I trust Mary? I know she can trust me. But does she know that? She's probably asking the same questions. We've always been straight with each other. Maybe we do a little tit for tat. I share a bit and then she shares a bit. Right. We draw each other's story out or as much as each wants to share.

"Suppose I tell you a little personal thing about me and then you do like-wise," he said. "I'll expand some more about me and you do the same. Let's see where we end up." Bull stuck a fork, loaded with garlic mashed potatoes, into his mouth.

"Good. But we gotta have a ground rule," she said. Her head sagged toward her plate, but she caught it before it landed in the bath of béarnaise sauce that her filet mignon swam in. She looked up at Bull with tears in her eyes and whispered, "Never breathe a word of what I tell you. *Please.* You gotta promise me, Bull."

"I promise. You promise too?" He delivered a practiced smile.

"Yes." She wiped her eyes with her napkin and forked a bite of green beans.

"Pinky swear?" *I hope she can stay awake for this. Her eyes are glassed over.*

That brought a lopsided smile to her face. And she took a swig of red wine.

"You know, Mary, I love my wife in many ways. But...ahem...she's never really been there for me, uh, I mean wanted to participate in...uh..."

"You talking about sex, Bull?" Mary seemed awakened from her stupor.

"Yeah. She doesn't like sex that much. Actually, she doesn't like it at all. I'm not talking about kinky stuff either. She doesn't go for it in any form. Never has. Guess I should have tried on the shoes before I bought them."

"Let's not get chauvinistic. But funny you should mention that," she said, "'cause you know I've been married to Robert for twenty-nine years. We stopped having sex twenty-eight years ago. I just don't find him the least bit attractive."

Okay, we're getting somewhere. "In my case, it's led me over the years to seek, shall we say, other sources to satisfy my needs." He paused to push the last bite of strip steak into his mouth. "For a few months, I found myself *in lust* with a young woman. Met her at an embassy party, and we began having clandestine rendezvous."

"Same thing happened to me. I was at a fundraising event, and I met this gorgeous girl...uh...I mean..."

"Don't hold back, Mary. You can tell me. I've known about your, uh, predilection for a long time. I don't care. Your secret's safe with me."

She rolled her head in a circle, working the kinks out. "Ah, thank god. I can't tell you how good it feels to tell someone that. It's been killing me. I started having a...lesbian affair with this redhead. Oh, I'd had other female encounters over the years, but this one was great. I was falling in love. She was beautiful."

"What do you mean she *was* beautiful?"

"Things ended badly, uh, violently. I don't know what possessed me, but I hit her with a lamp. ...Twice...hard. I ran from the hotel. Haven't seen her since."

"Is she okay?"

"I don't want to talk about that."

I was right not to tell about Dakota's demise. "Okay, my turn."

They'd pushed their empty dinner plates aside and leaned in toward one another, elbows on the table and chins resting in their open palms. A passerby would think they were having a lover's intimate conversation.

"I can't explain why," Bull said, "but I have a...scatological obsession."

"What's that?" Mary reached for her wine glass and another swig of the red.

"I like to watch a good looking woman...uh...shit on my bare skin. Okay?"

"That's so *gross.*" She closed her eyes, wrinkled her nose and shook her head.

"Hey, I didn't judge you. Don't judge me."

Properly chastised, she said, "I'm sorry, Bull. So what happened?"

"She was the best ever. I could have gone on with her twice a month forever."

"I saw Blaze, I mean the redhead, twice a month too."

"It wasn't cheap, mind you. This wasn't some gutter snipe. I paid eight grand a visit," he said. "But she was worth every penny." "That's what I pay, I mean paid."

"Huh. My relationship ended abruptly. Someone had shot video of us together and started...they began..." He closed his eyes, not able to speak the words.

"Blackmailing you," she finished his thought.

He nodded and pulled a handkerchief from his right rear pant pocket to mop his eyes. "I don't know how it happened. It's not like we hung out at a no-tell motel. We met at The Hay-Adams for crying out loud."

"You're not alone. They did the same to me. I'm still paying twice a month, at a Days Inn. And they dictate my actions in the Senate just like we discussed earlier in your office."

"I'm still paying them too, and I'm caught in their web. They've had me reverse direction on banking reform. Can you believe it? Did you meet a dyke, sorry, a lesbian named St. John?"

"I did, and she *is* a fucking dyke."

"You think Dale and Novotchin and the rest are..."

"I'd say we've got an epidemic."

They gave each other a long searching look.

25

Carrie and Melvin deplaned at Chicago O'Hare before noon and headed to the taxi waiting line outside the terminal. They hadn't spoken much that morning as Carrie mulled over Melvin's advice and contemplated possible interviews with politicians in D.C. She also dreaded her next conversation with Michael.

How can I get him to understand? I had to meet with Amici. It's my profession. My passion. Jeez, I don't tell him what kind of lowlife clients he can accept in his criminal law practice. Yeah. What gives him the right to tell me what to do?

It came time to board a taxi. Melvin stirred her from her day dreams with a slight nudge to the shoulder. "Ya gonna tell him where we're goin'?"

"Oh, sorry." Carrie gave the driver the address to her brownstone. "I thought we'd stash our bags in my home and go for lunch. You like deep dish pizza?"

Melvin gave her a big grin. "I'm up for anythin'. I may be seventy and a recovered gutshot victim, but I got a cast iron digestive system."

"Great. We'll go to Grassano's. They're pretty close, and they're the best. After, let's pay Brenda a visit. You'd like her. She's a nice girl…despite what she did for a living."

"Yeah. There was that."

Melvin settled into Carrie's guest bedroom while she checked her snail mail and home phone voice messages. Then they set out on foot for lunch.

"Ya oughta let this story die," Melvin said as they finished eating.

"Look. According to you, we just walked into the jaws of death in Las Vegas, came out unscathed, and here we are enjoying deep dish pizza in Chicago. How scary you think it'll be to spend time in D.C.? Interviewing *Members of Congress* no less. I'm gonna make sure Brenda's attacker gets what's coming to him."

"Don'tcha 'member what a *Congressman* did to Brenda? I can see why ya got problems with Michael. Sometimes you don't connect the dots too good."

Carrie clenched her jaw, facing yet another lecture.

"I'm gonna tell ya somethin' from what I know 'bout ya and what I learnt o'er time. You're headstrong, like a mule. And that's okay if ya wanna live yer life how ya want. It ain't okay if ya wanna partner with someone for life. People livin' together gotta bend a bit, like a reed. You're like a piece of rebar. Nobody hugs rebar."

Carrie furrowed her brow as she listened to Melvin. She crumpled the napkin in her hand. "Just because I'm a woman, you think I should only write about nursing babies and cake baking and bat mitzvahs? That's sex discrimination."

"It ain't got nothin' to do with yer sex. It's got everthin' to do with safety. How'd ya feel if Michael walked down dark alleys at night, huntin' for bad guys by himself? Why, you'd fear for his safety. You'd tell him to stop 'cause ya love him. And you'd be right. You'd be frustrated. Scared. Whatcha think he's goin' through?"

Carrie looked down and away, wringing the napkin in her hands. Twenty seconds passed. "I haven't thought about it too much from his point of view."

"Right. And when ya don't or can't do *that*, . . . whatcha call it?"

She dared meet Melvin's eyes, set deep in wrinkled sockets. "Self-centered?"

"Yup. Is Michael self-centered?"

"Not at all. He's wonderful. . . in every respect." Tears formed in Carrie's eyes.

"How'd ya feel if he was self-centered?"

"I'd. . . I'd. . . b-break off the relationship." A tear rolled down her cheek. She wiped it with her tattered napkin.

"Guess ya would at that. . . . Well, let's go see yer hooker friend."

Carrie phoned Brenda at home and on her cell and got voice mail on both. From a prior call to the hospital, she knew Brenda had been discharged. Carrie hailed a taxi, and they rode to Brenda's apartment building.

Halfway there, Carrie said, "You're a pretty amazing guy, Melvin."

"Yeah, that's me all right. *Mr. Amazing.*"

After pressing the button to Brenda's apartment several times, Carrie spotted the last name of the residents in the unit next to Brenda—Atwater. "Brenda said her neighbor, Susan Atwater, was going to help her. I'll buzz her apartment."

"Who is it?" Susan answered, sounding tense.

"It's Carrie Linden with a friend. I'm looking for Brenda Butler."

A loud buzz sounded and the lock on the building's entry door clicked. Melvin pulled the door open, and they walked into the lobby.

"Walk or ride?" Melvin asked.

"Let's take the elevator. I don't feel like hoofing it up five stories."

They ascended to the fifth floor. When the elevator doors parted, Carrie saw yellow police tape across Brenda's front door. Shocked, she turned toward apartment 51 and locked eyes with Susan Atwater who stood in her doorway, crying.

An hour passed and Susan's and Carrie's tears stopped flowing. Susan had finished relating all she knew about Brenda death.

"The police claim she committed suicide," Susan said. "I don't buy it."

"How did Brenda seem to you?" Carrie asked. "Depressed? Upset?"

"A little depressed…but it was like she had something to live for. Several times she said she was looking forward to talking with you about a career."

"Doesn't sound like someone preparing to take her life."

"I told the cops that too, but one of them mentioned she was a call girl. Maybe they didn't think it worth the effort to open up a homicide investigation on a…a…"

"It's okay," Carrie sniffed, "a dead hooker." She began crying again.

"Yeah." Susan coughed and wiped her eyes with a tissue.

For the first time, Melvin spoke up. "Carrie, why don't ya call Max? See what he can find out."

"Good idea. …Susan, there's a retired FBI guy we know, and he has friends in the Chicago PD. I'll get him to look into Brenda's death."

"My husband and I have really been frightened. We've never had a problem of any sort in this building. The cops said this was a one-off incident that wouldn't repeat. Still, all the residents are being extra cautious about letting people into the building and opening their apartment doors."

Carrie promised to contact Susan when she learned more about Brenda's death.

When Carrie and Melvin returned to her brownstone, she phoned Max.

Melvin sat on Carrie's oatmeal-colored living room couch, observing one side of the conversation, not commenting.

"Ms. Linden I presume. Home from safari?"

"Stop it, Max. I've got a big problem."

"When don't you?" Max asked, sounding annoyed.

"Brenda Butler's dead. The cops have called it a suicide, but I'm sure she was murdered. Max, she was thrown out her goddamn bedroom window!

"Her neighbor said she was talking about the future. She told me the people she worked for would kill her if she told anyone what she was doing and who with."

"Well did she?"

"Did she what?" Carrie asked.

"Tell anyone."

"Well, of course. She told me. But I didn't know the names of anyone she, uh, spent time with. And I only told Michael and you and, of course, Melvin."

"Melvin?" Max sounded surprised.

"He went with me to Las Vegas."

"So you involved old Melvin in your little quest, eh? I know the man is strong as an ox, but he's also seventy years old, Carrie. Don't you ever think about others before you put them in danger with your little crusades? Are you *that* selfish?"

"Enough. I've heard that twice today. I'm self-centered. Okay? Forget about me for a moment. Will you please contact your lieutenant buddy with the Chicago PD and see what you can learn about Brenda's death? Maybe they can take a closer look at her apartment or something. Please?"

"Sure, if you promise to call Michael and tell him everything that's going on. You have no idea the toll your behavior has taken on the lad these last few days."

"I will." They hung up.

"He gonna do it?" Melvin asked, arching his eyebrows.

"Yeah, but he says I'm self-centered too." She began to cry in earnest and buried her face in a throw pillow on the couch. She'd reached her stress limit.

Melvin lumbered into the kitchen. He grabbed a pair of Orangina's and avoided the bottle of whiskey, which he knew was collecting dust under the sink.

26

Just across the river from Georgetown University in Arlington, Virginia and minutes from the Smithsonian, Ruddock sat in front of a webcam in a Key Bridge Marriott hotel room. With interest, he watched a U.S. Senator engage in a full-on BDSM session. The degradation the Senator allowed and the pain inflicted, per his wishes, shocked even Ruddock. The Senator had first demanded the dominatrix bind his hands and feet with leather straps and lash his naked back, ass and genitals with the horse hairs at the end of a riding crop. They moved on to a golden shower, provided by the dominatrix, nipple clamps and more painful sado-masochistic activities. They managed to use every stick of furniture in the room for their games. *Ugh, I never want to stay in a hotel room again.*

Fortunately, the dominatrix didn't cover the Senator's head with a leather hood. She'd offered it, but he'd declined, saying something about claustrophobia. *Guess he has to draw the line somewhere. HA! Oh well, each to his own.* With his face in full view, no one could question *who* was featured prominently in the video.

While Ruddock packed up his techno gear after the rendezvous at the hotel, his cell phone rang. "Yes?"

"Good news, shit bird. We're now back up to fourteen girls, and we've hooked four more pols. Two more perverts to land and we'll be at full capacity."

"Good. I trust you received your expense money. Do I owe you more?"

"I received it, but I'm out another twenty-nine hundred and change."

"I'll put three grand in your post box tomorrow," he said.

"*So generous.* We've got the new johns lined up over the next three days. Unbelievable! Ellie May has seduced the lot of them. You know that whore from West Virginia? She's purring like an alley cat waiting for someone to open a tin of tuna."

"Good. I'll stay in the area to film them. Send me an email with the itinerary." *Can't wait to report this progress to Tony. Maybe I can squeeze extra cash out of him.*

"I suggest we move things along a little faster henceforth," she said.

"What do you have in mind?" *Why can't this broad just do her job?*

"We only need one solid video of these creeps to control them. Many of these pigs now only want to pay their fees and beat feet. They demand nothing in return. Guess their libido's shot. It's a cake walk for the girls. We could pay them a lot less if all they're doing is collecting pay envelopes. You and I could split the savings."

Greedy bitch, I mean butch. "I'll think about that. You know, very soon you'll be earning at the rate of three quarters of a mil a year—tax free."

"I love the sound of that."

"If all *you're* doing is running fourteen girls who collect pay envelopes, should I cut *your* pay and keep the rest?"

"You motherfucker. I'll slice your nuts off if you try to fuck me over."

"Then stick to the program. You're not exactly breaking a sweat as it is."

• • •

St. John threw her cell across her bedroom. It hit a deep purple cushioned chair and landed on the floor. She jumped from her king size poster bed, naked, and stomped around the room. That earned thumps on the condo ceiling below and some choice words from that neighbor about his right to quiet enjoyment of his property.

"What's the matter, honey?" the Georgetown coed asked with a whine. They'd taken a break from their evening of marathon sex for St. John to call Ruddock.

"I work so fucking hard. If it wasn't for me, that prick wouldn't make a dime. And he just threatened to cut my pay. MY FUCKING PAY! Sonofabitch. I'm the engine of this little cottage industry, and he has the audacity to *threaten* me."

"So is he going to cut your pay or not?" the coed asked.

"Not if I don't change the way the girls are paid." In a moment of bravado, St. John had shared with her Georgetown paramour how much she earned and how she made a living.

"Then don't fret about it. Your pay's intact. You make hell of a lot. My dad earns less than a quarter of what you bring in, and he spends much more time at it."

St. John looked at the coed, who'd come to a kneeling position on the bed, nipples erect. Naked, except for the ribbed, black strap-on dildo she sported.

"Come back to bed. I'm gonna take super care of you, you sexy devil."

St. John wiped away tears, smiled and rolled into bed beneath the coed.

• • •

One of Tony's cells chirped. He hoped it was Ruddock, calling to report, because he owed Shanghai a call with an update. *Too bad this operation will end soon.*

"Hello?" Tony answered, examining EZ-Bonds' paint-starved walls.

"It's Ruddock, boss. I'm calling to let you know we have the full complement of talent now and all but two of the targets are in play. I'll film four new ones over the next few days. My guess is we'll have all fifty-six targets in another week or so."

Tony sat in his executive chair, spinning around in circles. "Excellent, my boy, excellent! What news of our *pest* in Chicago? HEHEHE. I really like that term—*pest.*"

"As soon as I get these next four on film, I'll go to Chicago and treat the pest."

"Keep up the good work. Anything else?" *I've struck gold with this operation.*

"You remember the extra twenty large you gave me for recruiting? We only have two grand left. It's been costly. I'll put the surplus in your box when I get home."

"Keep it, kid. You've earned it. HEHEHE. Let me know when you've completed the work in Chi-town." Tony hung up, delighted in the report he'd now make to his Chinese clients.

Tony dialed the number in Shanghai, feeling justifiably proud of his success. As he glanced at his office, he wondered why he didn't take more pride in the space. *Maybe it's time to paint.*

"Report," the voice in Shanghai said. "We are quite eager to hear."

"All is in order. We have all but two targets in hand, and I'm sure those are right around the corner. Phase two of the operation is ready to proceed on your order."

"Superb. Keep us apprised." The line went dead in Shanghai.

Tony stood up and danced a quick jig around his office in his off-white custom linen suit.

27

Hundreds of billions of dollars and foreign currencies had poured into the worldwide stock markets, which were collectively up fifty-four percent in the past six months. Max set aside the *Wall Street Journal*. He cranked up the volume for the CNBC broadcast on the LCD screen in his living room. Maria Bartiromo was interviewing a small group of financial sages on the market's future. *According to these guys, I should be wearing a party hat. But these parties always fizzle. Pains me, but it's time to pull the plug.*

Max called his stock broker. Roland Ferguson had guided Max's investment portfolio for more than thirty years. Max trusted Roland's judgment but always reserved the right to reject Roland's advice, which he seldom did.

"Roland? . . . Max Foerce. I want out of the stock market. I want everything in cash or something solid like Treasuries. Maybe some gold and silver. Solid stuff."

"Are you kidding? We're in the strongest bull market for equities in history. All indications are the current run has legs that will continue through next year. You pull out now and you risk losing significant appreciation. My advice is wait another six to eight months, and then decide whether to sell. Do you need some cash?"

Max caught a glimpse of himself in a mirror as he paced in his living room. His knitted brow and frown told him everything he needed to know. "I'm afraid I'm not kidding, Roland. And I don't need cash at the moment. My portfolio's up close to sixty-seven percent year to date. I'm content with that, and you know the old saying about being a pig but not a hog when investing in the market. I don't relish becoming a hog when the slaughter comes. When can you fully cash me out of all equities?"

"Okay, I'll have you out by close of business today. I'll park the proceeds in cash reserves and have recommendations for you tomorrow about some safe alternatives. There are a few things better than Treasuries, yet quite conservative."

"Do it. Thanks Roland. We'll talk tomorrow." They disconnected.

That was painful. It'd be just my luck for my portfolio to climb another fifty points in the next six months. Well, like my daddy always said, "Appreciate what you have and don't whine over what might have been."

Max next dialed Lt. Jimmy Jablonski at his aging Chicago PD precinct.

He answered on the first ring. "Jablonski."

"Jimmy, it's Max Foerce."

"Hey buddy, I was thinking of you not two minutes ago."

"Why's that?"

"You remember your lady friend, name of Linden, who got attacked a few weeks back at Northwestern Memorial?"

"Yeah?" Max asked with apprehension. *Has something happened to her?*

"You'll recall Linden was visiting a patient when she was assaulted. There was a simultaneous murder attempt on that patient, name of Brenda, uh..."

"Butler," Max offered.

"Right. Brenda Butler. Well...Butler's dead. Took a flier out her apartment window a few days ago. The lame ass detectives assigned to the crime scene labeled it a suicide. Nice and tidy for the detectives, both of whom are close to retirement. Less leg work. Less paperwork. You know the story."

"Yeah, I've seen it before."

"Except for one thing. The ME found strangulation marks around her neck from someone with a very big hand. Said the bruising occurred *prior* to death."

Max glimpsed his image in the same mirror, nodding. "So she was murdered."

"Looks like. We've launched a homicide investigation. I hope your friend Linden will cooperate."

"*Believe* me, she will," Max replied.

"I've been babbling away here. What did you call for?" Jablonski asked.

"Nothing important. I'll call Linden and make sure she's available to you." They hung up and Max phoned Michael.

Michael's assistant answered, "Mr. Taylor's office. May I help you?"

"Cindy, it's Max. Is Michael in? I need two minutes for something important."

"That's about all he's got. He's walking into a client meeting."

A moment later, Michael picked up. "What's up, Max? I have very little time."

"Carrie called last night. She's home safe, but she learned Brenda Butler is dead. I just spoke with Jablonski in Chicago. Butler was murdered. Thrown out her apartment window. My guess is the doer's the guy who assaulted Carrie in the hospital." Max listened to silence for five seconds, imagining Michael's tension.

"Carrie's in danger," Michael said. "Can you babysit her right away?"

"I could, but Melvin Grimes is with her."

"Melvin? What's he doing there? . . . Never mind. . . . Forget Chicago for now. I'll ring her after I'm out of this meeting, and then we'll talk."

"She hasn't spoken with you?"

"No. Was she supposed to?" Michael asked.

"Go to your meeting. We'll talk later. Just know that she's safe for now."

When they hung up, Max phoned Carrie.

"Have you spoken with Michael?" Max asked knowingly.

"I've been struggling with what to say. But I'll definitely call him."

"Don't bother. He'll phone you in a few hours, so get your act together. In the meantime, I've made *my* call," he said sarcastically. "Jablonski confirmed Brenda's death was not a suicide. The medical examiner found strangulation marks on her neck that preceded her exit from the bedroom window. Expect a call from Chicago PD, and help them all you can."

"I knew it. I just knew it. Those lazy cops. I oughta. . ."

"You oughta take what happened to Brenda as a strong warning. The same could easily happen to you. Now get off your justice high horse and be aware of your surroundings at all times. Let Melvin know what I've told you, and tell him to be careful too. The cops have initiated a homicide investigation, and Michael and I will confer on steps to protect you."

Carrie gritted her teeth. "I'm fine. I don't need you guys to do anything."

"You don't get it. Maybe Michael can talk sense into you. I'm hanging up."

● ● ●

My stomach's in a knot. I can't treat clients like that. This has got to stop. Michael had pushed to finish the meeting in record time. He then phoned Carrie.

"Hi Michael. I was planning to call you today."

"For what purpose?" he asked.

"I, uh, I wanted to tell you about Las Vegas."

"So tell me." He rested his forehead in the crook of his thumb and pointer.

Carrie gave Michael the blow by blow story. "Melvin thinks Amici threatened us, but I disagree. Anyway, when we got home, we went to Brenda's apartment and discovered she'd been *murdered*. I guess Max told you. I'm so. . .so. . ." Carrie choked up and her voice broke.

"Carrie. Get hold of yourself and listen to me. I'm sorry about your friend, but she was involved in an illegal and very dangerous business. While she didn't deserve what happened, she knew the risks when she signed on."

"But Michael. . ."

"I said *listen*," he said hotly. "The police are on it. They're the *only* ones who should be investigating. That means *not you*. I gather you have no idea what you've stepped into, but I do. Don't forget. Every day I deal with people who've been involved in criminal, sometimes violent activities. You're in danger, believe it or not, because you got a look at the guy who assaulted you and Brenda. He's probably the same one who threw her out the window. And you've accused Tony Amici of masterminding the wholesale corruption of the U.S. Congress."

"But I…"

"I'm not finished. I'm flying out tomorrow for the weekend. When I get there, and not before, send Melvin home. I can't believe you involved that old gentleman again in one of your hair-brained schemes. You can risk your life if you want. But you don't have the right to put Melvin in jeopardy."

"I *didn't*. You're not being fair…"

"TONY AMICI IS A MASS MURDERER! …I don't know how else to explain it to you. Now please…buy some groceries and stay indoors with the locks thrown. I'll get there around mid-day tomorrow. We need to talk."

Michael slammed the receiver down. *This is the final straw.*

28

An *impressive list*, Carrie thought. From news reports, she'd cobbled together a total of 37 powerful U.S. Representatives and Senators whom the press had recently ridiculed for turning their backs on their long held and espoused principles. "Hey Melvin, the press have even hammered Senator Greg Chambers from Iowa."

Melvin picked up his morning mug of black coffee, got off the couch and stepped to Carrie's dining table to check her list. "Heck, I voted fer that guy every six years for thirty years. Thought he was on the up and up. Ya think he's one of 'em?"

She looked up at Melvin's downturned mouth and sagging jowls. *Maybe I shouldn't have said anything. Looks like I just burst his bubble.* "I may have gotten it wrong or perhaps the press did. Let's not condemn the man yet. He may be on the up and up as you say." *I oughta keep my mouth shut. Melvin's really been there for me.*

Melvin shuffled back to the living room, shoulders slumping.

Carrie followed him. "Thanks for all you've done, Melvin. I didn't have a right to involve you in any of this. Guess I wasn't thinking clearly. Maybe I was just feeding my obsession. You know, being self-centered."

"Ya did what ya had to do, and I kinda liked ridin' shotgun fer ya. I spent a decade doin' a lot worse things to child molesters."

"I know, but I don't want you to get hurt."

"I'm a big boy. I knew exactly what you was goin' up against, and I signed on fer the ride. I may be a country bumpkin, but I'm no fool."

Carrie walked around the back of the couch, wrapped her arms around Melvin's thick neck and kissed him on the cheek. "You are definitely not a fool. In fact, I think you're about the bravest man I've ever known. I don't want to take advantage of your generosity. You're like my foster dad, friend and confidant all rolled into one." She sniffed, and Melvin patted her arm.

"When's Michael showin' up?"

"Probably around noon, assuming his flight's on time."

"I should head out."

"I'm sure Michael wants to see you. Stay for lunch at least."

"Lil' girl, ya got an important life choice to make. I'm tellin' ya this like I'd tell my own kids. If ya wanna be with Michael, ya gotta quit this stuff. Write about somethin' else. Don't fool yerself into thinkin' ya can have it both ways. Life ain't like that. A sweet thing like you deserves a guy like Michael. But it's your choice."

Carrie sat in a side chair, listening to Melvin and massaging both temples with her fingertips. "It's just that I get all worked up about stuff like this, and I can't let it go. I'm sure Dr. Bernstein would tell me something like, 'This is characteristic of your self-destructive tendencies,' and he'd probably be right."

"Self-destructive or no, buck up and make a choice, kid."

They heard someone at the door working the Kaba Ilco heavy duty digital door lock on Carrie's front door. Max had installed it months ago after Carrie and Max were assaulted in her apartment. They stood up—tense, ready to...

Michael appeared in the open doorway.

Carrie ran to give Michael a loving hug, but he didn't return it in kind.

"You guys want some lunch?" Michael asked.

"I wouldn't turn down some more Grassano's pizza," Melvin replied.

Carrie and Michael stood on the sidewalk outside her brownstone apartment. They waved to Melvin as he started his old Chevy Tahoe and pulled away from the curb. "There goes a pretty special fellow," Michael said, "despite the fact that he's a serial killer of child molesters."

"Don't denigrate him."

"I'm merely stating a fact. He's otherwise decent, reliable and honorable."

They walked back into her apartment. Carrie grabbed two Orangina's from her refrigerator and handed one to Michael, already at rest on her couch.

"I'm not going to berate you for what you've done because you're intelligent, and you know everything I'd say about it."

"I'm sorry, I..."

"Save it, Carrie. There's something you don't know, but you should. I just learned myself a few weeks ago." He reached into a pocket of his roll-a-board luggage and extracted the hundred letters from Tony Amici to his mother. "Please read these in chronological order, and then we'll discuss the matter."

Carrie spent the next three hours on her couch, at the dining table and walking around her apartment fully engaged with the stack of letters Michael had handed her. After reading the final one, she inserted it back in its envelope and again examined the single photograph that accompanied one of the earliest letters. Without a doubt, it was a young version of the Tony Amici she'd just met in Las Vegas, only he had *ten* fingers showing. *How am I supposed to react to this?* Rather than commenting, she went to the bathroom to apply some makeup but mostly to buy time.

When she finally emerged, Michael asked, "Any thoughts?"

"It's a really weird coincidence," she said.

"To say the least. I found them in a box of my mother's possessions. It broke my heart when I discovered them and learned that a mobster had partly funded the first quarter century of my life. For all I know, he's still funneling clients to my practice."

"Oh Michael." Carrie approached him to give him a hug, but he turned away.

"So what if he's sending clients your way? You run a criminal law practice. Criminals need attorneys. You're handling your cases in a legal manner. Right?"

"Of course I am, but that's not the point. I can't continue my practice if I think I'm a lawyer for the mob. ...Being paid with mob money. Don't you see?"

What she *saw* were Michael's knitted brow, his reddened face and clenched fists. She sensed his anguish. *What can I say? This is so screwy.*

"I get it, and I'm sorry. ...Have you considered talking with Amici? From his letters, it's clear he's very proud of you. It's like he has affection for you from a distance. He obviously loved your mother...at least every letter was a love letter."

Michael arched a brow. "And maybe that drove my mother to alcoholism."

Ignoring the very touchy topic of alcoholism, she said, "You could ask him whether he's still sending you clients and, if so, tell him to stop."

"HA! I love you for your innocence, but your naïveté and penchant for getting into trouble are driving me nuts."

She ignored the dig. "Well it couldn't hurt to talk to him."

Carrie looked at her watch. "It's six-forty-five. Interested in dinner?"

"All right. Let's go to Roditys in Greektown."

Over a dinner of Greek salad, moussaka and Diet Coke, Carrie told Michael about the list she'd compiled of potentially corrupt politicians. "I'm going to D.C. on Sunday. I plan to interview as many of these folks as I can next week."

"Why do you think they'll talk to you? You think they'll admit they've been corrupted? How do you know you can even get an appointment with any of them?"

Carrie angrily set her pita bread and fork on her plate and looked Michael squarely in the eye. "Whatever you think about what I'm involved in, I'm a nationally recognized syndicated columnist and TV personality. There are men and women journalists who routinely risk their lives in war zones. I'm reporting from a different type of war zone. And I'm going to get this story. These jerks will make time to talk with me because of who I am. And I'll pull every trick in the book to make them slip up and spill the beans, even if it's only one bean they're hiding."

Michael shook his head. "I suppose if you're running around D.C., you'll be reasonably safe. Here, you're a sitting duck for the guy who killed Brenda."

They finished their dinner in silence. Carrie insisted on paying the check, and Michael deferred to her wishes. "I've made a decision, Michael. You and Max are officially off the hook. While I appreciate the things you guys have done for me, I absolve you of any responsibility for my well being. If you want to worry about me, that's on you. I'm an adult. I support myself. People care about what I say and write. And I make my own decisions about what I do, where I go and whom I meet."

Michael stared at her for several seconds. "Guess that's it then. I'll have to start thinking differently about you. I'm sorry it's come to this."

"Me too," she said regretfully, though she now understood Michael wanted a different type of woman—someone who played life safely from the sidelines.

They spent Saturday, mostly in silence. Michael prepared an opening argument for an upcoming trial while Carrie drafted her interview questions for next week.

29

En route to O'Hare, Carrie and Michael squinted at the morning sunlight through the Town Car's windows. Preoccupied with what now seemed a failed relationship, Their limited and businesslike conversation cast a chill over the forty minute ride. Michael counted down every minute of it, hoping Carrie would relent.

When they exited the cab and retrieved their luggage from the trunk, Carrie asked, "What flight are you on?"

"United six-ten. It leaves at ten-fifty-five. You?"

"Same, except you're probably in first. I'm in coach."

"Want me to try to upgrade you? I can…"

"No. I'm fine with my seat. See you." Carrie turned on her heels and left Michael standing curbside. She entered the terminal and disappeared from view.

• • •

Carrie boarded the airplane and walked past Michael in his first class seat without acknowledging him. As she navigated down the narrow aisle in coach she began to cry. A flight attendant stepped close and helped her stow her roll-a-board.

"Are you okay Miss? Can I get you anything?"

"I'll be fine thanks." Carrie plopped down in her window seat, buckled up and turned to face the window for the duration of the flight.

What have I done? I love him so much. Why can't I be like other women?

She recovered from her negative self-talk by planning the week ahead. Over the past few years, she'd interviewed a few of the Representatives and Senators on her list. It'd be a cinch to land meetings with them, particularly since she'd treated them fairly and pretty favorably in her articles.

But I can't dilly-dally with the rest. Can't afford to stay in D.C. for weeks. I'll need to hit the phone first thing tomorrow morning. Try to line up as many interviews as I can. I'll drop a few names. That'll help open a few doors.

The plane landed close to 2 PM. Carrie breathed a sigh of relief when she deplaned and discovered Michael had vanished. He hadn't waited for her. If he'd been there, she might have leapt into his arms and begged him to take her back. *I need time. The more time that passes, the stronger I'll feel about not having him in my life.*

Carrie boarded the yellow line Metrorail at Reagan National Airport. At the Gallery Plaza–Chinatown station, she switched to the red line and rode it the rest of the way. She arrived at the Bethesda Metrorail station on Wisconsin Avenue near the Bethesda Hyatt Regency. While not as posh as the Park Hyatt in Chicago, she'd previously discovered this comfortable business class hotel. It fit her needs perfectly, particularly its close proximity to inexpensive public transportation.

After a quick continental breakfast Monday morning, she first called the politicians with whom she could easily score interviews.

When executive secretaries asked the purpose of her interview, Carrie used a pre-planned cover story—she was writing an article, focused on the challenges of serving in high office today. Her readers would find fascinating the difficulty and hard work required to serve in Congress. The story played to every politician's ego, and their schedulers quickly realized that Carrie's column would run in every national and significant regional newspaper in the U.S. That meant free favorable press.

Five calls later, she had five interviews lined up, spread over four consecutive days. With the easy ones behind her, she continued dialing for interviews. Thirty-two calls later, she'd racked up seventeen more. This didn't exhaust her list of possible corrupt politicians, but it made a huge dent in it. Over the course of one week, she'd have a shot at twenty-two, and she'd put each one on the Linden interview grill.

Carrie changed into a cotton khaki skirt and jacket that covered a white cotton tank top. She slipped on a pair of chestnut brown Kate Spade flats, picked up her briefcase and headed to the Bethesda Metrorail station. Disembarking at Gallery Plaza–Chinatown, she hailed a taxi to Capitol Hill to begin her series of interviews.

Fifteen minutes into her first meeting, the interview hit a wall. Representative Bobbie McKay, a sixty-three-year-old politician who headed the House Judiciary Committee, went blank. He stared at a wall behind Carrie, not exactly crying though a few tears streamed down his face. Carrie had asked, "Why are you trampling on your long held principles? It's like you're being blackmailed. Am I right?"

Bobbie either wouldn't or couldn't speak. Was he in a trance? She waited three long minutes. "Congressman? . . .Congressman, would you like to continue?"

No response.

Carrie opened his office door and asked the secretary to check on Bobbie.

"Congressman? . . .Bobbie?" The secretary walked around his desk and touched his shoulder. "Bobbie, are you okay? . . .Bobbie?" She shook his arm.

He looked up at her and said, "Ginny, I'm not feeling well. I'm going home."

Ginny ushered Carrie out with a don't-even-think-about-coming-back glare.

The next three Monday interviews went south too. Carrie modified her questions to be less confrontational. But when she probed anything related to someone or some force controlling Congressional behavior, they clammed up, politely ended the interviews or, as happened in one instance, ordered her from the office.

Tuesday and Wednesday went mostly the same. Eleven consecutive smiling faces to start in eleven well-appointed offices with eleven enthusiastic comments about meeting a Pulitzer prize-winning syndicated columnist. All followed by various negative emotional reactions to her questioning. A few enraged, others distraught, another catatonic like Bobbie McKay. A few drew upon their slick political skills to terminate the interviews without seeming upset even though she'd disturbed their day.

Wednesday night, Carrie pondered her experiences of the last few days over salad and strip steak at Morton's in the Bethesda Hyatt. *I'm definitely hitting a raw nerve, but I'm not learning anything.* Then, eating a slice of cheesecake, she realized something. *Congress is a very small community. I've stirred up a lot of emotion with fifteen of these folks. But the word isn't out about me. Nobody's calling around saying, 'Watch out for Carrie Linden. Don't let her in your office.' You'd think by now they'd be battening down the hatches, but they aren't. What's it mean?*

As she brushed her teeth, preparing for bed, it dawned on her. *They're not talking about me because none of them know who in Congress is involved. They're all being individually blackmailed. They have no idea it's a coordinated strike.*

Representative Jimmy Novotchin from Chicago, initially happy to see Carrie, had his security detail escort Carrie from his office. But she'd hit the mother-of-all interviews. Throughout their brief meeting, and before things got hot, he chewed on a cigar and incessantly flipped open and snapped shut a solid gold lighter. Annoying, just like Brenda had said. "Where'd you get that good looking lighter?" she'd asked.

"Bought it in Vietnam when I was stationed there in the military," he'd said.

30

An article appeared in the *Washington Post* Friday morning, commenting about an impending meeting today about the stock market. The U.S. Treasury Secretary, Federal Reserve Chairman and Chairman of the Securities and Exchange Commission were teed up to consult with the chiefs of seven major Wall Street investment and banking firms.

Carrie read the article with interest. Her eyes came to a standstill when she saw a familiar name. One of the players included Archibald Graystone, CEO of Morgan Smithe and a former college fraternity brother and close friend of her father's. Uncle Archie, as she used to call him, periodically dined with Carrie and her dad when visiting Chicago. Graystone had risen to the pinnacle of his industry.

Carrie surfed the internet and found Morgan Smithe's corporate office phone number. She dialed it and was bounced to six different people until the sixth person, a woman with a British accent, asked, "What is your business with Mr. Graystone?"

"My name is Carrie Linden. My father, before he passed, was a very close friend of Mr. Graystone. Actually, Mr. Graystone was Uncle Archie to me while I was growing up. I'm now a national syndicated columnist, and I happen to be in Washington, D.C.. I saw in the paper that Archie's here today, and I wondered if I could get on his calendar for ten minutes. I'll be happy to show up anywhere in town at anytime." Carrie crossed her fingers as she listened to the pause in the conversation.

"I'm sorry. Mr. Graystone has a very full schedule. That won't be possible."

"Can't you call him and tell him I'm in D.C. I need only ten minutes. I'm certain he'll want to see me."

"I hesitate to disturb him over this. He's quite busy," she said in a curt way.

"Were I you, I'd hesitate *not* to call him about this. My father and I were very close to Uncle Archie." Carrie had no problem playing hard ball with gate keepers. These people shared one goal in common—protect the boss' schedule.

After a five second delay, the gate keeper said, "Please give me a telephone number where I can reach you. I can't promise anything, and you should not get your hopes up." After capturing Carrie's cell number, she disconnected.

Eight minutes later, Carrie's cell phone buzzed. "This is Carrie Linden."

"Mr. Graystone asked me to convey his apologies. Today is an extremely busy day. His calendar is overloaded."

"Never mind." Carrie was about to hang up.

"Allow me to finish." The gate keeper paused as if hating to deliver the message. "Mr. Graystone apologizes that he can give you only ninety minutes."

"YES!" Carrie exclaimed.

"Be at a restaurant named, Le Lion D'Or, at six for dinner."

"I'll be there with bells on honey. Thanks." Carrie disconnected and danced around her hotel room for several seconds. *I'll tell Uncle Archie what I think's going on with Congress. Maybe he can give me some guidance. Now, what to wear?*

They spent the first twenty minutes catching up and ordering dinner. "I'm very happy you called, my dear. I regret we didn't stay in touch after your dad passed, but I've been very proud of your success. I frequently tell people that I know you when they talk about your articles or see you on TV. Makes me feel close to a celebrity."

"Nonsense," Carrie replied with a smile. She studied the silver-haired slim man seated before her. Archibald Graystone fit the stereotype of a financial tycoon with his charcoal silk and wool hand-stitched suit, coifed hair and the dozens of heads that had turned to greet him in Le Lion D'Or. But when she looked at the playfulness in his hazel eyes, she remembered Archie laughing with her dad and playing hide-and-seek with her years earlier. He had a nice smile, though he'd never had his teeth veneered.

"Since we've not seen each other in years, was there a particular reason you wanted to get together, other than the fact we're both in the same city at the moment? Mind you, I'm happy to break bread with you in any event."

"As a matter of fact, there is." Carrie related the entire story about Brenda Butler, her contention about a scheme to blackmail members of Congress and Carrie's own research into dozens of Representatives and Senators who've been moving in opposite directions of late, compared with their voting and political histories. She also told him about the curious interviews she'd had the last four days and the few she had today that had ended in the same manner.

By the end of her tale, Archie's face had turned alabaster. He extracted a small silver pillbox from his breast pocket and removed a white tablet. With a trembling hand, he put it in his mouth and bit into it. He swallowed the ground up pill, throwing his head back with a swig of water.

"What was that?" Carrie asked.

"An aspirin. I started to feel heart palpitations. I took it as a prophylactic."

"I'm sorry if I've upset you. Should we get you to a doctor or hospital?"

"You haven't upset me, my dear, but your story has. I don't need medical attention at this time, but can we speak off the record?" He leaned across the table.

"Certainly." Carrie leaned in so she could hear Archie's voice, which had shrunk several decibels.

"The meeting I attended today concerned what's happening in the stock market. It's bloated. Money is flowing in at an unprecedented rate worldwide, and company valuations are skyrocketing. Many in government and the investment community worry another balloon is being created, and it will likely burst. That would devastate Wall Street and Main Street. We've speculated about the link between what's happening on Capitol Hill and how it affects the market, but we never imagined there might be a deliberate strategy to influence world markets. Until now."

"What do we do? I mean, what should I do? I know someone who's tight with the FBI. I could call him." She felt her heart racing.

Archie looked down at the uneaten medallions of veal the waiter had set before him. He then stared into Carrie's eyes. "You're like your father, you know. Always ferreting out the truth of things. He'd be very proud of you."

"Thanks, but what now?" she pressed.

"Now? You do nothing. I'll talk with people and call you in a day or two."

"I'm not very good at doing nothing," she said. "Last weekend I broke up with the man I love because he insisted that I not pursue this matter."

"Sounds like a wise man. He must love you a great deal because what you're digging into could mean your death, likely at the hands of some very unsavory characters. Please. Give me a day or two." He glanced at his watch—6:43 PM.

"Do you have to go? I thought we had until seven-thirty."

"In light of your revelations, I need to return to work immediately. We could be on the verge of a global calamity. If the U.S. develops a financial cold, the rest of the world will come down with pneumonia or worse."

31

Ruddock sat across from Tony Amici in EZ-Bonds. He marveled at the way Tony conducted business. Tony kept the details, even the most picayune, of every one of his nefarious enterprises in his head, categorized in some amazingly organized form. In an instant and when needed, he could download and verbalize dates, names, places, money matters and more. No one would ever find a slip of paper, containing one iota of information about Tony's illegal operations. At least not in Tony's hands or by his hand or in his vicinity. *If something ever happens to his brain, we'll be in a helluva mess. I probably don't know everything about the operation I'm running.*

He'd returned from D.C. after filming the latest politicians lured into their sex trap. After a few more episodes, Ruddock and St. John would confront the new johns with Tony's demands, and he figured they'd reluctantly comply as all the others had.

One of St. John's girls needed to land one last Senator, and they'd be at capacity. The Chairman of the Senate Committee on Foreign Relations, Senator Blane Merryweather, had been a challenge. He'd served in the Senate for thirty-four years and socialized very little, making access to him difficult. But a big event at the White House loomed on the horizon. Merryweather was scheduled to attend. At sixty-eight and, by all accounts, unhappily married to a cocaine addict, he made a perfect target.

"Where do we stand?" Tony asked, giving Ruddock *the look.*

"We've landed fifty-five of the fifty-six targets you gave us. The outstanding one, Merryweather, is in our crosshairs. I'd guess we're two weeks away from getting anything on him. I'll keep you thoroughly briefed."

"No repercussions? Nobody whining or threatening to go to the authorities?"

"Nothing thus far. They're all behaving like good little soldiers."

"I want to know immediately if you get a whiff of any threats."

"I'm on it, boss." *How much could it cost him to give me an at-a-boy?*

"What about our little pest in Chicago?" Tony smiled at the word 'pest.'

"I've checked many times a day every day for several days. Linden's not home. Don't know where she is. As soon as she gets back, I'll pay her a memorable visit." *I'm feeling like Rodney Dangerfield here. No respect.*

"All right. I've got a call to make. Go get coffee, and we'll reconvene in thirty minutes." He looked away from Ruddock—a clear signal to leave.

Ruddock slipped out the front door of EZ-Bonds and strolled down the street to a coffee shop two blocks away. *What's going on? Maybe if he'd let me in on a few details I could help out more. Maybe I could make more too. But Tony probably doesn't want that. Stingy bastard. . . . Some suit he has on today. Another custom job no doubt. Maybe I oughta have some suits tailor made. Dress up a bit more.*

• • •

Tony speed-dialed the number in Shanghai, and the man with the Chinese accent answered, "Report." The connection was clear as a bell. Tony felt anxious with every call. He was used to being the boss, the chief client, the arbiter, the final decision-maker. Now he reported to others. *Reminds me of my relationship with my father, the unforgiving prick. Good thing he's been dead for thirty-odd years.*

"The operation's running smoothly," Tony said. "All targets but one are under my control and performing as expected. No problems. I've kept abreast of their impact. The results are quite favorable." Tony sat on the edge of his chair at attention with his chest puffed out like a frigatebird's red throat pouch during mating season.

"Yes. We have seen a range of forty-nine to one hundred seventy-four percent growth, depending on company, industry and geography, of course. We are most pleased. The results have exceeded our projections. We are considering a bonus for you when this is over. Of course, we will need to verify that our forecasts are met in phase two. You have not launched yet, correct?"

"Correct. When will I receive your order to pull the trigger?" *C'mon you fucking gook, I want to know when to sell my stock holdings.*

"The growth trajectory is slowing. We expect things to crest in another month or so. We will let you know when to, as you say, pull the trigger."

All right. It's about time to cash in. "Can you advise me about, uh, you know... selling?" Tony asked.

"Were I you, I would begin now. Do it in waves to avoid notice. Do not share this counsel with anyone. If you do, we will definitely know, and you will not like the consequences."

Tony had no idea that the group in Shanghai had begun discreetly selling their holdings two months earlier. Unbeknownst to Tony, they owned tens of billions of dollars of equity in public companies around the globe through hundreds of separate brokers worldwide allocated to thousands of fictitious owners. No single stock position reached the level that would require filings with governmental entities such as the U.S. Securities and Exchange Commission. Liquidating their holdings and simultaneously preserving their gains required a discreet, smooth and stealthy selling protocol over a period of months. They'd launched a carefully choreographed sales dance to cash in gains without spooking the market as they converted their enormous global portfolio to U.S. dollars.

"Understood," Tony replied. "When should I be completely out?"

"Before we pull the trigger." The man laughed and cut the connection.

Tony picked up his EZ-Bonds hard line and dialed Fortuna Financial Advisors in Las Vegas. "Mario, this is Tony. I want out of the market. I've had a good run last year and this, but it's time to sell." *Hehehe, I'm making a shitload.*

"Tony, my friend. The market's really heating up. Selling's premature."

Tony smiled knowingly. "What do you care? You get paid whether I buy or sell. I want to deploy my capital in other ways. Sell everything in four equal blocks. Sell the first three over the next ten to twelve days. Use your own judgment on timing. Hold on selling the fourth block until you hear from me. Put it all in cash."

"But Tony, listen a moment..."

"Process my order, and don't argue with me," he said harshly.

"I'll convert one-fourth of your holdings to cash by close of business today."

Tony hung up and snapped his thumbs with a self-satisfied smirk on his face. *Knowledge is everything. My portfolio's up two million and counting. Wonder how the guys in Shanghai are doing? Those fucking gooks are probably raking in tens of millions.*

• • •

Ruddock rejoined Tony forty minutes after he left for coffee. "What's next boss?" He didn't know what else they could possibly discuss at this point.

Tony adjusted his diamond studded cufflinks. "What's next is this...maybe I shouldn't tell you so soon, but I want you to be mentally prepared. Do not, under any circumstances, speak a word of what I'm about to say to St. John."

"By the way, boss, how do you know St. John?"

"She was referred to me. That's all you need to know. And stop interrupting. What I have to tell you is vital."

Ruddock leaned forward, eyebrows raised.

"In a few weeks, you'll deliver new demands to our friendly politicians. You'll give the same specific demand to each one. You will *not* deliver their orders until directed by me. Clear?" Tony stared a hole through Ruddock.

"Yes sir." Ruddock sat up straight as a board.

"You will direct them to take up where they left off before you turned them."

Ruddock sucked in a deep breath. "You mean I'll ask them to flip flop?"

"Correct."

"That should make them very happy."

"I don't give a good goddamn whether they're happy, sad or dead for that matter. When I give the order, be prepared to turn the herd back the opposite way."

32

Sunday morning, Carrie packed her bags to catch a late afternoon flight to Chicago. Uncle Archie had frustrated her. *Another man telling me what I can and can't do. Well, maybe I can't do anything about a global financial meltdown, but I can put Jimmy 'the torturer' Novotchin in prison. Maybe the jerk had Brenda killed too.*

In a huff, she called Max.

"Hello Ms. Linden. I'm surprised to hear from you," he said sarcastically as he sat on his living room sofa, watching CNBC report on the market's continued rise.

"Cut the crap, Max. Just because Michael and I've split doesn't mean I can't have a civil conversation with him or you for that matter."

"Okay, okay. What can I do for you?"

"First off, don't think about it that way. I don't want you to do anything for me. I want you to help me do something for the sake of justice, for the sake of America. I need you to help me remove a piece of slime from the U.S. Congress."

"Which slime ball on Capitol Hill did you have in mind?" he chuckled. "There are so many, it's hard to know where to start."

Carrie related the gist of the twenty-two interviews she'd conducted. She told Max how she all but accused each one of being blackmailed. She detailed their reactions. Carrie offered her hypothesis that someone's blackmailing all of them individually.

"Hmm, I'm impressed you were able to connect with so many of these folks in such a short period. I'm not surprised they gave you the bum's rush, given what you accused them of. But I do think you're onto something. Still, what you've got is pretty thin. …The FBI will need something more concrete to work with."

Carrie didn't share her discussion with Uncle Archie. He'd asked her to keep their exchange off the record, and she'd agreed to maintain his confidence.

"Okay, I'll zero in on one slime ball in particular. Brenda specifically told me, while she was lucid, that she was having sex with a senior level Congressman who smoked Cuban cigars and carried a gold lighter he bought while serving in the military during the Vietnam War. Said he had an irritating habit of constantly snapping it open and shut. In my presence, Representative Jimmy Novotchin chewed on a cigar and he fiddled with a gold lighter in exactly the same way."

"Ahem, uh Carrie, coincidences like that are insufficient. I can't go to my old buddies at the FBI..."

Carrie interrupted. "Max, shush and listen. ...I complimented Novotchin on the lighter and asked where he'd acquired it. He said, and I quote, 'I bought it in the 60s when I served in Vietnam.' I bet there'd be a match between the bits of tobacco they plucked from Brenda's back and the brand of cigars that pig smokes."

"Oooo, you've piqued my interest, girl," Max said. "That's practically death-bed testimony from Brenda and possibly concrete forensic evidence, albeit circumstantial. Hmm...maybe someone can place him at The Drake Hotel on the same date when Brenda was attacked. I bet they still have security video available. I'd better get to the Chicago PD before Drake security erases what they've got."

"Novotchin may have had her killed too," Carrie said, breathing excitedly.

"Mmm, maybe. From my experience, that'd be a stretch for a Congressman, but he could have outsourced it. You know, hired it done."

"Yeah. ...Well, where do we go from here?" Carrie tugged at her hair.

"*We* go no place. This is a matter for the authorities, local and Federal. Local because it involves assault and battery and murder. Federal because a Member of Congress is the person of interest. I'd like you on the phone when I call Jablonski on Monday. But I'll need to think about whom we call at the Bureau. If they can build a case against this bastard, they'll bring him down. The Feds hate corrupt politicians. Me too. Taking one out of circulation, especially one from Chicago, would be a rush."

Carrie paced her hotel room, listening to Max's energy rising at the prospect of nailing a Congressional felon. He had the bit in his teeth along with her.

"You think we can nail this guy in the next few days or weeks?" she asked with a smile on her face as she jabbed the air like a prize fighter.

"Realistically? No. But we might take him offline in a few months. Trust me. I'm all over this now."

"So we're good, eh?" She stood with her fingers crossed.

"Yeah. You did good, kid. Let's go get 'em.'"

33

Ruddock arrived in Chicago late Sunday morning. With little to do for the next few days vis-à-vis the politicians, he holed up at Airport Hilton, ready to deal with Carrie straightaway if she appeared. He phoned her again. No answer.

He checked into the hotel, turned on the TV and watched *Mission Impossible III* on demand. While his escapades didn't involve the high tech and outlandish action sequences of the film, his challenges often seemed close to impossible. When the movie ended, he called Carrie another time. No response.

A look at the room service menu made him gag. And none of the restaurants advertised in the hotel guide appealed to him. *Oh what the hell, I'll train into town and dine at NoMI's. It was great the first time.* He dialed the restaurant for reservations and scored a table at 7 PM.

Ruddock dressed in all black. A Tommy Bahama silk tee with chinos, soft leather shoes and a lightweight Polo jacket. He caught the train to downtown.

The next order of business concerned determining the kind of message to deliver to Linden. It'd be violent. But how violent and what type of violence?

Throughout his late teens and throughout adulthood, he'd perpetrated diverse acts of savagery on men and women alike, including murder. *Tony told me to deliver a message. That implies she should survive. Don't know why he won't let me kill her. That'd permanently solve the problem. It'd add to my headcount too. . . . Oops, I forgot. I decided to stop counting after twenty.*

She obviously can take a punch. I laid her out pretty good in Brenda's hospital room, and she came charging back after that. Could slap her around a little to get her undivided attention and have a very hard talk with her. Then again, melius abundare quam deficere. Better too much than not enough. Perhaps it should be enough to put her in the hospital. Hate to mess up that pretty face. Could rape her. . . . Naw, that'd probably piss her off. Break a bone or two? Hmm, lots of options.

Before he sat down for dinner, Ruddock made another call to Carrie's home. She answered on the second ring, and he immediately hung up.

He ordered a glass of the expensive Opus One Cabernet that he enjoyed on his last visit. After reviewing the menu, he selected fois gras and kumquat terrine as a starter, followed by prime beef filet with sides of roasted acorn squash and steak cut fries. The dinner order behind him, he stared out at Lake Michigan from his table next to the wall of windows in NoMI's. *Time to get down to business.*

During dinner, Ruddock made two important decisions. First, he would not inflict any permanent physical damage, although she'd likely never forget what he'd do. The impact on her psyche *would* be permanent. *She'll crawl into a mental cocoon to avoid thinking about me. She'll fear leaving her home or picking up the phone for months. I can always return to escalate the message if needed.*

A beating. That's what it'll be. A methodical, punishing beating. I'll deliver verbal warnings between each round of blows. The message? . . . 'Stop investigating anything related to Brenda Butler.'

Simple enough. With his size and strength, he knew he could knock her out with one punch, so he'd have to pull his punches to prolong her agony and drive the message home. *Open hand. That's it, a lot of open hand blows. Maybe some body punches thrown in for good measure. That's the ticket.*

Second decision: he would not give Carrie or the authorities any way to identify him as the perpetrator. She'd seen him with Brenda, but his image must not have registered because she bumped into him at EZ-Bonds and looked him straight in the face without reacting.

He patted the breast pocket of his Polo jacket to confirm the presence of the folded balaclava he'd brought to cover his head. The thin leather gloves in another pocket would ensure no fingerprints. They'd also prevent cuts to his hands that could leave pesky blood traces behind. The good folks at the Nevada State Prison had taken his DNA without his consent when he'd spent ten months in a six by eight foot cell as their involuntary guest. It wouldn't do to leave blood evidence.

Dinner ended with a snifter of Chambord liquor over ice. *Time to go.*

• • •

Carrie had finished unpacking her suitcase and briefcase when the phone rang. No one was on the line. *Wrong number,* she figured. After plowing through a week's worth of snail mail and mentally exhausted, she took a shower, dried her hair and dressed in a *Boyz N The Hood* t-shirt, jeans and cordovan loafers. *Wish Melvin was here. We could go to Grassano's together for pizza. Guess I'll bring his share home.*

She closed her apartment door behind her. The Kaba Ilco digital lock automatically secured the door, but she also threw the two deadbolts that Max had installed last year with the high tech lock. *No point making it easy to break in.*

At 8:30 PM, the streets turned dark and empty. Carrie set out for Grassano's with a spring in her step. Tomorrow morning, she'd brief the Chicago PD about Novotchin as well as someone from the FBI. They'd start building a case on the pervert. Her D.C. fishing expedition wound up a good investment. She'd caught a whale. Carrie smiled as she walked on a trodden path through a heavily treed city park that took up an entire city block. Crossing through the park was a shortcut to the pizza parlor. A block later, she stepped into Grassano's, unaware someone had followed her.

Ruddock sat on a bench outside and across the street from Grassano's, observing Carrie through a plate glass window. When she made to leave, he high-tailed it back to the heavily treed park she'd traversed on her way to the restaurant.

Carrie left Grassano's, carting four slices of pepperoni pizza in a box. She ruminated over how to stay active in the Novotchin case. Everyone would try to block her participation every step of the way. She smiled as she imagined the headlines she'd write. *It'll be a fitting eulogy for Brenda and a shot across the bow to the rest of those creeps on Capitol Hill. Now for a good night's sleep and an exciting day tomorrow with the PD and the FBI. I can't wait.*

• • •

Ruddock waited for her in the park, which stood devoid of any human traffic. Darkness had consumed this hot summer night. The absence of a moon weighed in his favor, and the trees blocked any view of the ground from neighboring apartment buildings. He pulled on the balaclava and slipped into his black gloves, pushing the leather snugly into the crooks between his fingers. The leather creaked as the gloves stretched over his large fists.

As Carrie ambled through the park on her way home, a large dark form unexpectedly appeared in her path. "What's..."

Carrie didn't utter another word. Couldn't. A right hand slap with an upward trajectory struck the left side of her face. It lifted her off her feet, and she went soaring. The pizza box flew in the opposite direction. She landed on a patch of grass.

Then he was on her. Squatting over her upper chest and neck, kneeling on both her biceps. He pinned her to the ground. Ruddock put a gloved hand over her mouth. Carrie tried to bite him, but he clamped her jaw shut. She wriggled beneath him. Lifted her legs to knee him in the back. He was too far up. No leverage.

"Pay close attention. *Stop investigating anything related to Brenda Butler.* Otherwise, I'll return. And you won't survive my next visit."

He removed his hand from her mouth. She started to scream, but he back-handed the right side of her face. Blood streamed from her mouth and nose, which now tilted to one side. The opposing nostril had torn a little from her upper lip. Holding her hands against the ground, he rose up and dropped his knees onto her biceps with considerable force. She winced and sucked in a painful breath.

He slapped her face and neck. He leaned toward her head and reissued the verbal warning, *"Stop investigating anything related to Brenda Butler."* Ruddock worked his way down her torso with his palms and the backs of his hands, striking her breasts, rib cage and stomach. He paused a few ticks to see if she was conscious. Confirming she was, he continued the beating. When he reached her hips, he balled his massive hands into fists and laid into the tops and sides of her thighs.

Ruddock interrupted the beating for two seconds. He swiveled his head in a 270 degree arc to check the area. *Deserted.* He placed his heavy hand on her forehead and used a thumb to pry open an eyelid. She blinked and moaned. *Still conscious.*

He whispered in her ear, "You think we're done here? Oh no. I've only tenderized *one* side. Remember. *Stop investigating anything related to Brenda Butler."* He rolled Carrie onto her stomach and straddled her. Using his fists, he pounded her shoulders and back, kidneys, buttocks and thighs. Precise strikes to cause severe bruising, some internal bleeding and a multi-day stay in whatever hospital she landed after the EMS guys scraped her up off the ground.

After punishing her backside using his fists as meat mallets, he flipped her limp body over. She was out, but breathing. Ruddock stood. For good measure he kicked the bottom of each foot soccer style, like driving in game winning fifty yard field goals. Carrie lay sprawled on the ground in an awkward heap. As he strolled out of the park, he removed his balaclava and gloves, prideful of the pain he'd inflicted.

He dialed 911, refusing to identify himself, and briefly summarized Carrie's condition and location. After all, Tony ordered him to deliver a message, not whack the chick. And she really needed medical attention.

Ruddock then lifted his wrist to eye level and examined his Rolex Submariner. High on adrenaline, he thought, *Huh, am I good or what? A skilled, surgical beating in less than ninety seconds. Plus another thirty seconds for the 911 call. Masterful. That bitch will be pissing blood for days. . . .I oughta get a bonus for this. Tony? Message fucking delivered!*

34

Monday morning, Max's cell phone rang. He stood and turned off the CNBC stock market report he'd been watching, regretting he'd not hung onto his portfolio of stocks a little longer. Snagging his phone off the fireplace mantle, he examined the caller ID and answered.

"Max? Jablonski here."

"Hey Jimmy. I thought we were on for this afternoon."

"We were. You know your friend Linden?"

"Yeah?" Max caught his reflection in the mirror over his fireplace. His brow already bunched together with a grim look on his face.

"She got any relatives?"

"Not that I know of. Why?" His heart started pounding.

"Well, somebody better get out here. EMS picked her up late last night. Looks like a couple of pricks practically beat to death."

"Holy shit!" Max closed his eyes and clenched his jaw.

"Yeah. Sorry. She's back in Northwestern Memorial."

"How bad?"

"She'll live. Plenty of heavy bruising all over her body. A few lacerations. Maybe a busted rib or two. Listen. This wasn't a mugging. Her purse still held money and credit cards. Jewelry's intact. It wasn't your garden variety beating either. . . .I'd say she was tortured. In a frigging *decent* part of town. Maybe two or three perps."

"Damn it! Any witnesses? Evidence? Statement from Carrie?"

"No, no and not yet. It happened out of sight in a neighborhood park. Whoever these guys were knew how to inflict pain and cover their tracks. Linden's unconscious. My guess is when she *can* give a statement she won't have much we can work with."

"This is gonna rock her boyfriend. Ah. . .we'll be out later today. Before we sign off, I'll brief you on what we would have told you on our call today." And he did.

"Huh. Never liked Novotchin. Guy's a liar and a general prick. Can't believe that creep's still in office. I'll call The Drake. Head of security there was a former Chicago cop. I know him. If there's anything on their video history, he'll find it. He hates Novotchin even more than I do, so he'll really scrutinize their database. We're gonna get these sons of bitches. I don't like this kind of shit goin' down in my town."

"Just remember, we're looking for a clear image of the Congressman entering or leaving The Drake on the same day and around the time of Brenda Butler's ordeal."

"Got it." They disconnected.

Holy hell. This'll be a blow to Michael. He took a few seconds to gather his wits and prepare for the call. *No time to brew over this.* Max dialed Michael's office.

Michael's anger was palpable. "Look, Michael. Finish up whatever you're doing. I'll make reservations for us to Chicago this afternoon. I'm sorry to say, but I think her trip to Las Vegas caused this. Too bad she didn't listen to us."

"Tell me she's going to make it," Michael said in a voice tinged with anguish.

"Jablonski says she will. She's a tough cookie. She'll pull through. I'll see you at Reagan National about two o'clock in the United terminal."

Max made travel arrangements and packed two bags, anticipating an extended stay in Chicago. Then he called an old friend at the FBI's Washington Field Office.

"Maximum Force! Man, we sure miss you around here. We were just talking about you the other day. How are you?"

"Personally? Quite well. As a private citizen, I'm very disturbed."

"Uh-oh, I know that tone. What's up?"

Max briefed John Wyatt about Carrie's mishap. Then he backed up and gave Wyatt the background—all the way from Brenda Butler's hospitalization through Carrie's visit with Tony Amici and interviews with Representatives and Senators.

A twenty-four year FBI veteran, Wyatt had co-investigated many cases with Max before Max retired. Now as Assistant Director in Charge of the Washington Field Office, Wyatt mostly managed people, data and budgets as opposed to investigations. But he still had passion for fieldwork. He also had his finger on the trigger for assigning resources. He'd had a distinguished career at the Bureau, climbing the ranks through outstanding performance and personal sacrifice, year after year. Wyatt blended into the general populous with his off-the-rack blue suits, white shirts, red ties, black shoes and graying hair. A black professional with an encyclopedic knowledge of the Bureau—its protocol, staff, cases and high profile criminal targets. Moreover, Wyatt had the gift of insight into the criminal mind, and he knew how to harness the Fed's resources to exact justice in decisive ways. A straight arrow.

Wyatt patiently listened to Max's precise, concise and unadorned summary. "I recall you worked with Dick Snyder on a case in Arizona last year."

"Right. We broke up a body parts harvesting ring. Amici was at the heart of it, but we couldn't nail him for it. Carrie Linden was the person who initially glommed onto the existence of the illegal ring. She's got a real nose for bad business."

"Amici's been a thorn in our side for years," Wyatt said. "Very clever guy. When the heat comes down, he always manages to have several cut-outs who insulate him from prosecution. Manages his communications and financial dealings well too. Very slick. And he's hyper-aware of any surveillance.

"I follow Linden's columns. Never met her though. Sounds like a great gal. This matter about Novotchin and other politicians concerns me greatly. I'll need to brief Director Parr about this as soon as I hang up. It's got political implications written all over it. I'll assemble a team and put them to work. See what we've got going on Amici, if anything. If your buddy Jablonski finds anything on video, let me know immediately. Any idea what they're trying to do by gang banging Congress?"

"No."

"Hmm, it's probably time to take another run at that asshole Amici anyway."

"Thanks. I wouldn't waste your time unless there was fire beneath the smoke."

"I'd follow you to hell and back old friend. You ready to saddle up for this?"

"Count me in, partner. I'll be in touch."

Max made a final call to Northwestern Memorial and learned that Carrie lay semi-conscious in the ICU, her status no longer critical.

Max arrived at the airport first. Michael showed up, sweating from the D.C. August humidity. He moved fast and was grinding his teeth. "Ready? Let's go."

"Calm down, man. We've got an hour before departure time. Let's head to our gate, and I'll fill you in on what I've done since we spoke this morning."

Max brought Michael up to speed on his talks, first with the hospital and then with Jablonski and Wyatt. "The Chicago PD's all over this, and the Fed's interest is more than merely whetted. I'll say one thing for Carrie. When she gets a bead on criminal behavior, she goes right for the jugular. If she hadn't poked around, I doubt the authorities would be in pursuit."

"Yeah, right. If she hadn't poked around, she wouldn't be in the hospital," Michael said angrily. Tears formed in the corners of his eyes.

Max observed the pain registered on the face of his friend and surrogate son. "You're right, but we each choose the course for our lives. Naïve though

Carrie may be, this is the path she's selected. Neither of us likes it, but we should respect it."

Michael gave Max a quizzical look. "I thought you disapproved of Carrie. You've been after me to dump her. Now you're sticking up for her. What gives?"

"I've never disapproved of Carrie as a person. I have consistently said she flies too close to the flame, and that's extremely dangerous for her and you. I've tried to discourage it to protect you both. Otherwise, it's good for others. She's an amazing public servant."

They didn't speak during the flight. Three and a half hours later and after dropping their bags at the Park Hyatt Hotel, they entered Northwestern Memorial Hospital. A volunteer at the information desk gave Michael a room number for Carrie.

Michael fast-walked to the elevator with Max following on his heels. "At least she's out of the ICU," Michael said. They boarded the elevator alone, and Michael touched a button for the fifth floor, his hand noticeably shaking.

"Michael, look at me."

He did. Distress written all over his face. He'd begun hyperventilating.

"I want you to get hold of yourself. Carrie's sustained a bad beating, and it won't be a pretty sight. You need to be brave here. Keep it together for Carrie."

Michael hung his head and nodded. "I'll do my best." He instinctively choked off an impending panic attack.

"Good. I promise you. We're gonna nail the bastards—one way or the other."

35

Thirty minutes after popping a Viagra tablet, Senator Blane Merryweather, Chairman of the Senate Foreign Relations Committee, sat in a Four Seasons hotel room chair, naked. He observed Ellie May lying on the bed on her back, knees up but spread, wearing only her red panties and cupping her double-D breasts in her hands.

He'd treated her to an early dinner at the hotel, eating and drinking lightly in preparation for the tablet he would consume. They engaged in some under-the-table touching and sexual innuendos. After coffee, he paid the check, and they retired to the hotel room. Merryweather noted how timid Ellie May behaved with their first kiss, but she quickly relented, opening her mouth wide and sliding her tongue into his. With a bashful look, she'd disrobed except for her red bikini panties while he stripped and swallowed *Mr. Blue*. The pill had done the trick, and he now stood at full attention—something he'd missed for a couple of years. *Hooray for the Pfizer-riser!*

At sixty-eight and with a miserable marriage, he'd become obsessed with his Senatorial work and tending to his constituents. Nothing else mattered, or so it seemed until he met Ellie May at the White House dinner. He thought about his body—completely out-of-shape and sexually out-of-practice. He knew he was balding and gray, wrinkled and marginal in the looks department. Eyeing Ellie May, thoughtfully, he was astonished he was in this room at this time with this gorgeous bombshell of a girl. Merryweather wondered whether this innocent girl from West Virginia could give him a new lease on life or at the very least some desperately needed periodic relief.

He said, "Okay darlin', remove those itty bitty panties."

"I'm really shy," she said, but she shed them in an instant. "Oh my, I've never seen such a huge pee pee before. Whatcha gonna do with that big thang, Blanie?" She made a moue with her lips and raised her eyebrows as if frightened.

Merryweather grinned. As he stepped toward the bed, he sucked in his gut and puffed out his chest a bit. "Why darlin', I'm gonna do whatever I want." And he did. In multiple positions, multiple times, until after hearing her moans and groans and feeling her body spasm, he erupted.

He rolled off Ellie May, panting, sweating and wheezing. Breathless, he said, "You have no idea how good that was for me."

"For *you?* Blanie, I only been down this road once before. With my high school sweetie after prom. He don't hold a candle to you. You rocked my world."

The Senator smiled inwardly. *I've still got it.* "I want to see you again."

"I can't wait, Blanie. You done things to me…I never 'magined I'd feel. How 'bout two weeks from now? We can meet in the lobby."

"I'd prefer sooner."

"Me too, but I gotta visit my mama in Romney. She's feelin' a bit poorly."

"Oh, all right. But two weeks from tonight without fail. Right?"

"I'll be here waitin' Blanie," she said, giggling. "Maybe you can do that thang with your tongue again." With that, she stroked his flaccid penis. "Tell me 'bout that big job you do on the Hill." He did, in excruciating detail.

Two hours later, they departed the Four Seasons, headed in different directions. He offered her a lift, but she declined, saying she lived nearby and preferred to walk. *A few more visits, and she'll invite me into the rest of her life.*

• • •

Doubled over laughing at the Senator, Ruddock couldn't contain himself. He chuckled while he gathered his electronic gear and pulled the same from the room where Merryweather had enjoyed his romp with Ellie May.

Don't know why St. John was so negative about this girl. Said she was stupid. Hell, she got Merryweather to spill the beans on a bunch of issues, inner workings and personalities in his Senate committee. She had him sharing inside, uncomplimentary and really embarrassing shit about foreign dignitaries, Senators and the POTUS.

I've got so much meat in this one recording, I'm going to send St. John in right away with our demand. Get the ball rolling with this guy.

• • •

Relieved that Ruddock had taken her advice to move sooner with targets than previously, St. John confidently marched up the steps of the Capitol building with a smirk on her face and her laptop under her arm. Waves of summer heat rippled before her eyes. *Nothing compared to the heat Blanie's gonna feel.* St. John belted out a laugh. She didn't personally know Senator Merryweather, but his executive assistant, Darlene, had been her former lover a few years earlier.

"What are *you* doing here?" Darlene hissed, apprehensive.

"Got nothing to do with you, sweet cheeks, unless you don't let me in to see Merryweather. And I mean right now," St. John threatened.

"He's on the phone and jammed with meetings today. How long you need?"

"Figure ten to fifteen minutes at most."

Darlene closed her eyes for several seconds. "Okay. As soon as he's off the phone. Promise this has nothing to do with me. I need this job."

"Like I said, it doesn't concern you."

Four minutes later, Darlene escorted St. John through the door to Merryweather's office. "Senator, this is Ms. St. John. I understand she's one of your constituents, and she needs a few minutes of your time." Darlene quickly exited the office and quietly pulled the door shut behind St. John.

Senator Merryweather stood and walked around his modern cherry wood desk to greet St. John. "I'm sorry, but I don't believe I've had the pleasure." He shook her hand vigorously. "Please, call me Blane and have a seat." They sat facing each other in two chocolate-colored leather Scandinavian chairs.

"What can I do for you Ms. St. John? Lovely name by the way."

"Well Blane, or should I call you Blanie?" She let out a big belly laugh.

"What?" he asked with apprehension. Nobody called him that, except…

"That's a good question—what. Sit still a minute, Blanie, and I'll show you the what." St. John opened her laptop, keyed a portion of the video from two nights earlier and showed Merryweather a clip of one of his rounds with Ellie May, followed by one of his most egregious comments about the President and two fellow Senators.

By the end of the video, Merryweather sat hunched over in his chair, elbows on his knees with his face in his hands. Then he sat up straight and looked St. John straight in the eye. "I should have known that little tryst was too good to be true. I made a mistake. But I guess you're here to extract something in return for my error."

"You're smart, Blanie. Here's what you're going to do for us…"

"STOP! If you're smart, St. John or whatever your name is, you'll leave my office immediately. I don't give a damn what you've got or whom you share it with. My wife doesn't give a shit, and I'll apologize to anyone who gets offended. As soon as you walk out that door, I'm calling the FBI. My advice? Run for the hills, *bitch*."

St. John bolted from her chair and sped from the Capitol building.

On the third ring, Ruddock answered his cell phone.

"Where are you?" St. John asked.

"Reagan National Airport. Why?"

"We've got a major problem."

"Tell me."

Once she'd explained what happened in her meeting with Merryweather, he said, "Go home. I'll call you in an hour or two and let you know how I'm going to solve this problem."

● ● ●

"YOU FUCKING IDIOT!" Tony screamed. "You rushed the mark. You didn't give time for his feelings to build for the girl and for him to dig a deeper hole. You fucked it up. This is a goddamn cluster fuck."

"Not me, boss. I was set to build a much deeper case on the guy, but St. John ran with what we had. She broke protocol without my knowledge or approval."

Ruddock could almost hear the gears grinding in Tony's mind. The thing with Merryweather was very bad news, and he wasn't about to take responsibility for any of it. He waited a full minute.

Finally, "I fear Senator Merryweather has little time left on earth. Finish it. Quickly…carefully…no traces. Put St. John on ice somewhere. We're very close to the finish line. Once we turn our herd back to their original positions, get rid of her."

"Understood." They hung up, and Ruddock set off for the Hyatt Regency, close to Senator Blane Merryweather's Bethesda home. *Wonder what'll happen to me after we cross the finish line?*

36

Dr. Hugh Kaptur, the hospital's top internist, stood in Carrie's hospital doorway, studying her chart, as Michael and Max approached.

"Are you gentlemen here to visit Ms. Linden?"

"Yes," Michael said. "We're close friends from out of town."

A moment later Dr. Leo Goldstein arrived with Hank Greenbaum. The four of them conferred with Dr. Kaptur. Leo had been Carrie's psychotherapist. A short, avuncular fellow in his early sixties with a preference for tweed suits, rumpled shirts and floral bow ties. Dr. Goldstein had helped Carrie overcome her drinking problem, at least temporarily, and confront her psychological demons. His friend, Hank Greenbaum, was still publisher of the *Chicago Tribune* where Carrie previously worked. Also in his sixties, Hank had been very close to Carrie's father and served as a father figure for Carrie for many years after her dad suddenly and unexpectedly passed. Given his penchant for being a clothes horse and though portly, Hank could pose with Max as older models for *GQ* magazine. Dr. Goldstein was on record with the hospital as one of Carrie's physicians. He was notified of her admission and had, in turn, phoned Hank.

Dr. Kaptur stopped his summary of Carrie's medical condition with Michael and Max and rewound the tape so he could brief them all at once.

"Ms. Linden is fortunate to have survived the torture she experienced. And I mean torture. The bottom line is she'll live. We often see patients who've sustained beatings. Usually a bloody nose, a broken bone, a few bruises. Ms. Linden has been systematically beaten up and down both sides of her body. I've never seen anything like it. The people who did this must be maniacs...psychopaths. We've set her nose, reattached her right nostril to her lip, bound her two fractured ribs, but the numerous bruises will need time to heal. We're keeping her hydrated and medicated for pain."

"Can we see Carrie?" Michael asked.

"I'd prefer not until tomorrow. We just moved her out of the ICU, but she's still incoherent. There's nothing you can do for her at this time. Going in now may disturb her and will certainly upset you, with the possible exception of Dr. Goldstein."

The four visitors looked at one another. Finally, Leo broke the silence. "Gentlemen, this is a frightening and highly emotional situation. I recommend we accept Dr. Kaptur's counsel and let Carrie rest tonight. She is in good hands."

Hank said, "I concur, as hard as it is to pry ourselves away from here. It's dinnertime. Let's eat together. My treat. And we'll discuss Carrie's situation."

"I agree," Max said. "But I have a quick call to make before we dine." He put his hand on Michael's shoulder. "All right big guy?"

"Yeah." Michael's head hung low, eyes closed.

Nine minutes later, the four of them boarded Hank's stretch limousine. His driver had parked near the hospital on stand-by. "Take us to Eddie's," Hank ordered.

En route, Max made his call to Jimmy Jablonski. "Jimmy, it's Max. Any news on the Linden attack?" The other three watched attentively as Max nodded, grunted responses and eventually hung up. "The cops have nothing and may never get anything on the perp."

They arrived at Eddie's and were immediately seated at Hank's usual table.

At the turn of the twentieth century, a former prize fighter named Eddie, opened "Eddie's" in a space close to the *Tribune*, founded in 1847. Another Eddie purchased the bar and grill over fifty years ago from the first Eddie and continued the establishment's reputation as a lively haven for reporters, business people and politicians. Numerous signed photographs hung on every wall, depicting famous historical figures who'd visited the bar, including many movie stars. Several booths and other nooks and crannies served as quiet spots where small groups gathered for private conversations and deal making. While Eddie Number Two had performed some updating of the premises, largely painting the walls, he worked to maintain the early 1900's feel of the place. The original ornately carved wooden bar took center stage in the establishment and contributed to its ambience.

"Happy to see you Mr. Greenbaum. What can I get you gents?" Eddie asked. He attended personally to certain regular customers. Hank had been one for decades.

"Unless anyone objects," Hank offered, "I'd like Eddie to bring us a bottle of his nineteen year Cadenhead's. The circumstances call for a single malt scotch."

Over dinner they discussed Carrie—her penchant for endangering her life for justice, which Leo claimed provided self-gratification, her routine success in her quests, their feelings about Carrie and how to handle her current situation. Michael and Max shared what Carrie had been working on and their joint belief that her visit with Tony Amici had precipitated her attack. Max reported on his talk with the FBI.

Twice during their discussion, Michael nearly broke down. But he managed to control his emotions. Michael's tortured state of mind was obvious to everyone.

As dinner wound to a close, Leo said, "There is much to work on. If I may, I have a suggested division of labor." No one objected. "First, telling Carrie that what has happened to her resulted from her visit to Las Vegas is a waste of time. I suspect Michael is not in a position to counsel Carrie, nor are you, Max and Hank. That has been my job in the past, and I propose to reassume that role." No one objected.

"Next, Max is best qualified to singularly pursue anything with the authorities, and I recommend he do so and report as appropriate to the rest of us." Hearing no objection, he continued. "Hank, I believe Carrie may need a little financial support while she recovers. She dislikes taking charity, so perhaps you can route a few assignments to her. But they cannot be make-work projects. She has to feel they are worthy of her talent."

"Count on it," Hank said, his jowls swaying a bit as he responded.

"Michael, my friend, this is perhaps the most difficult role among the four of us. But it is probably the most important one for Carrie. I know you love one another, and loving Carrie has its challenges. If you are up to it, I ask you to show her love, patience and understanding. There should be no recriminations, no revisiting bad history. Focus on the future."

Michael stared at Dr. Goldstein for several seconds.

"Ahem, just to clarify, I am not asking you to marry her," Leo said. "Only to show her love. Does that make sense?"

"Yeah. I will. I'm also going to call Melvin Grimes. Given the risks he's taken for Carrie and his affection for her, he has a right to know what's happened."

Everyone agreed.

"And one more thing," Michael said. "I'm going to pay Tony Amici a visit."

A chorus of "what's" and "no way's" resounded around the table, coupled with three faces with deep frowns.

I have matters to discuss with him. Some having nothing to do with Carrie.

37

"Why can't we get naked?" the coed asked St. John.

"Shut the fuck up or get out. I'm waiting for a call." She ran a hand over her face a few times as she sat at her kitchen table, staring at a cell phone and thinking about what had happened with Merryweather, wondering if he'd called the FBI. *Are there security cameras in the Capitol building? Absolutely. Did they capture my image? Without a doubt. Can they find a photograph of me someplace? Most likely. Jesus, I'm fucked!*

Wait a minute. Nobody recorded what I said to Merryweather. It's his word against mine. Where's the proof? . . . Oh. I've gotta erase all that shit on my laptop. Wouldn't do for anyone to see the videos.

St. John stomped into her second bedroom where she plopped down next to a small glass and aluminum-framed desk. The girl quietly followed. St. John booted up her laptop and opened a folder, containing scores of videos Ruddock had sent her since the beginning. She deleted the video folder and emptied her computer trash basket. Then she scoured her laptop for anything else connected with the operation. In her email outbox, she found two incriminating emails. One linked her to Brenda Butler. Another she'd sent to the dominatrix. *Why'd I keep these?* After hitting the delete key twice, St. John emptied her trash bin again.

"What are you doing?" the coed asked innocently.

St. John hadn't sensed her presence. She wheeled around in her chair and faced the girl. "Look, bitch, I don't have time to explain. You gotta go. This thing between us?" She searched the coed's face. "Well, it's over."

"But I thought you loved me." The coed began to cry.

"Get your shit and get out." St. John stood and took the girl by the arm, hauling her around the condo to pick up her belongings. She grabbed the coed's toothbrush from the glass on the bath sink and jammed it in her hip pocket.

At the front door to the condo, the girl turned to St. John in tears. "But I love you. What have I done? Can't we..."

St. John pushed her through the door, slammed it in her face and threw the locks. *Gotta concentrate. Why hasn't that shit bird called me?* She replayed the episode with Merryweather over and over. *What went wrong? ...Ah, that shit bird told me to go ahead and confront Merryweather. Too soon.* She shook her head. *That West Virginia bitch Ellie May. She's partly at fault. I'm so screwed.*

What now? Should I bug out? Cash in all my securities and savings? Put it all in a bag with my jewelry? Maybe throw in some other valuable shit I can carry? How long would that last me? What about my condo? Damn, this is the end.

Nah. What do they have on me? Nothing. I dare them to get in my face. I'll bring them all down. Then she realized. In her agitated state, she hadn't thought things through rationally. She'd just deleted all the evidence she could use to bring anyone down. *I'm really fucked.*

Her cell phone rang and she grabbed it. "Yes?"

"It's me," Ruddock said. "I've thought about your problem and discussed it with my partner."

"What partner? You have a partner?" She looked around the kitchen and rubbed her face.

"Shut up and pay attention. Merryweather probably didn't do anything after you left his office. You didn't succeed in turning him so why should he embarrass himself? We figure eight-twenty you've got nothing to worry about."

"So say you. And who's *we?*"

"In the off chance he contacted the authorities, you need to take some action. Get rid of any evidence immediately."

"I just erased everything on my laptop," she said, breathing heavily.

"Destroy your laptop, idiot. They can get into it and find deleted files."

"Okay." Her mind was racing. Perspiration ran down her temples.

"Next, collect and hide the cash you've earned. You don't want any pesky questions about how you've accumulated hundreds of thousands of dollars."

"Right. I was planning on doing that tomorrow."

"You didn't put money in a bank or the stock market. Right?"

"Uh, actually, uh, the market has been doing so well, I invested..."

"Dumbass! I told you from the start. No traces."

Sweat trickled down her chest between her breasts.

"Leave town. Take a vacation. The Carolina's, New Mexico, Canada. Stay in a cabin or a bed and breakfast. Pay cash. Don't charge anything. No traces. Got it?"

"What about the girls and my cut of future fees?"

"I've got their contact information. I'll keep things running."

"But they rely on me." She sucked in a hopeful breath. Ten seconds passed.

"Not anymore. You're out."

"You set me up. You fucking set me up!"

"Not true. In a month or so, if conditions are right, you go home."

"And then what?" she asked, running her free hand over her face.

"Nothing. Get on with your life."

"And if things aren't right?"

"Then you're screwed. You knew the game. You understood the risks."

"But you *told* me to confront Merryweather," she said accusingly.

"Did I say that? I really can't recall." Ruddock chuckled.

"Damn it, you prick, you think I'm gonna let you fuck me over while you make out like a bandit? I'll bring you down and whoever else's with you." She gritted her teeth and stomped around her living room.

Ruddock laughed. "Pray tell. How will you do that?"

The full weight of her predicament landed on St. John with full force. She knew of no one other than Ruddock who was involved in the blackmail operation. He alluded to a partner, but this was the first she'd heard of one. He'd introduced himself at the start as *Jeremy Blevins*. Was that his real name? He'd probably destroy his throwaway cell after this conversation. She hung up and stared at the phone.

Thirty minutes later, she thought, *I'll cash everything in and bug out. Maybe I'll take my little friend along for company. Have to apologize to her first. I'll keep my laptop. If I can recover the files I deleted, I might have some leverage.*

St. John sat down to make a to do list—unaware that two men, dressed in off-the-rack business suits and white shirts, sat silently in an unmarked Crown Victoria parked across the street in front of her condominium building. They waited for Julie White, *AKA* St. John, to leave the premises so they could install court-ordered surveillance devices.

38

Over bacon, eggs and hash browns the next morning, Max told Michael, "I'm headed to Jablonski's office. We're meeting with the security guy from The Drake. We'll see if he's found anything that would put Representative Novotchin on premise when Brenda Butler was attacked. Afterwards, I'll talk with my FBI buddy and see where things stand with their investigation."

Michael set a crust of toast on his plate. "Sounds good. I'll call Melvin and then pay Carrie a visit. I hope Bernstein can get through to her."

"Hope so. Listen. I know you're intent on confronting Amici, but please take my advice. Amici won't change. You can't trust anything he says. You'll walk away from the meeting disappointed. And you may put yourself directly in the firing line."

"I know those are possible outcomes. But I have to try. If there's one bit of rationality in the man, one ounce of decency..." Michael's voice trailed off.

Max shook his head. "You're thinking about him as Michael Taylor would think, not as Tony Amici thinks. You've got to crawl into *his* mind. I've hunted and brought down creeps like Amici my entire career. I'm not being fatalistic or biased or provincial when I tell you, they're all the same. His type views anyone who doesn't support or, more importantly, endangers his interests as a threat. And threats are routinely dealt with in the harshest ways."

"I don't think he'll harm me. I'm his son."

"Blood relations don't mean spit to a guy like Amici. Didn't you ever see *The Godfather?* They didn't make all that shit up for the movie. You know? I'm asking one last time. Please let the FBI chase the fucker. They get paid to do that, and they're much better qualified and equipped than you."

"I'll think about it."

They left the breakfast table, and Michael took the elevator to his room while Max departed for his meeting with Jablonski.

Michael considered Max's admonitions. *Most say never gamble in a casino because the house odds are stacked against you. Even still, some come out winners. I've got to try.*

He picked up his cell and called Melvin.

"Hullo?"

"Melvin, this is Michael Taylor. How are you?"

"Good."

"You'd better sit down. I've got some bad news."

Michael paced his hotel room while he related what had happened to Carrie.

"Sonsofbitches! She gonna make it?"

"Yeah, she'll live. I'd like you to tell me about your visit to Las Vegas. From your view. And don't leave anything out, no matter how minor you may think it is."

When Melvin finished, he said, "No doubt. Amici had somebody beat her up."

"There's no way maybe you misinterpreted his intent or didn't hear him clearly?" Michael asked, hoping for a "yes."

"Nope. Guy's evil. Needs to be put down like a rabid dog. Needs to be put outa everyone else's misery. I gotta mind to do jes' that..."

"Don't do anything like that Melvin, the FBI's involved now."

"Right. Jes' like they were with that body parts racket. I know yer a big shot criminal mouthpiece, but the justice system don't work on pieces a shit like Amici."

A few seconds of silence slipped by. Then, "I'll call you with updates on Carrie," Michael said. And they hung up.

• • •

Gino Maglieri walked into Jablonski's office a few minutes after ten, dressed in polyester blue slacks and a red jacket with The Drake Hotel's emblem on the breast pocket, black socks and shoes with thick rubber soles, and a white cotton shirt with a navy clip-on tie. Gino had the watery bloodshot eyes, washed out face and ruddy nose from broken capillaries of many confirmed alcoholics.

Jimmy had warned Max about Gino's appearance and that he was a juice freak. Max decided to hear the man out before passing judgment. In his experience, the job often led to alcoholism, or maybe some with the tendency to be alcoholics became police officers. Chicken or the egg? Who knew? And why did it matter anyway?

Gino fought to catch his breath—short due to heavy smoking and his hike from The Drake to the precinct to avoid paying taxi fare. He put his hand to his chest. "Give me a minute." With a heavy smoker's cough, he cleared his throat.

Jablonski poured a cup of black coffee and set it in front of Gino. After taking a sip and calming down, Gino pulled a DVD from his inner breast pocket. "Throw that in the computer." He coughed heavily again and settled down.

Jimmy slid the DVD into his laptop, and they gathered around the screen. As clear as day, Representative Jimmy Novotchin strolled into The Drake at 8:02 PM on the night of Brenda's attack, lighting a cigar with a gold-colored lighter as he passed by lobby cameras. At 9:11 PM, he departed, in what seemed a hasty stride with hair mussed and tie dangling loose with no cigar or lighter in evidence.

"What time did EMS receive the call?" Max asked Jimmy.

Jablonski hit several keys and brought up the report. "Says here 9:05 PM."

Max looked at Gino. "How long would it take someone moving fast to get from Butler's room to the lobby? Don't think. What's your top-of-mind guess?"

"Five minutes or so," Gino said. "Depends on whether the guy's dressed, whether he runs into maid service, how long the elevator takes to arrive, how many stops it makes on its way down to the lobby. But five is a good guess."

Max's and Jimmy's eyes met. "Gino," Jimmy said, "I'm going to see you get a commendation for this. Good job."

"I'd go so far as saying, great job," Max said, smiling. "While you're waiting for that commendation, take this." Max reached in his pocket, pealed a hundred dollar bill from his roll and stuck it in Gino's jacket pocket with the emblem. "Have a big steak on me, my friend. You've just done your country a big service."

They shook Gino's hand, and he left the office, walking a little taller, with a big grin on his face and what appeared to be a renewed sense of dignity.

"I need three things, Jimmy. Make me a copy of this DVD. Two, keep this under wraps for now. The Feds will come in on this like gang busters, but I'll make sure they work with you. After all, this is *your* town. Third, answer a question."

"I can do the first two. What's the question?" Jablonski had a puzzled look.

"Why do you guys have such a hard on for Novotchin?"

Jablonski laughed. "Oh that's an easy one. The Chicago PD supported the fucker in his initial run for Congress. You know, posing for photo ops, giving testimonials, all so he could tell voters that the cops were behind him. Once he was in office, he threw us under the bus. Didn't fulfill any promises to help with funding. In fact, he eviscerated us routinely in the press for police brutality, insensitivity to minorities, corruption, and on and on. None of which were true. Guess he decided he needed another voting block more than he needed us."

"Well, that'd do it," Max said. "What a creep."

When Max left the precinct, he dialed John Wyatt in D.C. "You'll never guess what I have in my hand, John." He turned the DVD over in his hand.

"Uh, let's see. Your dick?" Wyatt chortled.

"You're a funny man. The Chicago PD and Drake security came through big time. I'm holding a DVD. I've got date and time stamped images of Novotchin entering The Drake prior to Brenda Butler's attack and of him beating feet a few minutes after someone dialed 911. On his way in, he lit a cigar with a golden lighter."

"Holy crap! After we last spoke, I briefed Director Parr, and he's royally pissed but, in a way, he's gratified about the possibility Novotchin did the deed."

"Why gratified?" Max asked.

"Because Mr. Novotchin makes a habit of putting the screws to the Bureau."

"Not smart. Chicago PD's got the same problem with him. I'll email the file to you. Any news about other corrupted politicians and Tony Amici?"

"No and no. The Arizona office has chased Amici so many times and come up empty that I suspect no one is up to the task. Not good, but I understand."

"Maybe you need to get fresh blood on the scene with enthusiasm for the task."

"Maybe. I'll be in touch." Wyatt signed off.

Max caught a cab to the hospital. *This is news that'll perk Carrie right up. Unfortunately, it may reinforce her risky behavior too. We'll see.*

39

Senator Robert Gleason sat in Bull Bullock's office after business hours. The staff had long gone. Both were on their third cocktail when Mary Grendel joined them.

Bull rose and stepped to his bar. "Scotch, rocks. Right Mary?"

"Please. Hi Bob."

"Hello Mary. I wish this meeting involved a different topic."

She took the offered drink and said, "Yeah, we all do."

Bull said, "Mary, I've told Bob everything I shared with you over dinner a few weeks ago. And he's told me some private things about himself. I think it would be best if the two of you aired your own dirty laundry with one another while I finish up some paperwork. That done, we can proceed with planning a course of action. And I believe we're agreed the required action will be dramatic and painful."

While Bull worked at his desk, the two Senators revealed their dark secrets of sexual corruption and how their Senatorial actions had been compromised.

Gleason headed the Senate Select Committee on Intelligence. At 53, he'd just been reelected to a fourth term. His family had amassed a fortune in the coal mining industry, and his enormous wealth exceeded Bull's by a factor of two. Bob physically resembled Cary Grant and exhibited Cary's class and sense of humor—most of the time. That made him popular with his constituents, particularly female voters.

Bull penned his name to a final letter and rejoined Bob and Mary at the two opposing couches. "Feels good to get this out in the open." Bob and Mary nodded their heads. "I bet we could compose a pretty accurate list of our colleagues who're in the same boat with us."

"I'm sure we could," Bob said, "but these blackmailers have us by the balls... oh, sorry Mary." He took a pull from his glass of rum and coke.

"Forget it. Bob's right, Bull. What would we do? What could we do?"

Bull stared at his associates for a few seconds. "I've got an idea. But let's first assemble the list. Once we have it, I'll tell you my plan. And I think the merits of it will speak for themselves when we examine the list." He offered a toothy grin.

Thirty-five minutes later, they'd written down forty-six names of Members of both Houses of Congress. "I wish we had a few Members of the House with us right now," Bull said. "I think the list would be more accurate and maybe longer."

Mary spoke up. "We tried to rope Dale Bennett into this, Bob, but he wouldn't even acknowledge there's a problem. I'm damn certain he's involved. He's hiding."

"No doubt in my mind," Bob said. "Assuming this list is reasonably on target, and I think it is, what's your plan Bull?"

Bull stood and slowly paced his office in his stocking feet. The silk and wool Isfahan carpet felt good under his footfalls. "I'm thinking four steps. First, we each speak with two people on this list with whom we're very close. We get them to confess, just as we'll self-disclose to them. We'll instantly triple our ranks, adding a few folks from the House. That'll set us up for step two."

"This is very risky," Bob said. "If just one of these..."

Mary interrupted. "Bob, no guts, no glory. If you've got a better idea, speak up. Otherwise, I want to hear the rest of Bull's plan."

Hearing no objection, Bull continued. "Step two is a repeat of step one. We use our larger contingent to expand the circle. If the first step yields a force of nine, I think we can haul in another twenty, maybe thirty in step two. We might wind up with two-thirds or more of this list. That's a lot."

"That's a powder keg, if you ask me," Bob said.

"Hey Bob," Mary interjected. "This is just the kind of thing that pisses me off about men. I'd tell you to grow a pair of balls, but balls are delicate and sensitive little things. So I'll just say, grow a vagina. Will you? 'Cause those things take a pounding."

Everyone laughed. Mary had broken the tension in the room—momentarily.

"Point taken, Mary." Bob had laughed so hard, he'd sloshed some of his drink onto his custom charcoal trousers. "Tell us the rest Bull."

"All right. In step three, we meet. Offsite. Secretly. Maybe at night. Everyone who's in the circle. We'll all know why we're there. At the meeting, we get the group to identify any others and who's best to contact them and bring them into our circle."

"I'm good with that," Bob said.

"Me too," Mary added. "Then what?"

Bull flashed his trademark toothy smile. "Why, isn't it obvious? ...We all resign or retire."

Bob dropped his glass, spilling rum and coke all over himself and Bull's couch. Mary began to cry. Bull sat staring at the other two.

When Mary regained her composure, she said, "You're right. There's no other way. I've thought about doing just that to get out from under this blackmail threat."

"What about our party?" Bob asked. "We'll likely lose both Houses."

Bull leaned forward, aggressively pointing a finger at Bob, "WE DON'T FUCKING DESERVE TO CONTROL EITHER HOUSE! Every goddamn name on that list is a member of our party. We owe our nation probably more than our precious positions. Shit! We've voted to send young kids to war, but what? Are we unwilling to take what amounts to a soft bullet? If I have to hold a goddamn press conference and out every fucker on this list whose been corrupted, I will!" Bull glared at Bob.

"Wait, wait, wait," Bob said. "Don't do that. I'm with you Bull. Let's follow your plan. No press conferences. No public confessions. We'll all just fade away. There are scores of folks who'd jump at the chance to take our positions."

"Right," Mary agreed. "And it isn't like the people on this list need their jobs in Congress to support their families."

They examined the list again. "Mary's got a point," Bob admitted. "I hadn't thought about the backgrounds of these folks. We're all filthy rich."

"When do we start?" Mary asked.

"Now," Bull answered. "Let's each pick two names, so we're not calling the same folks. Tomorrow, we'll start dialing for recruits. I'll make a copy of this list for you before you leave my office, but guard it carefully. No more copies. Next week, we'll meet here to share results. Warn these people that any leaked confidences will result in a public revelation about them. Nobody will want that."

Having identified their contact names, Mary and Bob accepted a photocopy of the handwritten list. Sodden from the alcohol, they wobbled out of Bull's office.

Bull poured himself another Jack Daniel's and plopped on his couch. *Hoped I'd spend another twenty years in this office. Not gonna happen. And just 'cause I like watching a good looking broad shit on me. Oh, and of course, the matter with Dakota. How could I have killed her? Is she really dead? What a fucking dope I am. Wonder what St. John will do about Dakota if I retire?* He took a big swig of bourbon. *I'll think about that tomorrow.* He stretched out on his couch and closed his eyes.

40

At 4 PM Pacific Standard Time, 7 AM China Standard Time, one of Amici's phones made its distinctive "pinball" ring. Tony watched as the cell lit up on his desk.

The ring always reminded Tony of the twenty-five cent a game machine at the back of his father's bar. Those were good times—playing pinball with his friends, that is. He spent the balance of his youth in constant fear of his father, a capo in the Gambino family back east, seconded to Las Vegas to oversee certain family interests. His dad hated being away from the east coast action and power base of *La Familia*, but he nonetheless persevered and built an infamous business for himself in Vegas.

The elder Amici used his bar to launder money. His wife and son, young Tony, never lacked for anything. But the elder constantly leaned on his son to behave in church, mind his mother, make good grades, stay away from girls, mow the lawn and more. All reasonable requests to be sure, except the requests routinely took the form of demands at the end of a slap or a punch or, literally, a kick in the ass.

The junior Amici was expected to follow in his father's footsteps. After all, he was a full-blooded Sicilian, and it wouldn't take much for him to become a *made man*. He'd inherit his father's illicit ventures, mob connections, and, importantly, inside ties to the justice system. With proper tutelage, it'd be difficult for Tony to do anything but maintain or grow the family enterprise. He'd grown it—tenfold.

No one had ever asked whether he wanted to do anything other than run circles around the law. He'd secretly hoped to become a life insurance actuary. Tony excelled at math. At the early age of twelve, his father enlisted his help with various accounting tasks. Not only could the kid count, but he didn't need to write anything down. He stored it all in his twelve-year-old brain. No way could young Tony be allowed to run off to college. How would the business survive without him? It couldn't.

As the Feds broke up the Gambino family, piece by piece, back east, the Amici contingent in Vegas prospered and diversified their activities with young Tony taking an ever increasing management and, then, leadership role. When Tony turned twenty-four, his father suffered a fatal heart attack, leaving Tony the business and a trajectory for what would be his life long illicit career. His father also left him a permanent reminder of his brutality a few years before he died. Tony's physical deformity had healed by the time the elder passed, but the psychological damage had been done.

"Yes?" Tony answered the phone, wondering about this unscheduled call.

The Chinese-accented voice filled the air waves. "It is time to have your puppets change course back to their original point of origin. Do this today."

"Don't you think we should give it a bit more time? The market's on fire."

"Are you arguing with me?" the Chinese man challenged.

"No, no. Just making an observation. So that I understand clearly, you want me to have them completely reverse the positions they've recently taken."

"You understand our command. We demand complete obedience."

Command? Obedience? You fucking Chink. I'd like you to kneel at my feet, you prick. Gathering his wits, Tony asked, "What about the other matter?"

"Do not pursue it at this time and until further notice. Tell your contractor not to take any action whatsoever. We will contact you if and when we wish to launch."

"What do you mean by *if?*" Tony asked, genuinely curious.

"Do you not understand the English language? Try thinking about synonyms: assuming, in case, on condition of, supposing, whether. Do you comprehend? Did you not go to grade school?" the Chinese man asked in an extremely condescending tone.

Motherfucker. Who are you to insult me? I'm doing all the work, and you're reaping all the benefit. I ought to fuck up your action. Tony groped to control his emotions. "Of course I know the meaning, I was just wondering…"

"Do not think. Do not question. Just perform. This conversation ends now."

The line went dead and Tony dropped the phone on his gray metal desk as if he'd been handling a garden slug. He felt blood rush to his face, and he breathed heavily. He gritted his teeth and rubbed the knuckles on his left hand where he often felt phantom sensations of his missing fingers—that they were still attached and moving appropriately with the rest of his hand. He'd lost them at the age of eighteen.

Tony took a deep breath and stormed out of his office.

On his way out, one of his office thugs said, "Hey boss?"

"NOT NOW!" Tony yelled, and he left EZ-Bonds for a stroll down the Boulevard. A half hour later, he returned to his office. Realizing he'd already made more money on this one venture than all his other businesses added together for the last two years, he calmed down. *It's just business. And it will soon end.*

Tony dialed Ruddock. "Where are you and what are you doing?"

"I'm in the D.C. area preparing to take care of our errant Senator."

"Forget that. Turn the herd around. Do it right away. Issue new orders today."

"Boss, I'll do my best, but some might not be reachable until tomorrow."

"DO IT!" Tony screamed in the phone and hung up.

Tony took a deep breath and massaged his left hand again. Then he called the mechanic. On the second ring, Tony heard the man say, "Speak."

"Do you know who this is?" Tony got to play boss yet again.

"Affirmative."

"Listen carefully. Continue your preparations, but do *not*, I repeat, do *not* take any action until I notify you. Understand?"

"That was our understanding, and it remains so," the mechanic responded.

Tony sat in his office, sulking. Then he reached for another phone and dialed his financial advisor. "Mario, this is Tony. Don't argue with me. Cash out all my remaining stock holdings today without fail." He cut the connection.

• • •

Sitting on the edge of his hotel bed, stupefied, Ruddock pondered the call from Tony. It had been a few years since he'd seen or heard Tony lose his composure. Had he done something wrong? He didn't think so. He surely hoped not. Those on the wrong side of Tony didn't have futures. Even if you were on his good side, you never knew for sure. *Guess I'd better start dialing.*

Ah, as Brother Joseph used to tell us on the field, "Nolite te bastardes carborundorum." Don't let the bastards get you down. And Tony's a real bastard. Ruddock examined two pages filled with fifty-five names and cell numbers.

His first call went to Dale Bennett.

"Do you know who this is?"

Through slurred, drunken speech, Dale said, "Uh, yeah. Whatdya want now?"

"Immediately, you will reverse all the positions I've ordered you to take. Start tomorrow without fail. It'll be easy. And I'll be watching. So don't screw up."

Dale asked, "That mean I'm off the hook? I can go back to being normal?"

"You're free for now. But, hey, don't start thinking you were ever normal."

41

Three days into her hospital stay, Carrie sat at a seventy-five degree angle in her bed while Michael tipped a spoonful of warm tomato bisque between her lips. Every part of her ached, including opening and closing her mouth. Ordinarily, she liked soup, but consuming anything, presently, caused her to use multiple parts of her body—lips, jaws, tongue, throat, esophagus, chest and stomach—all of which screamed with pain, despite the narcotics she took.

"I know you hurt, sweetie, but you've got to eat."

Carrie let the soup flow onto her tongue, let it swirl around in her mouth and, closing her eyes, gingerly swallowed it. A tear appeared at the corner of her right eye, and Michael dabbed it with a tissue. She'd resorted to whispering. "Thank you, I don't deserve you being here. I did this to myself."

"It's okay. I like having you under my control for a change." He smiled.

She laughed, but immediately caught herself as pain registered in her rib cage, generating a raw moan. Dr. Kaptur and the nursing staff had done everything medically possible to ensure her comfort. But the key recuperative ingredient no one could administer or control was time. Time for each bruise to go through its healing cycle. Time for the lacerations to her skin to mend. Time for Carrie to realize she'd survived. Time to sort out how she'd move forward with her life after the attack.

Carrie could feel each area of her body toiling away, fighting every local traumatized part. She imagined tiny crews of white-coated technicians with tools and ladders and paint cans hard at work on each sore spot. That included her feet. *My god what happened to my feet? They said I had no broken bones, other than the ribs, but my feet are so frigging sore.*

Michael slipped the spoon into her mouth again. Then he offered her a straw to sip some tea the dietician aide delivered with her sparse lunch tray— tea, soup, juice, and a few saltines to let sit in her mouth until soggy so she could swallow them. *Jesus, my neck hurts too. Not inside but outside. But when I try to do something inside like swallow, the outside kills me.*

"Here's a bit of good news," Michael said. "I spoke with Dr. Kaptur this morning, and he said you're making good progress. I realize it may not seem so, but he said you're fortunate that you're in good shape and don't smoke. Otherwise, your recovery would take much longer." He smiled again, but she didn't take much encouragement from Michael's words or facial expressions.

Right. I'm so happy I don't smoke. What I really need now is a bottle. Why don't you serve me up some Jameson and soda. No. Forget the soda. Get me a liter with a straw. She daydreamed about the 750 ml bottle gathering dust under her kitchen sink. *Maybe when I get home. I'll have...* The phone in her room rang, disrupting her alcoholic fantasy.

Michael answered. "Yes, yes. ...I'm Michael Taylor. Right, a good friend. ...Yes, she's recovering well, but still in a lot of pain. ...I'm glad you spoke with Hank. ...Well, it's difficult for her to speak, but I can put the receiver next to her and you can speak to her. ...Okay. Hold a minute." He turned to Carrie and raised an eyebrow. "I've got Archie Graystone on the line. Says he's your uncle. Isn't he CEO of Morgan Smithe?"

Carrie closed her eyes, smiled and tilted her head back, signaling she recognized the name and wanted to speak with him.

Michael placed the receiver next to Carrie's ear.

"Carrie?" Graystone began. "I know you can't talk easily, darling girl. I'm so sorry about what happened to you, and I wish you a speedy recovery."

"Uh huh."

"I tried multiple times to reach you at home and on your cell phone. Finally I resorted to calling Hank Greenbaum. He told me where you were and why. Sounds like your in good hands, especially with Michael there."

"Uh huh."

"This may not be the right time to tell you this, but I think it will please you. After we met in D.C., I conferred with my top executives about our conversation. There's nothing else that explains market conditions other than the plot you outlined."

"Uh huh."

"We've made hundreds of calls. Very quietly to avoid spooking the markets. Calls to top execs among all our competitors as well as major banks. We've had in-person and webcam meetings with every executive team of every major stock exchange around the world. I've also met with key figures in the Treasury Department, the President of the U.S. and several foreign leaders. Even though we have nothing concrete, everyone's on alert."

"For what?" Carrie managed to ask.

"For any unusual buying or selling patterns. Any trades involving significant volumes by single sources that can't be traced to valid individuals or firms. If anyone spots an irregularity, we might yet nip this in the bud and avoid a meltdown of the global markets. It would be catastrophic for large and small investors."

"Ah."

"It'll be difficult because of the global complexity of the equities markets. But we're working hard on this. I thought you should know as you work to recuperate. The world market owes you a debt of gratitude for your insights, bravery and perseverance. Even if the safeguards we're putting into effect don't pan out.

"My dear, the barbarians may have penetrated the gate this time, but we have to force them back out."

"Tell Michael all," she whispered. Carrie closed her eyes and signaled with her head to Michael she could no longer continue the conversation.

"Mr. Graystone? Michael here. I don't know where you left off in your conversation with Carrie, but she needs to rest."

"We were done, Michael. And please, call me Archie. Greenbaum told me who you are, and I had one of my assistants run a profile on you. I'm very impressed and pleased to have my adopted niece in your company. Thank you for taking care of her. We should meet sometime."

"Thank you, I'd like that."

"Carrie asked me to bring you up-to-speed on a matter." Archie related the dinner meeting he'd had with Carrie and the actions he and others had taken as a result. "A moment ago, I told Carrie the world markets are in her debt. But, alas, we may be powerless to halt the bubble from bursting. The hell of it is, the rise in the global equity markets has not resulted from a series of smart, productive activities around the globe. Rather, it's likely deliberate sabotage by some yet unknown entity. While a group of Senators and Representatives may have started this problem, I seriously doubt they could have formed a cabal to run up the U.S. and other markets."

"What group do you think is responsible?" Michael asked.

"We've no way of knowing. We can't predict what they'll do next or when. And if everyone began taking clients' equity positions down around the world, it would cause a stampede. The entire market would crash through *our* deliberate acts. Last week, I told Carrie that when the U.S. becomes financially ill, the rest of the world suffers a great deal more. That's not just a bumper sticker statement. Large and small businesses in some hemispheres would collapse, leading to high unemployment and greater loss of capital. But it'd get worse. In some parts of the globe, people would literally *die* from shortages of water, food, medicine, electricity, and on and on. Whoever did this and any who make it worse would have blood on their hands."

Michael's mouth stood open. "My God! What about all the checks and balances in our government?"

"What about them? You know the story about a few rotten apples?"

"They spoil the barrel."

"Right. It takes only a handful of corrupt or dysfunctional individuals or groups to bring the world market down. Look at Enron, WorldCom, AIG, Bernie Madoff. Think about Greece and a few other European countries. The tsunami in Japan. The world's now inextricably tied together economically."

"What can I do to help?" Michael asked.

"For now, help our girl get well. She's done more good than a company of marines to right the wrongs that have been perpetrated by a few."

The call ended on that note.

"Sweetheart?"

Carrie opened her eyes halfway.

"You did it, babe. You busted this mess wide open. I'm proud of you. Action's being taken around the world to head off a financial disaster."

"Not enough," she whispered.

"Sometimes good efforts aren't enough when the bad guys have had months or years to devise and execute their plans. But that doesn't diminish your good efforts." He held her hand in both of his. "You, my dear, must now concentrate on recovering."

A few tears trickled down Carrie's face. She murmured, "I've conflated good efforts with extreme personal risk. I've gotta stop this."

"We can work on that together. For now, let's focus on getting you healthy."

Max walked in. "Uh, sorry, I'll be outside."

"Stay," Michael said. "What's up?"

"I think we'll be able to nail Novotchin for attacking Butler, thanks to Carrie's initiative in interviewing him. The FBI is chomping at the bit. We've got video of him at The Drake the same night as Butler."

"That's super," Michael said. "Right Carrie?"

The corners of her mouth inched up.

"Somebody called 911 to report Carrie's incident," Max said. "Maybe he was a concerned citizen who didn't want to get involved. But maybe he was the perp."

"There was only one," Carrie whispered.

"I was thinking," Max said, "as soon as we can, Carrie, you need to listen to the 911 tape. See if you can identify the voice."

Carrie began to cry softly.

"It's too soon, Max," Michael said.

"I'm sorry, but this can't wait."

42

At 8 AM the next morning, Carrie's hospital room door opened and closed quietly. She couldn't see the visitor through the curtain that had earlier been drawn around her bed. Whoever entered made no noise, which raised the hair on the back of her neck. She gripped the bed sheet as the curtain slowly opened, revealing Melvin Grimes.

"Crap, Melvin. You scared the heck out of me. Make some noise, will you."

"Sorry. Didn't wanna disturb ya."

"I'm sorry. It's just…I'm on edge after what happened."

"Michael called me. Let me know you was here. I 'preciate him doin' that."

"I'll have to thank him, but you shouldn't have come all the way. Such a long drive and all. But now you're here, it's good to see you."

Melvin took her hand in his big mitts. "I shoulda stuck with ya after we went to Vegas. Ya needed round the clock protection."

"Hey, don't think that way. You're not to blame in the least. And if you had, you probably would have gotten hurt."

Melvin grinned. "I'm a might good at protectin' myself. Besides, I'm an old geezer who's pretty much run his circuit. But you? You're a youngster who can still make a big mark on this planet."

Carrie frowned. "That doesn't mean you should risk your life for me."

Changing the subject, Melvin asked, "When ya gittin' out?"

"I'm kind of on a wait and see schedule. Maybe a few days from now. In the meantime, Michael and Max are here. Max doesn't think the guy who did this will return unless I dig deeper into Brenda's death and what she was involved in."

"Huh. Ya gonna follow his advice?"

"I haven't though much about anything but getting well."

Melvin looked around the hospital room. "Nice digs."

Carrie smiled. "Melvin, you're a pip. You crack me up."

"How's things with Michael?"

Carrie smiled again. "He's his usual wonderful self. I'm sure being out here is costing his legal practice, but he insists on sticking by me while I recover. That's pretty special."

"You betcha."

"Everything fine with you and your family?"

"Yup. Grandkids in college. Makin' good grades so's I hear. Son and daughter are doin' good with their better halves. ...You know, I'd like to git my hands on the creep who hurt ya." His eyebrows bunched in look of sincerity over his blue eyes. He gave her hand a little squeeze.

"It's okay. The cops are investigating, and they may find him. I bet the guy was behind what Brenda was doing with that Congressman."

"Honey, there's no doubt in my mind that Amici sent him to hurt ya. It's too big a coincidence. We go to Vegas, get threatened by Amici, and next thing ya know, you're on yer back here, hurtin' bad."

Carrie's lips made a moue. "I don't know about that."

"Nice quality ya have, sweetie. Willing to give Amici the benefit of the doubt. I'm not that tolerant."

Michael entered the room. "Hey Melvin, nice to see you."

They shook hands.

"Don't get up," Michael said.

"I was jes' checkin' in on our girl. Pretty banged up, huh?"

Michael nodded. "Yeah. Hopefully for the last time. How long are you in town for?"

"Thought I'd stay 'till t'morrow. Then head back. It's 'bout a half day drive."

"Can I offer to put you up at my hotel or take you to dinner?"

"I'm fixed at a Motel 6 jes' fine, but I'll take ya up on dinner? Sure liked that Grassano's pizza we had my last visit."

• • •

Over pizza, Michael asked Melvin's advice about his relationship with Carrie.

"You're pretty close to Carrie. What can I do to get through to her? She can't continue the life she's leading or she'll get killed."

Melvin polished off the last bite of a slice and gave Michael a long look. "Ya know, I own a small farm. Don't operate it now. Used to have a few horses and other animals. A lesson I learnt long time ago was ya don't change the nature of the beast. Goes for people too.

"I know ya love Carrie, and she really loves ya back. But, she's the way she is. It's her nature. She's gotta wanna change. Or, you gotta accept what she is."

Michael ran a hand through his hair. "But she's in danger."

"Ya have choices to make 'bout yer lives. Maybe she'll change, maybe not. Maybe you can take her as is, which is pretty good, maybe not. Son, ya gotta decide."

Michael shook his head. "Jeez, this is so hard."

43

"Just grand," Wyatt said sarcastically. "Another example of government incompetence. The left hand doesn't know what the right hand's doing."

Max had shared what he'd learned through Michael and Carrie about Archie Graystone's global actions to head off a global stock market collapse. Naturally, the key financial arms of the Federal government were in the loop, but no one had thought it prudent to involve the FBI, except Max Foerce.

"Director Parr will shit a brick. He's met multiple times with the SEC Chairman and the Treasury Secretary about other matters in the last few weeks. They can't say they didn't have a chance to read him in on the problem. And here we are in the middle of a related surveillance effort on multiple Members of Congress—approved by Attorney General Wayne King no less."

Max sat across Wyatt's desk in D.C., checking his manicured nails. "John, you want to run around your office a bit and let off a little more steam?"

"You know what I mean, damn it."

"Of course I do. It's the nature of the bureaucracy. Why do you think I retired? My friend, what we need to do now is to keep on the backs of these miscreants you've been tailing and be the adults in the room with a few other agencies."

Wyatt gave Max a hang dog look, clenching and unclenching his fists. "All right. I agree. I just had to blow my stack because now I have to share this with my investigative team. They'll be rightfully pissed." Wyatt sat back in his executive chair and rolled his head around in circles to get the kinks out.

"Tell me," Max said. "What have you guys been up to?"

Wyatt took a deep breath. "Okay. I've got a team going. Several agents are concentrating on selected elected officials. I've got a few zeroed in on Novotchin.

"After you gave us Linden's list of the Members of Congress she interviewed, we took a hard look at all members. Checked out news reports in the last six months for any unusual behavior. Spoke discreetly with some Congressional insiders about inexplicable voting and any other out of the norm behavior. Based on that, we expanded the helpful starter list that Linden assembled to a total of forty-one whom we believe are involved. Maybe there are more we should add, but we're erring on the conservative side. We'll get our ass handed to us if we falsely investigate a Senator or Representative and have little basis for it.

"Four people are working twenty-four hour surveillance on each of the Members of Congress on the list."

Max liked what Wyatt said. This was precisely why he'd told Michael and Carrie to let the authorities handle the matter. The FBI employed an army of well-trained personnel to throw against a problem of this magnitude. "Found anything?"

"Oh yeah, sorry to say. The folks on the list have *all* met at least once in different seedy hotels with hookers—really beautiful, classy ones, like Linden talked about. Take a look." He handed Max a file containing pictures of a dozen different women. Ravishing beauties one and all. "Interestingly, most of these meetings are short. Several lasted a few seconds. In and out, so to speak."

Max examined the photos. "These girls look like they stepped out of Escada."

"What's that?"

"A very high end boutique." Max pushed the file back across Wyatt's desk.

"Each of these working girls is serving a handful of politicians. Maybe there are more of them. So far, all we have are sightings of politicians showing up for clandestine meetings, backed up with photographs. We have no evidence of money changing hands. But we've made inquiries with the hotel managers. All they know is someone books and pays for the rooms in advance. The girls show up, pick up the keys and that's it. No one has complained about any disturbance or room damages."

Max said, "It'd be political suicide for you guys to nail politicians for heeding the call of nature. You need more, even if you get evidence of them paying for sex."

"Right." Wyatt stood and stretched. He walked over to a white board next to his desk and drew a diagram including circles, squares and diamonds, connected with lines and arrows. He inserted names, actions and decisions in the various shapes. Across the bottom of his images, he drew a time line. "This is the game plan."

Max watched as Wyatt sketched the FBI's investigative plan. He almost missed being on the inside, but quickly remembered how good a life he now led. "So your next step is to turn the girls and use them to trace backwards to their employer?"

"You've got it. And here's a recent development." He told Max about the attempt to blackmail Senator Merryweather. "I don't know if this connects with the others, but we're investigating. We've got a pic of the accused blackmailer. Name's Julie White, a former Senator's daughter. Told Merryweather her name was St. John. We've got her condo under surveillance, phones tapped. Nothing yet."

"John, you're brilliant. What about Novotchin?"

Wyatt smiled. "I've got four agents on him. Not only does law enforcement hate him, but he's pissed off his own party members. I don't know how he keeps his position. Must have pictures of his colleagues in compromising positions with goats."

"HA! It wouldn't be a first time."

"Novotchin's hooking up too, and he's drinking very heavily. We've known he's an alcoholic, but he's drunk all the time now. We're checking his personal and Congressional financial records. Parr wants in on the Novotchin bust."

"Why's that?" Max asked with raised eyebrows.

"Says he wants to make sure we do everything by the book and to his satisfaction. That's a cover. The Director wants to get even with Novotchin for all the years of embarrassment and extra work he's caused the Bureau for no good reason."

"Huh. Malcolm's good. Pays not to piss of the Director of the FBI."

"Max, as soon as Linden's healthy to travel, I'd like her here with you to work with us. Since she's talked with many of these suspects and has a holistic view of the scheme, she'd be a great resource. You think she'll cooperate?"

Max began laughing. "Cooperate? I'd say wild horses couldn't stop her from coming here and trying to *take over* your investigation."

• • •

Michael picked up Carrie's hospital room phone when it rang.

"It's Max," Michael told Carrie. "Hold on Max, I'll pass the phone to her."

"Hey," she said a bit more easily than the words she'd spoken the last few days with others: Dr. Kaptur, nurses, Michael, Melvin, Archie, Hank and Leo.

"How are you?" Max asked.

"Better, but still sore. They're gonna discharge me tomorrow, but they want me to rest a few weeks. It'll take time for my bruises and ribs to mend." Carrie looked at Michael while she spoke with Max. She saw love in his eyes. He'd been a godsend, sitting bedside from morning until night, even while she napped.

"Ahem," Max cleared his throat. "I know you've got some appointments coming up with Bernstein and you need to rest, but...uh..."

"Out with it, Max," Carrie said.

"Could you rest here in D.C.?"

"Why there?"

"The FBI wants you in on their operation to bring these politicians down, including Novotchin. I told them you probably weren't physically up to it."

Carrie rolled out of bed. Her feet hit the floor and she instantly recalled her bruised feet as pain shot up her legs. "AH," she moaned. "Sorry, Max, I just put some weight on my feet. Damn they hurt." She gathered her wits while the pain subsided. "The answer to your question is YES. I'll find a way to get around without too much pain. Plan on me being there tomorrow, maybe in the late afternoon."

Michael snatched the receiver from Carrie's hand. "What are you talking about? She can't go anywhere to do anything. Are you nuts?"

Max shared the FBI's request, and Michael negated it. Before he could disconnect, Carrie wrested the phone from Michael. "Max, there are two things I must tell you." She was speaking more to Michael than Max. "First, I've got this wonderful, protective guy sitting next to me whom I love. But second, you can tell the FBI I *will* be there tomorrow to help them bring these bastards to justice."

Carrie hung up, and she saw the angst in Michael's face. "Sweetheart, I won't be in danger. I'll be rolling around in a wheelchair during the next several days. I'd rather be doing something productive than hanging at home. I've got to do this."

Michael stared at his feet, shaking his head. They didn't speak for a few hours.

44

They flew to D.C. in adjacent seats. Michael had booked two first class United Airlines tickets for a mid-day flight from O'Hare to Reagan National Airport. Max would greet them at the airport, drop Michael at his residence and put Carrie up at his home while she worked with the FBI in Washington. Despite Michael's offer to stay with him, Carrie politely declined. Given the state of their relationship, she wanted to create some distance between them.

During the flight, their small talk felt forced. After a few minutes, they kept quiet, both pondering what had become of their love for each other.

Jablonski had called Carrie's hospital room so she could listen to the 911 call that followed her assault without going into the precinct. Time was of the essence to get Carrie's reaction to the caller's voice. After three re-plays of the recording, Carrie said, "It's him. It's the guy who beat me. I'm sure of it. Why'd he call 911?"

Jablonski had replied, "You ask me? He's a sicko. And we're gonna do our level best to put this guy away."

"I'm certain it was him," Carrie firmly restated.

When she'd hung up, Michael said, "They'll get a voice print from the 911 call and compare it with that of any suspects they dredge up."

Upon exiting the terminal at Reagan National, Max greeted them and took hold of their bags while Michael pushed Carrie's wheelchair. Max directed them to his 1969 restored red Pontiac Bonneville convertible equipped with its 360 horsepower engine. He stowed their luggage and the wheelchair in the massive trunk. They drove out of the airport in silence. Due to the humidity, Max kept the convertible top up and the AC on full during their trip through the District and northwest into Maryland.

When they reached Michael's building, Max said, "I'll call you tomorrow."

"Please do," Michael replied. And he disappeared into his building.

"Well that was an entertaining ride," Max said to Carrie as they drove away.

"Put a lid on the sarcasm, Max. Let's focus on the task."

"Sorry. You're right, kid. We've got some bad guys to catch."

• • •

The following morning, Max introduced Carrie to John Wyatt who, in turn, introduced them to a team of twelve FBI agents in a large conference facility at the J. Edgar Hoover Building. Everyone took a seat. Carrie sat in her wheelchair. "We'll have to repeat the briefing this afternoon because not every agency could make this morning's session. Just as well. This'll give us a chance to ask our questions now."

"What other agencies are you bringing in?" Max asked.

"Being the cooperative government agency we are, we've invited several you might suspect—Treasury, SEC, NSA, CIA and a few others related to Homeland Security. We want to ensure everybody who needs to know is read in on this."

Several agents mumbled under their breaths to one another. "If you have something to say," Wyatt said, "spit it out. No secrets here folks."

A tall and skinny red-headed agent stood and said, "I was remarking, uh, aren't you the one people refer to as Maximum Force? You're a legend around here."

Max gave the agent a hard look and responded, "Max will due just fine." Redhead abruptly sat down, properly chastised.

Another agent, an athletic looking Hispanic woman, said, "I was saying that I know a bit about you, Ms. Linden. I'm honored to work with you."

"Thanks for the compliment, but I'm just one of the team here. Please call me Carrie. You'll need to tell me how I can help you put these bad guys away."

Wyatt glanced around the room. "Okay, this isn't a love in. Let's begin."

Carrie briefed them on the entire case from Brenda Butler to her encounter with Tony Amici, her Congressional interviews, her meeting with Archibald Graystone and her assault. She voiced her theory that the politicians involved had been individually compromised, though with all the negative publicity, some might suspect others of being turned. She distributed copies of her list of suspected corrupt politicians. It riveted everyone's attention though they'd seen it.

After the questioning ceased, Wyatt assigned two agents to follow-up with Lt. Jablonski. Their task? Get a copy of the 911 recording about Carrie's assault and whatever additional data Jablonski could supply, like a sample of the bits of tobacco left in Brenda Butler's back. The Hispanic agent and Redhead would work with Carrie to run through her story again in greater detail, particularly the content of her Congressional interviews and the need to match Carrie's list with the one Senator Merryweather had composed as well as the one the FBI had generated.

Two agents were tasked to meet with Graystone to collect his statement. Another pair would travel to Phoenix the next day to partner with their fellow southwest agents on a new surveillance effort, targeted on Amici in Las Vegas. Briefing fellow agents now in the field, like those watching elected officials, Julie White (*AKA* St. John) and Senator Merryweather, fell to the remaining three agents.

"I don't know whether you're up to this, Carrie," Wyatt asked, "but are you open to wearing a wire and talking with these politicians again? In particular, I'm thinking about Representative Novotchin. But there will likely be others."

"You bet I am," Carrie said with a gleam in her eye.

"I'd like to work with Ms. Linden, I mean Carrie," the Hispanic woman said.

"You've got the job, Mara," Wyatt said. "Mara Gonzalez will partner with you on this task. In fact, she'll be your permanent partner during the course of this work."

"Fine by me." Carrie smiled at Mara.

Wyatt looked around the room. "This may be the biggest case of your careers, people. Let's get it right and get it done. Any questions?"

Silence filled the room. Then…

"Ahem, just one," Max spoke up for the first time in three hours since his minor reprimand of Redhead. "How do you wish to deploy me?"

"I knew I'd forgotten something, old friend. If you're agreeable, I want you to honcho our team. You know what that means. Does that work for you?"

"Delighted to serve," Max said, adjusting the half-Windsor knot in his tie.

The agents present grinned from ear to ear. Wyatt said, "When Max speaks to you, he speaks for me. Any questions?" Hearing none, he adjourned the meeting.

When the agents had filed out, Wyatt huddled with Carrie and Max. "You gave an impressive briefing, young lady. Our investigation is better off for it."

"That's just the reporter in me." Carrie smiled.

"And that's what I need to discuss with you. I know you want to be part of this team, and we need your participation. But I want your word you won't write or speak about the workings of this team until the investigation concludes. I'll want to review and approve anything you write or say about it afterwards. Agreed?"

Carrie stared at Wyatt for a long moment and said, "Deal."

45

At Dulles International Airport, Michael boarded the first of two United Airlines flights to Las Vegas. Unfortunately, a non-stop flight wasn't an option, and he risked a quick forty-five minute layover in Houston to avoid what would have been more than a seven-and-a-half hour trip. He arrived in Las Vegas at 9:27 PM.

Throughout his journey, Michael thought about Tony Amici and his deceased mother, Jeannie. He considered Max's advice not to confront Amici. But he also remembered the content of the one hundred love letters Tony had written to Jeannie—love letters that included warm feelings for him. *It brings an old saying to mind*, he mused. *I looked down my sleeve and saw my father's hand.* He shuddered at the thought of his blood ties to this devil. *Wonder if I have half-siblings?*

He needed to meet his father if for no other reason than to satisfy his biological curiosity. But he had two other big reasons for meeting the mobster. Michael wanted to strike two simple deals.

How to do it? That's the question. If I show anger, he'll probably get defensive and become angry too. Not a good way to negotiate. If I pretend affection for my long lost father, I'll appear weak. Tony's used to living in a hard world where the weak are trampled underfoot. I've got to find a middle ground. But what?

A chauffeur flagged Michael down in the baggage claim area of McCarran International Airport. He took Michael's bag and ushered him to a waiting Town Car. At that time of night and on a weekday, it took thirty-five minutes to reach the Palazzo Hotel on the strip. Michael had stayed there often and knew it to be a relatively quiet, luxury hotel.

During breakfast the next morning and probably for the twentieth time, Michael mulled over the conundrum of how to approach Amici. No matter how he played it, he couldn't walk in with a speech. It'd fall apart for a host of reasons he couldn't begin to predict. One thing he knew for sure, based on FBI reports, Tony Amici predictably sat in his office at EZ-Bonds from eight to five, except Sundays.

At ten o'clock, as Michael headed to the taxi line in front of the Palazzo, he stumbled in the lobby when a wall of nausea hit him. He hugged a pillar in the hotel lobby to steady himself as his head swam and he struggled to catch his breath. Though disoriented, he recognized the symptoms and fought off the panic attack. Fifteen minutes later, still a bit weak-kneed, he boarded a taxi for the short ride to EZ-Bonds.

"You sure you wanna get out here, mister?" the Hispanic driver asked when they arrived.

"Yes. Here's an extra ten for you."

"Uh, you wanna me to wait? Take you back? You know, make sure you come outa there okay?"

Michael stared into the driver's brown weathered face a moment longer. "I'll be fine, but sure. Wait for me, and there'll be an extra fifty in it for you."

He stepped from the cab into the bright August sunlight and walked into EZ-Bonds. As his eyes adjusted to the dim light of Amici's offices, he noticed the hanging wanted posters, the scuffed, green linoleum floor and the flaking paint on the walls. *And this is where the king of the Vegas underworld lives and works every day?*

Next he spotted two gargantuan thirty-something-year-old men sitting in the tiny reception area. They appeared no taller than he, but they were twice as wide and heavily muscled with thick necks. One sported a white wife beater that contrasted with his brown skin and the tattoos that adorned his neck, chest and arms. His close-cropped jet black hair matched his partner's. A toothpick sticking out of the other one's mouth was comfortably lodged between two front gold teeth. Two teardrop tattoos showed clearly beneath his left eye—a two-time loser. Probably state prisons.

"Whatcha want honey?"

Michael turned to face a short, pudgy receptionist behind a peeling Formica countertop. He checked out her hot pink strapless jersey dress, two sizes too small and three inches too short, and what appeared to be heavy stage make-up.

He thought, *Maybe I overdressed.* Like usual, he wore one of his standard Wearhouse for Men's blue blazers with gray slacks, loafers, a blue button-down shirt and a striped tie. He carried a soft black leather Coach briefcase in his left hand.

"I'm here to see Mr. Amici. My name's Michael Taylor."

She blew a chewing gum bubble, popped it and continued masticating. "Just a sec, hon. I'll see if I can bother him." The receptionist sashayed from behind her desk around the corner and into an office. A few seconds later, she emerged and said, "Go on in…but hit me up after, handsome. I'd love to show you the town." She gave him a suggestive wink.

Michael returned the wink with a half-smile and walked into Tony's office.

46

Amici stood up behind his desk, a few inches shorter than Michael, but as handsome in his way as Michael was in his—only Tony dressed far better. They stared at each other for several seconds but didn't shake hands. Finally, Tony cracked a big smile and spoke.

"I wondered if I'd ever meet you in person." He nodded. "This is unexpected. If I'd known you were coming, we could have met somewhere, uh, more fitting."

"It was a spur of the moment decision. I won't take much of your time."

"I've got plenty of time. Shut the door and have a seat." Tony took his and adjusted the razor sharp creases in his slacks. "What can I do for you Mr. Taylor?"

Michael took one of the orange chairs. "For openers, please call me Michael? You did in your letters to my mother." With that, Michael lifted his briefcase. Tony quickly leaned forward and reached into an open desk drawer.

"Don't worry, Mr. Amici. I'm only carrying paper." He extracted his mother's one hundred letters and arrayed them on the desktop in front of Tony. "I suppose one thing you can do for me is to explain these." Michael gave Amici a half-smile.

Tony eyed the letters. He scooped them up and rifled through the pile, opening and examining a few random letters. He dropped them on the desk, leaned his head back and closed his eyes. A minute later, having gathered his composure and shaking his head, he responded, "What's to explain? Isn't it evident? I'm your father."

"I'm not sure about *that*. You see, I grew up without a father. You certainly were a donor of sorts and a benefactor, but I never really had a father."

Tony closed his eyes again. *This is my son. The good one. The one I'm proud of. The one I hoped to have by my side. Not that little prick I raised who's always in trouble for drug possession. Maybe. . . If only. . .*

"Did you really love her? My mother?" Michael pressed.

Jolted from his reverie, Tony nodded as he answered. "Very much. More than you'd believe. I can't tell you how many times..."

"Why didn't you marry her?" Michael asked in a sincere tone.

"Ah," Tony looked into Michael's eyes, nodding, "that's a long and complicated story."

"I've got time for the abridged version." Michael sat very still.

How can I explain my life? It's not the one I chose for myself. And look at him. Good looking, educated, legit. And what balls he has coming here. Kid's got guts.

Tony leaned back in his chair and straightened his suit jacket. "A little history. ...My father owned and operated a bar. ...Oh, let's be honest, shall we? It was a money laundering operation. He was tough and very abusive. Put me on his payroll when I turned twelve. At sixteen, I fell in love with a Mexican girl—a sweet little thing as I recall. When my father learned about it, he claimed I'd sullied the family's honor and beat me severely. It wasn't the first time or the last."

Michael asked, "And what does that have to do with my mother?"

Tony smiled and waved a hand. "Be patient. ...The girl and her family disappeared the next day. I don't know what became of them. I was searching for love—something absent from my entire youth. Two years later, my father arranged a marriage for me to the daughter of a Gambino family member. I trust you know who and what the Gambino family is, or at least was in their hey-day."

Michael nodded.

"The wedding was set to take place a year following high school graduation. Late in my senior year, my class took a trip to D.C., like so many other high school graduating classes.

"I met your mother, quite by accident, next to the Washington National Monument and spent the next few days with her—not with my class. Those were glorious days." Tony paused and closed his eyes for three seconds, recalling the past. Then, "No subject was out of bounds. We were two peas in the same pod. Jeannie was an extraordinarily warm and captivating young woman. I'd never met anyone like her and haven't since."

"I guess you know she became a chronic alcoholic," Michael said.

"Yes. She wrote me about it. Very sad." Tony grimaced and shook his head. "Michael, most of us become things we never anticipated being. Hopefully, you'll be all you want to be in life. Anyway, Jeannie and I fell in love. Would my presence have made a difference? Perhaps. But not in the way you think. I'll explain."

Michael relaxed a bit in his chair.

Tony took a deep breath. "I called my father for permission to stay in D.C. for two weeks extra to explore the historical sites. Of course, it was just an excuse to spend time with Jeannie. We fantasized about getting married and building a life together. I promised Jeannie…" Tony choked up. After collecting himself, he continued, "I promised her I'd return home and tell my father the arranged marriage was off, that I was marrying Jeannie and quitting the family business."

"How did that work out for you?"

"Ah, you didn't know my father. A month after I returned, I was still working up the courage to speak with him when I received a letter from Jeannie. She was pregnant with you. She needed me, and I felt honor bound to go to her.

"So I mustered the courage and made a short speech to my father in his bar in front of a half dozen of his thugs." Tony bit his lower lip, remembering the incident.

"My father roared with laughter, and his men laughed with him. Then he got serious. He said, and I'll never forget, 'You stupid shit. You'll get married as planned, and you'll forget that little whore in D.C.'

"I stood my ground. I was angry. He'd insulted Jeannie. I told him I didn't have to obey him. I was a man. He said, 'You need a life lesson.' This is what I got for my impudence." Tony held up his left hand and splayed his three remaining fingers.

"My loving father ordered his men to grab me. They held my hand down flat against the bar. 'Give me the hatchet,' he ordered his bartender. 'I'm going to remove your little pinky. You don't really need it in life, but it will remind you to obey me in all things.'

"I screamed and begged, and then the hatchet came down—three times to finish the job. They wrapped my hand in a bar rag and drove me to the hospital."

Michael blew out a breath of air and blinked in horror.

Tony rotated his left hand for Michael's viewing. "As you can see, his aim wasn't true. He took two instead of one. Of course, he was right about one thing. This hand reminded me every waking moment that I had to obey him until, a few years later, the happiest day of my life arrived—he died. Otherwise, I would have lost an appendage or maybe worse. You see, blood relations didn't count much to him if they interfered with his business. And my arranged marriage was all about his business."

Listening with his eyebrows bunched, Michael asked, "Couldn't you have just left and taken my mother with you?"

"Huh. I guess you haven't learned a few things in your criminal law practice. They'd find us wherever we went. I was afraid for your mother. My father would have sent someone for Jeannie if I'd given him trouble. I didn't want her harmed or killed.

"So I obeyed my father and married. Years passed. I corresponded with Jeannie, secretly. My arranged marriage was one of duty, not love. But I always loved your mother," Tony sniffed. "I provided what support I could. More as I grew older."

Tony pulled a maroon silk square from the pocket of his grey pinstriped suit jacket and dabbed a few tears in the corners of his eyes.

Michael shifted in his seat. "Did you ever see my mother again after you returned from your senior class trip?" he asked evenly.

"Never. We agreed to write every three months, and what you see before you is evidence I kept my end of the bargain."

"Some deal. We barely survived from month to month," Michael said.

"I often wished I had taken Jeannie and you directly under my wing."

"Why didn't you after your father died?" Michael's voice remained calm.

"Simple. To give you a chance to be legit. Mind you, I'm committed to my, uh, industry. Have been for decades. But there was no reason for you to be any part of it."

"Thanks for that, I guess. Did you grease the skids for my scholarships?"

"No. You did that all on your own. I was very proud of you. Jeannie was too."

"Did you help get me into Harvard Law?" Michael asked.

"You should be happy to have received help. Of course I pulled some strings." He pointed at Michael with the index and middle fingers on his left hand. "If you hadn't made good grades and scored well on admissions tests, my influence would have counted for nothing."

"Did you funnel clients to me when I set up my law practice?"

Tony chuckled. "Criminals need attorneys. What can I say?" he shrugged.

"Do you still refer clients to me?" he asked with a raised eyebrow.

Tony gave Michael *the look*. He thought, *This may be my good son, but he hasn't the right to interrogate me*. Michael glared back.

"On occasion, I give associates your name because you're a good attorney. And that's the last question I'll answer." Tony frowned. "Who do you think you are, barging in here, uninvited and without an appointment and interrogating me? After all I've done, you should be shining my shoes or kissing my ass." Tony sat upright in his chair, leaned forward with a menacing look and tugged at his jacket lapels. What made him even angrier was Michael's affect. He appeared relaxed, sitting in the same chair in which so many hard cases had cringed in meetings with Tony.

"I'm grateful for your early support Mr. Amici, and I appreciate that you loved my mother. I can tell from your letters that you had deep feelings for her and, to an extent, for me."

Tony unclenched his jaw, let out a breath and sat back in his chair.

"Since you had the heart to help me in the past, I ask two favors from you going forward. Neither will cost a cent." Michael offered a sincere, measured smile.

"What are they?" Tony asked gruffly, shooting his cuffs.

"First, don't refer any more clients to my law practice. Agreed?"

Tony thought for five seconds. "Done. Your second request?"

"Do not harm or cause to be harmed Carrie Linden ever again."

"HEHEHE. That's one good looking girl you've got. But that bitch keeps putting her nose where it doesn't belong. I'm afraid she may lose it or worse."

"I'd hoped we could come to terms on this. It would cost you nothing, and she can't harm you. If you have even imaginary affection for me, then leave the ones I love alone," he said with a determined look.

Tony raised his voice. "If she interferes with my concerns, she risks everything. Understood?"

"You've made me understand one thing. . . . You're just like your father."

"WHAT!" Tony exclaimed.

"Let me put this in a way you might better understand. If Carrie is harmed in any way that I can trace back to you, I'll kill you with my bare hands." Michael stood up with his briefcase in hand and gave Tony a curt nod. "Thanks for you time." Leaving the letters behind and Tony with a hanging jaw, Michael casually left.

Tony seethed with anger. He stepped to his office doorway and watched Michael saunter out of EZ-Bonds. *I did so much for that kid. Loved him like I tried to love my other son. And he treats me like this? Threatens to kill me? NOBODY threatens me! . . . I'm like my FATHER? He's got no idea who he's fucking with, but he's gonna find out.* Tony banged his fist on his office door. The two thick-necked thugs in the reception area jumped to attention. Tony raced out of EZ-Bonds and onto the street, trailed by his goons, just in time to see a taxi pulling away from the curb.

47

The mechanic stood next to the swimming pool at his Palm Springs compound. It would likely reach one hundred ten in the sun today, but the heat had not yet built. He'd spent part of his latest contract fee installing a solar system on his desert home, and he watched with interest as the workmen set up in the early morning hours.

In addition to the solar panels and the inverters needed to convert the variable direct current from the panels' photovoltaic output to alternating current, the mechanic had purchased forty lead-acid deep cycle batteries. The batteries would hang from an exterior wall of his home and store electricity for use. The mechanic smiled at the idea of being energy self-sufficient. *This is such a great place to live.*

Last night, he'd dined at a new Spanish restaurant in Rancho Mirage, called Catalan—twenty minutes from home. Between courses, he received an odd call from a man who spoke English with a heavy Chinese accent. He contemplated it as he observed the solar crew in action.

The caller had spoken the right codes to which he'd given the appropriate responses, certifying both parties to the call. The Chinese man wanted to commission a hit. While the target appealed greatly to the mechanic, he found the assignment troubling. Never before had someone requested he assassinate one of his clients—in this case, Tony Amici. He found Amici base and lacking in honor. But Amici presently employed him, and the mechanic felt a conflict of interest—an ethical dilemma, not a moral one. The Chinese man had given him thirty days to consider.

Time to check in with my shooters. I'll think about Amici next week.

He dialed the Israeli, sipping gourmet Columbian coffee he'd just brewed.

"When can I proceed?" she asked. "It's taking too long."

"Patience, please. Remember, the fee is higher than usual. I await instructions just as you. I will be in contact." He disconnected and called the Cuban ex-Ranger.

As the phone rang, he studied the Washingtonia Robusta palm trees in his back yard. *Hmm, a half foot taller than last year. And the cacti have blossomed. Yellow, red, white. I so love the desert.*

The Cuban picked up, and the mechanic had the same conversation as with the Israeli woman, except the Cuban began haggling again about his fee.

"Sí, I got the advance payment. Thank you, amigo. But I know you're makin' out really good. Lot better'n me right?" the Cuban asked in an accusing tone.

"Your fee is more than you normally receive, and you have received fifty percent of it up front. You also do not have to travel as you always do. I could have selected someone else for this highly profitable assignment, but I chose you. Do not make me reevaluate my decision."

"You gotta come up with more, hombre. I got family responsibilities."

"Manage them. Do not manage me. If we have this conversation again, I will visit you and take more than your advance fee from you. Do you understand?"

"Hey, hombre, I was just negotiatin', you know? Gotta try."

"Do not try again." The mechanic hung up. *Prick.*

He'd been unable to contact the black ex-Navy Seal, despite multiple calls throughout the day. Worrisome. Although the former Seal was a great shooter, the mechanic wondered about his mental stability. He was a loner, a recluse. *Has he flaked out? It isn't like him to be non-responsive. I'll try again tomorrow.*

48

Michael answered his office phone early-morning.

"It's me," Max said. "Have you checked the financial news this morning?"

"I've been tied up with clients."

"You remember those Members of Congress who on Friday announced reversals on their newfound business orientation? The DOW has already dropped over seven hundred points this morning. Great way to start a week."

"Is the impact U.S.-centric or...?"

"Asian markets are down about nine percent, pretty uniformly. Remember, their markets open and close a day ahead of us. European markets will close in a few hours, but they're down eight-and-a-half points so far."

"Let's hope it ends there."

"I doubt it will." Max hung up and walked into a massive amphitheater for the start of a multi-agency briefing at FBI headquarters. Carrie sat in her wheelchair on the dais at the front of the room, surrounded by various agency heads. There was standing room only in the space that sat two hundred, theater-style. Max leaned against a wall next to the exit—a good place to observe the speakers and the audience.

A minute later and facing the audience, John Wyatt brought the meeting to order. "Thank you all for coming," he said into a live mike. The room hushed. "Each of you has top secret clearance, and I remind you that you signed in when you entered this room. You'll receive a copy of the sign-in sheet before you leave so you'll know who was here. Nothing said in this meeting can be shared with anyone else at this time. If there's a leak from this room, we'll find out and you'll be prosecuted." Shaking his head, Wyatt added, "I admit, that's not a friendly way to start a meeting, but, shortly, you'll understand why I've put that fact on the table front and center."

A Deputy National Security Advisor to the President (code for political appointee) sitting in the fifth row raised his hand. "What if I need to tell..."

Attorney General King cut him off. "I'll clarify for Mr. Wyatt. Anyone in this room who shares anything about this meeting with anyone not in this room at this moment, without first getting approval from Mr. Wyatt, will be prosecuted to the full extent of the law. Get it? It won't just be a career ending move. Any questions?"

Way to go Wayne, Max thought. *That should control most of these nitwits and make the few who'll leak anyway think twice before they do.*

The Deputy National Security Advisor slumped in his chair, red-faced.

"As I was about to say," Wyatt continued. "We have a conspiracy on our hands of epic proportions. It began in the U.S., and it has begun affecting the rest of the world. Hopefully, the impact will be minimal and short-lived. I've asked two civilians to join us today." He gestured to Carrie in her wheelchair. "Carrie Linden is a noted syndicated columnist who uncovered the conspiracy and brought it to our attention. The reason she's in a wheelchair is that people at the heart of this conspiracy savagely beat her and almost killed her to shut her up." Most of the audience nodded in recognition of the reporter. A few grimaced. Probably, Max imagined, at the thought of a reporter sitting inside their top secret tent.

"The other is Max Foerce." He pointed to Max who raised an open hand and gave a short wave. "I'm sure you remember Max—one of the FBI's all-time most successful agents." Smiles around the room greeted one of their own.

"In a moment, I'll ask Carrie and Max to brief you. They're both working directly with my investigative team. They're also best positioned to tell the story of this conspiracy in layman's terms. I'll then brief you on what the FBI's doing. Afterwards, we'll have a Q&A session. ...Throughout this briefing you need to ask yourself one question." Wyatt paused for effect, then pointed to the audience. "What should you do in your role in government to help? ...When you have an answer to that question, call me or come see me to discuss it. DO... NOT...WRITE...TO...ME.

"Attorney General King has appointed me *mission coordinator* for the mess we're dealing with. That means I'll be synthesizing, collaboratively with you, the possible actions we might take. In turn, I'll give them to the AG to discuss with various agency heads and the POTUS."

Just then, a huge screen at the front of the room came to life. The image of the President of the United States appeared. President Mark Stine had a commanding presence. At six foot five, ably built from his days as a rancher and cattleman, and with a full head of silver hair and tanned complexion, he gave off an aura of vitality and high energy, even on video, despite the fact he'd just celebrated his 70th birthday. "Am I on time Mr. Wyatt?" he asked with his Texas drawl.

"Yes sir. You have the floor."

"I'll make this brief y'all 'cause I'm heading into a meeting with some key advisors and then the heads of the G-eight countries about this new strategic threat. I've been read in on all you're gonna hear. We need your best work on this, people, individually and collectively. And you need to maintain strict silence outside this group until you're given permission by Mr. Wyatt to speak with others. I'll leave you with one fact. In the last half hour, the DOW has shed another five hundred points. The trading day isn't over, and the market's down thirteen hundred points. Good luck, y'all, and God bless America." The screen went blank.

Jeez! That gave me goose bumps, Max thought. *But what a clusterfuck!*

Carrie gave the audience a concise and to the point summary. She was so articulate and had such great poise, even sitting in her wheelchair, that she held the entire audience spellbound. From memory, she ticked off facts, dates, names of politicians and events in a cohesive, well-delivered speech. She also shared a few of her hypotheses that made eminent sense to anyone paying attention.

Hmm, a hard act to follow, Max thought. But he followed anyway, and his authoritative demeanor, coupled with his knowledge of the various agencies present, lent credibility to his portion of the briefing that centered on evidence gathered to date.

Wyatt shared the actions the FBI had taken and their plans going forward. After the Q&A session, he concluded by asking the FBI investigative team to remain. Then, he adjourned the meeting. Those leaving filed out, mostly in silence.

Turning to Max, Wyatt muttered, "I'll bet within fifteen minutes a few Members of Congress will receive calls about this meeting."

"I know," Max said. "But you had no choice. You had to deliver this briefing to get our behemoth bureaucracy working together. It's a double-edged sword."

• • •

At 4:05 PM Eastern Standard Time, Archibald Graystone stepped into the Oval Office. He shook hands with the President, the Treasury Secretary, the Attorney General and the Chairmen of the SEC and Federal Reserve. Standing, he said, "Mr. President, throughout the day I've spoken with colleagues around the globe. The DOW lost over seventeen hundred points today. Overseas markets have dropped precipitously—worse than in the U.S. Consensus? Everyone expects an unprecedented run on the global markets over the next few weeks. No one can fathom the level where the markets will bottom out and what will happen afterwards."

"Gentlemen," the President began, "you'll excuse me, but I'm an ex-cattle rancher. I didn't major in economics, and I'm no financial wizard. I've got a dumb question. Somebody explain to me why this is affecting the rest of the world as it is. Give me a crash course here."

"Ahem," Graystone spoke. "Think of it this way, Mr. President. Countries around the world trade goods and services with one another. When the global market is robust and there's confidence in economies around the world, corporations and consumers buy more things. That, in turn, creates more confidence. The buying behavior feeds the attitude of confidence and vice-versa. As a result, the value of companies generally increases, hence the rise in the stock market."

"Makes sense," the President said, nodding.

"If corporate success is based on solid fundamentals like strong balance sheets, good customer bases, predictable cash flow, favorable regulatory climates, then the rise in price of a particular company's stock is justified."

The President nodded. "Okay."

"Because of our global interconnectedness, stock markets tend to rise and fall together. They're correlated. Not perfectly, but they're correlated enough so that you see similar patterns in price movements globally.

"Now, think about the debacle in Greece and how that tiny country has depressed the markets around the world, simply because they might default on their debt. And theirs is a small fraction of the U.S. debt."

"We've all taken that in the shorts." The President shook his head.

"Right," Graystone said. "Imagine what happens to the rest of the world when bad things happen in a huge economy like ours." Graystone paused to let that sink in. "Suppose stock market prices are artificially inflated. In other words, the value of corporations is *not* based on solid fundamentals. When elected officials alter the corporate playing field through their legislative and regulatory actions and their allocations of capital, analysts factor those actions into corporate valuations, which they report to those buying stock. When the analysts make those calculations, they take what Congress does at face value. No one assumes they're gaming the system."

"Wait. I get it," President Stine said. "This handful of miscreants in Congress have boosted the U.S. market with a bunch of fake rhetoric and action, and they've now removed that support structure from the market. Investors are fleeing the market 'cause they can't count on continued success, and that's created fear and ripple effects around the globe. Those effects have hurt weaker markets a lot harder than the U.S."

Everyone in the room smiled. "I couldn't have said it better, Mr. President," Graystone said.

"Gol dang it!" President Stine exclaimed. "Folks, we got some cattle in Congress that need castratin'."

49

Max stared in the face of each FBI agent present and then addressed the team. "You guys are doing a great job dogging the Members of Congress on our list. But we need to move from watch-mode to action. We need to provoke a mistake by one or more of our targets. Any ideas?"

No one spoke for a half minute. Then, Mara Gonzalez raised her hand. "You know how Carrie interviewed seventeen Members of Congress on our list and came away with evidence on Novotchin?"

"Yeah?" Max raised an eyebrow.

"Suppose we wired Carrie and had her meet with a few other politicians on our list. Maybe that'd shake something loose. If Carrie's willing, that is."

"You betcha." Carrie practically jumped from her wheelchair. "That's a rockin' idea." She launched into a speech about how it would work.

Max interrupted. "Carrie, you and Mara work out the details. Mara, pick two other agents to help with the tech stuff and logistics. Stay close to Carrie in the field. Let's see what we can learn. Good idea, Mara. Anyone else?"

Redhead raised his hand. "Yeah?" Max asked, eyes narrowed, remembering the kid had previously referred to him as *Maximum Force*.

"I'm dating an aide to a Congressman on our list."

Everyone laughed. One agent asked, "How are things *under cover*, Red?" Another, "Are you sure you aren't dating the CongressMAN?" A third, "Did you say aide or intern?" The team hee-hawed.

Red's complexion darkened, and he looked down at his notebook.

"Go on, Red. Let's hear it," Max urged. "Maybe the rest of you could use your craniums instead of your rectums and offer some constructive ideas."

The laughter instantly died.

"Over pizza last night, she said her Congressman plans to attend some secret meeting two nights from tonight. She doesn't know the agenda for the meeting and said it sounded mysterious. When I asked who else would attend, she rattled off a half dozen names. ...I checked. They're all on our list. Maybe we should stake out the meeting and see who shows up. Maybe we could even listen in."

Everyone remained silent, waiting for Max to react. Max asked, "What do the rest of you think of Red's idea?"

One agent spoke up and said, "I think that's politically dangerous because..."

"WRONG!" Max exclaimed. "Red's idea is brilliant. That's just the kind of go get 'em thinking we need. Red, put a team of four together. Find out where they'll meet or follow your friend's boss to the venue. Get video of who comes and goes as well as license plate pics. Audio record their meeting, although I'd prefer full video if you can swing it. Look up their asses and get something we can use."

Red beamed. "Yes sir. I'm on it."

Another minute went by. Max was about to adjourn the meeting when one of the attorneys in the room spoke up—a tall and lanky, pasty-white fellow with limp brown hair. "I'd say it's time to press Novotchin. Hard. Let's yank the drunken fucker from his office in handcuffs. Make a big scene. We'll grill the bastard and see what information we can squeeze out of him about the rest of Congress."

"Hmm, an interesting proposition," Max said. "But he's a pretty cagey guy. Let's go with your suggestion to press him, but inject a little finesse. We don't want him to clam up and lawyer up."

Another attorney raised his hand. "Let's do this. I'll work with Charles to develop a loose script. Then, the two of us will approach Novotchin as he leaves his office. We'll show him ID and ask him to come quietly with us to headquarters. Tell him we need to discuss a matter concerning time he spent at The Drake Hotel some weeks ago. We'll say something like 'I know you don't want a nasty public display.' Show him a pair of handcuffs. Then, we'll bring his ass in for a discussion with you."

The lanky attorney asked, "So we shouldn't rough him up a little?"

Max shook his head. "I said go get 'em. I didn't say beat them up. Do it smart. We're going to make him think that ratting out his colleagues in Congress on the conspiracy will get him off the hook on the Drake matter, which it won't. Be nice. Be firm. Be scary. Act like you're holding back incriminating information. Good idea guys. Work together on this, and remember—finesse."

"Okay." The tall attorney sat back in his chair, likely disappointed he wouldn't be kicking down doors. The second attorney leaned forward, visibly excited.

"All right folks. That's enough to get started. Let's hit the bricks."

As Max wheeled Carrie from the amphitheater, she said, "I liked the way you handled the team. They're pretty fired up."

"Thanks. Your briefing was inspired. I think you earned your stripes with them this morning. But when you do the wired interviews, I want Mara or another agent on your heels in case one of these creeps goes off the rails and tries to hurt you."

"That's not gonna..." She turned to face Max, and he gave her a stern look. "Okay, okay."

50

As he shaved, Ruddock smiled into the mirror at how quickly his fifty-five corrupted politicians responded to his orders. *And they say leading Congress is like herding cats. I turned them like a Marine marching band. On a fucking dime! They're just a bunch of cheap suits.*

His cell phone rang. "Hello?"

"Do you know who this is?" Tony asked.

"Yeah boss." *Wonder what he wants?*

"Now that you've turned the herd, I want you to monitor them. Make sure they don't change their positions."

"Will do." *That's easy.*

."I also want you to complete the assignment I pulled you away from."

Ruddock thought for a moment. "Uh, you mean dealing with the one who refused to play?"

"Right. No one refuses, and we can't risk any blowback. Do it right away."

"Understood."

"After that, I've got a few other matters for you. Your colleague needs to go."

"Permanently?"

"Right."

"Boss, when you told me to have her bug out the other day, I did. She'd already set up appointments for our, uh, employees for several weeks going forward. Then, she split. I don't know where she went, and she's not answering her cell."

"IDIOTS! That's who I have working for me. IDIOTS! Just because you go into hiding, you're not incommunicado."

"Sorry boss, I didn't have time..."

"Time? No, you didn't have the brains to figure it out. ...If and when you get hold of her, end it."

"I will. And I'd like to say..."

"Don't say anything. The last item concerns a man named Michael Taylor. He's a successful Maryland criminal attorney. I'll text you his cell and office phone numbers. Find him and have a hard, heart-to-heart talk with him."

"Like the one I had with that pest in Chicago?"

"Not that hard, but make it memorable. The message is, 'No one threatens Tony.'" That said, Tony hung up.

PRICK! He wants his orders followed to the letter. When I color outside the lines, he goes berserk. Now that I didn't, he's raining shit on my head. I gotta get out of this business. Then, Ruddock remembered, *Nolite te bastardes carborundorum. I won't let the bastards get me down.*

That night, Ruddock sat in his rental car a half block from Senator Blaine Merryweather's home in Bethesda. At 9 PM, in what likely was an upstairs bedroom in the Senator's home, the last light extinguished. Ruddock had seen only two persons entering or exiting the home in the last three hours—the Senator and his wife. Ruddock badly needed to piss.

He'd dressed in black attire for this job and pulled on his black leather gloves and balaclava. Seeing no one on the street, he quietly exited the car and walked in darkness toward the Senator's house. The half-acre and heavily treed lots in this neighborhood provided ample cover, making it near perfect for a home invasion. Ruddock sidled up to a rhododendron bush next to the back door.

Time to drain the lizard. It felt good to relieve the pressure that had built. Now he could conclude this business in comfort and move on to his next assignment.

He easily picked the single lock on the door. Seeing no evidence of an alarm system, Ruddock slipped into the house and closed the door behind him. He listened. No sounds. Among other things, that meant no dogs. He hadn't seen any in his earlier reconnaissance of the property, and no one had walked a dog before bedtime. *Perfect.*

That afternoon, he'd picked up a United Kingdom Special Forces knife at an Army Navy Surplus store. Its black epoxy powder coating the blade and black handle made it near invisible in the dark—its 6.22-inch blade adequate for the job at hand. He carried it in his right gloved fist as he moved further into the house.

Ruddock made his way around the first floor, acquainting himself with the simple layout of this fifty-some-year-old house—kitchen and family room at the back, living room and formal dining room at the front. He unlocked the front door in case he needed to make a speedy exit out the front. Then, he slowly ascended the stairs, stepping on the far edges of each stair tread to avoid creaking sounds.

At the top of the staircase he spied four doors—one a double door on the right at the end of the hallway, presumably the master bedroom. He stepped slowly down the hall and carefully grasped the solitary doorknob on the double doors.

WHAT THE FUCK?

Someone switched on the bright hall lights. The doors to the other rooms crashed open, and three men pointed handguns at him. "DROP YOUR WEAPON! DROP YOUR WEAPON! KNEEL DOWN!"

Multiple voices screamed at him. It was surreal. For a second, he couldn't believe what had happened. How could he be in this situation? The voices continued pounding in his ears. "DOWN MOTHERFUCKER OR WE'LL SHOOT."

Ruddock dropped his knife. It clattered to a stop on the wooden hallway floor. As he moved to a kneeling position, the door to the master bedroom opened. "And whom do we have here, visiting at this late hour?" Senator Merryweather asked.

• • •

An hour later, Ruddock sat in an FBI interrogation room, having been strip-searched. The only items he'd brought with him to Merryweather's home included the car key and the knife. At some point, the FBI would let the local cops in on the bust. For now, they held him as an accessory to an ongoing FBI investigation. Minimally, he'd be charged with breaking and entering. The pigsticker he'd brought along and his behavior in the house suggested attempted murder. But the FBI wanted more.

That's it. I'm fucked. There's only one thing I could do to fuck myself permanently—rat out Tony. That'd be a death sentence. Maybe not the first or second night behind bars, but soon after. Jesus, how could I have let myself down like this?

Since Merryweather's call to the FBI after St. John's visit, agents had taken up residence in the Senator's home, their cars parked around the corner. For three hours, they'd watched an unidentified vehicle parked a half block away with someone sitting behind the wheel. They'd stood alert, waiting for the car to leave. Instead, the driver had exited the vehicle and walked toward the Senator's house. Showtime.

Ruddock understood the Miranda rights they'd read to him, but he had nothing to say, except to ask for a phone call per his rights. He knew of one local attorney.

A minute later, Michael Taylor answered his cell phone.

51

"What was that all about?" Carrie asked.

Michael rolled back into bed underneath the sheet and gently pulled Carrie to him. "The FBI has some guy in custody at headquarters for breaking and entering a Senator's home. Says he needs an attorney. I don't know how he got my number."

"That's odd. Why would the FBI be involved in a B and E?"

"I don't know. Because it was a Senator's house?"

Carrie frowned. "Doesn't make sense."

"I'll find out all about it tomorrow. Right now I'm concentrating on something far more critical in my life."

She laughed and asked, "Oh? What might that be?"

"You."

Michael had picked Carrie up from Max's home in a friend's SUV. His Jaguar convertible wouldn't accommodate her wheelchair. They'd eaten early at a restaurant in Great Falls, Virginia, called the Serbian Crown—a long-established D.C. area eatery for French and Russian cuisine. At the end of dinner, Carrie asked to check out his kitchen remodel to which she'd contributed input but never seen the final results.

Once in his Chevy Chase condominium, one thing led to another, and they found themselves in a passionate embrace. The next thing they knew they'd made love twice in a row. It had been tricky due to Carrie's bruises, but they quickly found positions that allowed pleasure with no pain—mostly involving Carrie on top.

Lying on her side, she gave Michael a little jab on his shoulder. "I thought you weren't interested in my crazy life. Or do you just want to get me into bed?"

"It's definitely all about bedding you," he said in jest.

She laughed and then became quiet. "Do you know how much I love you and love being with you?"

"I believe I do. You've got to know I feel the same way." He kissed her forehead and softly ran his hand down her arm.

"Then why can't we make this work? We're both smart, professional people who've never been as attracted to anyone else as we are to one another, and..."

"And don't forget about the sex," Michael added.

"I'm serious about this, Michael. I'd...I'd be happy with something more permanent, if only we..."

Michael kissed her hard on her lips, and she reciprocated.

"I want you in my life so much, but..."

"But what? You don't want me to be what Max calls a justice-junkie? You want me to write about coming out parties and flower arranging? That won't happen."

She stared at him. He turned on his side to face her and returned her gaze.

"It doesn't bother you to put your life in danger repeatedly? I've only known you two years, and you've come close to being murdered three or four times during that period. I don't know anyone with that kind of record. Even the hardest criminals I represent lead far less dangerous lives."

Carrie propped herself up on her elbow. "If you read the articles I've written, beginning fifteen years ago and continuing forward until today, you'd see I have an ongoing love affair with justice. I didn't realize it until I went through psychotherapy with Bernstein. But as I examined the patterns in my life and the events that likely drove me to be who I am, that's the result. I don't think I can change it. The more I think about it, I don't want to change. I love what I do. And it pains me greatly that who I am doesn't work for who you are because I adore you. We're perfect for one another in so many ways."

A tear rolled down Carrie's cheek, and Michael reached up to wipe it away. "During my youth, I lived in constant fear of something happening to my mother. I only had one parent, no other relatives and no other adult figures in my life. So if something had happened to her, I would have been in trouble. She had grave self-destructive tendencies and no redeeming qualities like you have, even though she loved me. Those tendencies exacerbated my fears. No doubt that's colored the way I think about our relationship. And despite that little self-insight into my psyche and no matter how great I feel about you, your love affair with justice makes me cringe."

"I'm still here, aren't I?"

"Of course you are. If you ceased to exist for whatever reason, it would break my heart. But if we were married with a day-to-day life together, I think I'd die if anything permanent happened to you."

Carrie sat up on the edge of the bed. "Michael, let's not get melodramatic. We're all going to die at some point."

"Yes, we are. But there's such a thing as taking chances that hasten the end. Forget about my interest in you. You're too lovely a person to die young."

Carrie reached for her bra and panties that had fallen on the floor next to the bed. "I think you'd better return me to Max's house before I turn into a pumpkin. Besides, I don't want any funny looks from him."

"I'd hoped you might stay the night."

"Tomorrow's a busy day for me, and you have an appointment with the FBI."

En route to Max's home, Carrie asked, "How did your trip to Las Vegas go?"

"So Max told you about that, eh? Is nothing sacrosanct with that guy?"

"He was concerned."

Michael turned off Wisconsin Avenue and into Max's Bethesda neighborhood. "Well he needn't have been. I met my father, learned a little about my mother and him and we reached a little agreement."

He pulled into Max's driveway.

"What agreement?"

"He won't refer any more prospective clients to me. I followed your suggestion."

"That's great. Will that put a big dent in your firm's revenue?"

"I have no idea, and I really don't care."

"Sounds like you could have done that by phone, instead of schlepping to Vegas. Or did you need to see him face-to-face?"

"Looking him in the eye was a good thing. I'm certain I made a few points that he'll think about for a long time."

Michael helped Carrie into her wheelchair and wheeled her into Max's house.

Max lowered the volume on his TV. "You two have a good time tonight?" Max asked.

"Indeed we did," Michael said. "Serbian Crown."

"Ah, one of my favorites"

52

The checkout clerk at Ralph's grocery store eyed the two obvious lesbians. "You guys visitin' for a while?" she asked.

St. John said, "No, we moved here a few days ago."

The clerk noticed the younger woman didn't respond, but she'd wrapped her arms around the other one's waist.

As the clerk continued to scan their groceries, she said, "I'm glad to meetcha. Name's Roselinde, but friends call me Rosie. Nice to see new ladies movin' to town."

"We're looking forward to a quiet life here," St. John said.

"HA! It's quiet all right. But we got some fun things goin'. What's yer name?"

St. John replied, "I'm Gwen, and my partner is Brittany."

The clerk began to bag the groceries while St. John/Gwen pulled cash from her wallet to pay. "Where you guys livin'?"

Brittany spoke up. "On a hilltop at the end of Piedmont Road."

Gwen glared at her.

"That's off Kit Carson Road, southeast of town, isn't it?"

"Right," Gwen said.

"Piedmont ends with a gate to the National Forest. We used to call it the Forest Service Road. Ya don't live in the forest do ya? Hehehe."

"No, we've rented a house."

The clerk took Gwen's cash and placed the groceries in their basket. "Hope to see ya around."

Heading to their Jeep Wrangler, Gwen said, "You got recto-cranial inversion?"

"What?"

"Are you fucking stupid or what? I've told you over and over again. We're hiding out from some bad guys. Don't go around telling people where we live. Get it?" Gwen gave Brittany a little smack on the back of her head.

"Sorry."

Before leaving D.C., St. John had arranged new identities for the two of them with a contact she knew. She also cleaned out her bank accounts and cashed in her securities—just before the market crashed. They took a series of Greyhound buses from D.C. until they landed in Taos, New Mexico. Brittany argued they should stay in Santa Fe because her parents had taken her there a handful of times on vacation. But Gwen insisted they needed someplace more remote. An hour-and-a-half north of Santa Fe and with less than five thousand population, Taos felt sufficiently remote to Gwen.

Another advantage to Taos was its tiny airport—if she ever had to get out by plane, and if she wanted to leave on a day when Taos Regional Airport was open for business, and if weather permitted small aircraft to take off and land. Very remote.

Using her new ID, Gwen purchased the three-year-old green Jeep Wrangler when they arrived in Taos and was studying with Brittany for their New Mexico driver's licenses. They paid cash to rent a small two bedroom modern house, fully furnished. It sat on three wooded acres at the top of a hill. Two sides of the lot backed to the National Forest. The other two sides abutted two other three acre residential lots. From this perch, they enjoyed a 360 degree view. They could also hear any approaching vehicles on the tenth-of-a-mile long gravel driveway. Good and remote.

Upon moving in, Gwen had said, "Welcome to the wilderness, sweet cheeks."

In their great room, Brittany had opened the blinds to the wall of windows that yielded a breathtaking view of Taos Mountain. "I love it," she said.

At one grand a month in rent and minimal carrying costs, Gwen figured they could hide out a decade or more before her money ran out. Aside from the art galleries, the only main places to shop in town included a couple of grocery stores, pharmacies and a Wal-Mart. Good for stretching their funds for a lengthy period.

After stowing their groceries, Gwen gave Brittany a hug and said, "I'm sorry for smacking you at the store. We've got to be super careful. Guard our identities, where we're from, where we reside, how we can afford to live without working. You know? We've been over this many times. You said you understood."

"Sorry, I momentarily forgot. Rosie seemed really sweet, and she's only a grocery clerk. I'll get better at this hiding out thing."

They plopped onto the sofa facing Taos Mountain. "I'm not worried about Rosie," Gwen said. "I'm concerned about the people who might come to town and happen to ask Rosie questions about us. Get it?"

"Yeah, yeah. ... What say we go out on the town tonight? Have some beers."

"Brittany, there are only two or three places to go."

"So let's go to one. Maybe we'll meet some people. Make some friends."

Gwen rubbed her eyes with her fists. "Okay...but only if you promise to stick to our script. Don't get all boozy and forget who you're supposed to be and why we're here in Podunkville."

Brittany smiled. "I promise. ...We're gonna make some frie...ends, gonna make some frie...ends," she chanted.

"Jesus. Put a lid on it."

53

The two of them sat in a windowless FBI meeting room—no cameras, no listening devices. After Ruddock's allowed phone call the night before and unaware of who Ruddock was or his possible connection with the corruption of Congress, Michael agreed to meet this prospective client at 8 AM the next morning. Ruddock sat back in a chair with his hands behind his head, fingers interlaced. Michael faced him across a table on which lay a folder with Ruddock's rap sheet and FBI report plus a legal tablet.

"How'd you come to call me?" Michael asked.

"Friend gave me your number."

"Who?" Michael's brow wrinkled.

"It doesn't matter. You're here now." Ruddock smiled.

"Where's your home?"

"Don't have one."

"Have any relatives?"

"None."

"What do you do for a living?"

"Rob houses." Ruddock smiled.

"Nice." *This isn't getting anywhere fast,* Michael thought. *Guy seems to be enjoying this.* "So, you admit to breaking and entering the residence of Senator and Mrs. Merryweather."

"Didn't know it was theirs. I just picked a random house. Nice neighborhood. Older folks. Figured I'd boost some valuables to keep me going a while."

"What about the weapon?"

"Oh the knife? That's just a tool I take with me on jobs. Helps me pry open locked desk drawers, cabinets, things like that."

"It's brand new. They said you carried it like you meant to harm someone."

"I've never harmed anyone." Ruddock's face showed indignation.

"Really?" Michael rifled through the manila file in front of him. "How about that manslaughter conviction in Nevada you served time for?"

"Oh...well there was that. An accident, but I paid my debt to society. Let's focus on the present. I admit, I invaded the old folks' home, and I'll plead guilty to a B&E. Cut me a deal will you? I'm willing to do a year—two if I have to."

Michael chuckled. "You think you're in control, but you aren't. You don't get it tough guy. The Feds want you for something else, something much bigger."

"Don't know what they're talking about. I did the B&E, and that's it. Guilty.""Have you ever heard of attorney-client privilege? You can tell me the full story, and I'll hold it in confidence."

"HA! Look. Just help me take the rap for the B&E. I've got resources, and I can pay you handsomely."

Michael stared a hole through Ruddock. "I've handled hard cases like you before, but I'm not sure I want to represent *you* now. You've got a really bad attitude."

"I admire you. You've got big cojones," Ruddock said.

"What makes you say that? And how do you know me to admire me?"

"Let's just say there's a heavyweight I know in Vegas who claims you recently threatened him. Now that took balls. Got to admire a man like that."

"What are you talking about?"

"It's whom I'm talking about."

Michael's heart began racing. His breathing became short and difficult. Vertigo set in, making it hard to sit up in his chair. He struggled to control it.

Finally, he said, "I'll think about your case. Maybe I'll be back, maybe not."

As soon as he closed the meeting room door behind him, he leaned against the wall, tugged his necktie loose and unfastened his top shirt button. A minute later, with his panic attack under control, he walked down the corridor to a drinking fountain.

He's Amici's man, not just a burglar. Merryweather tipped off the FBI about the corruption scam, and they had him under their protection. Was Ruddock tasked to deliver payback? By Amici?

Max appeared behind him. "Make a new friend?"

"I...I can't represent him."

"Why's that?"

"Can't say. Attorney-client privilege."

Beads of perspiration had formed on Michael's brow. Max said, "Hey buddy, it's okay. You know, that sonofabitch would have killed Merryweather. Wife too just for good measure. He's not talking, except for the B&E. Based on where he went to prison, I'm trying to connect him with Amici."

Michael gulped. "I can't say anything. But I won't represent him."

"I don't blame you, but you might want to kill him."

"What?"

Max took Michael by the elbow and directed him around a corner to an empty hallway. "I thought it wouldn't hurt to do a voice analysis of him and compare it with what we got in Chicago on the nine-one-one recording. If there's a match, we'll level assault and battery and attempted murder charges against him for Carrie."

Michael dropped his briefcase. This time the panic attack slammed him hard. He weaved on his feet and fell into Max who laid him down on the carpeted floor. Max shucked his silk jacket and balled it up under Michael's head. He bent Michael's knees and put his feet flat on the floor. Then, repeatedly lifting Michael by his belt buckle, he said, "Just breathe buddy, breath in slowly. Everything's okay."

Five minutes later, he helped Michael to his feet.

"I'm sorry. I'm so embarrassed."

"Don't worry about it, I'll send you the pressing bill for my jacket."

"When will they have the voice analysis completed on Ruddock?"

"End of day, probably."

• • •

Tony had made a dozen calls to Ruddock's cell phone. No answer. The national news reported a break-in at Senator Merryweather's home, but no one had said anything about the perpetrator even though the FBI had foiled the burglary.

He never fails to answer my calls. Tony drummed the three fingers on his left hand on his desk. *Was it him? Did they get him? Damn it, answer my calls!*

Two hours passed during which Tony made three more calls. No answer. *That's it then. Got to get rid of this cell. Cut all ties. Wonder if he got to Michael before he tried to do Merryweather?*

Tony's Shanghai phone rang. "Hello?"

"Cancel phase two. I repeat, cancel it altogether."

"But I've already paid..."

"I do not care about what you have paid. Cancel it."

"Of course. I will. May I ask why?"

"Phase one was incredibly successful and it continues to pay dividends. We have no need for further action. As a matter of fact, we may need the talent who would have been part of phase two to help steer their enterprises into a brighter future."

"Makes sense. But what about the money to set it up?"

"Keep it. This is our final conversation. Do not attempt to contact us again."

The line went dead. Tony instinctively dialed the Shanghai number he'd been using, fearing there'd been an accidental disconnect. The robotic message stated, "This number is not in service. Please check the number and dial again." He hung up.

Hmm, what to do?

An hour passed, and Tony called the mechanic.

"Speak."

"Do you know who this is?" Tony asked.

"Yes."

"The job is cancelled."

"Really?"

"Do you have a hearing problem?" Tony asked.

"Fine. The job is cancelled."

"Now we have to talk about money."

"What about it?" the mechanic asked.

"Since you haven't completed the job or taken any risk, I'll let you keep one-third of the deposit I gave you for your troubles. Send the rest back to me. I'll expect it in three days." *God I love sticking it to this Nazi prick.*

The mechanic laughed out loud into the phone. So loud that Tony pulled the phone away from his ear.

"Allow me to explain something to you, Amici. The up front deposit is non-refundable. Period. You will simply have to eat it as a cost of doing business."

"This is robbery! I'll never use you again."

"Amici, I do not need your business." He disconnected.

Motherfucker, the audacity of that guy. I'm gonna have somebody find him, whack his nuts off and stuff them in his mouth—right before I kill him. This one I want. At least I get to keep the other two million the Chink paid me. Some consolation.

• • •

What to do? The mechanic watched as the solar techs put the final touches on the system at his Palm Springs compound. *This will piss off my colleagues. I know they looked forward to these hits.*

He took another pull from his Cohiba Espléndidos cigar, and the idea came to him. *I collected three million up front and paid them $225K each. I will give each another $75K as a bonus. Three hundred K is a nice round number. I am still left with more than two million, and all I did was make a few phone calls. That will buy good will, and they will be indebted to me. A win-win all the way around.*

The mechanic contacted the Israeli and the Cuban shooters. They were satisfied with the payday. Everyone likes to be paid for doing next to nothing. But the ex-Navy Seal remained unreachable. *May have to pay him a visit in New York.*

He then dialed the number he'd been given for the Shanghai contact. After the proper codes were spoken, he said, "If that Vegas job is still open, I will take it."

"Good. Look for the advance fee that we discussed. We will let you know when we want it done."

54

Over eighty FBI agents followed their respective, Member of Congress to a Community Center on Rockville Pike in nearby Maryland. Bull had asked his executive assistant to find a venue, outside of government, for a highly confidential evening meeting and to secure the key to the building. When she identified and booked the Center, she assured Bull it would be deserted at 9 PM.

The Congressman, whom Red's team of four had tailed with two unmarked vehicles, arrived early at the Center. From a block away, they spotted other Members of Congress approaching with their FBI tails in pursuit. It looked like a parade. Red instantly realized the predicament the FBI was in. He quickly radioed his colleagues, informed them of the situation and ordered them to back off, less they be spotted.

Red took up a parked position close to the entrance to the Community Center. He and his partner slumped in their seats in the dark. His colleagues in the second car stopped at the entry point to the Center's parking lot.

"We'll video the folks entering and exiting the building," Red said. "You guys shoot pics of the inbound cars and their license tags. This is a bonanza guys. We've got these bozos red-handed. As soon as they're all inside, we'll try to gain entry to video the meeting."

"Roger that," the agent in the other car responded.

Members of Congress continued to arrive until 9:10 PM. With the last arrival, the entry door to the Center closed and the exterior lights went out.

"Let's get on it," Red said.

They jogged to the entry door with their equipment only to find the door locked. "Shit! Let's see if we can get in another way." Racing around the building, they found two other doors, both locked. "Okay, let's get back to that bank of windows where the lights were on."

"Won't be able to see anything," Red's partner said. "The drapes are drawn."

"We'll audio record whatever's said. I checked out that new spy mike we've begun stocking. It's supposed to be best in class. It's got a contact element that lets you hear through brick walls. We'll be fine up against the window."

• • •

"Now that we've had a little reunion of sorts," Bull said, standing in front of the seated group, "let's get down to business. No one's in the Center tonight but us, and we're not being recorded. If my tally is right, we have forty-nine Members of Congress here. That's more than I expected and, hopefully, there are very few who aren't here though they should be."

"I'd like to bloody well know why we are here," a twenty-seven year veteran of the House stood, voicing his objection. "I had to leave an important dinner to attend this…this…whatever you call it."

Bull glared at him for five seconds and the Representative sat down. "Senators Grendel, Gleason and I contacted several of you and brought you into this circle. Those folks recruited others and so on. If you're here, it's because, like the rest of us, you've been a bad boy or girl. You know exactly what you've done. I know my misdeeds as well. We have each failed in our sworn duties to our constituents and our nation. Each of you damn well knows what I'm talking about." He surveyed the faces before him.

A Senator asked, in a conciliatory tone, "Bull, I'm not sure what you have in mind, but aren't we pushing things? Everything seems to be returning to normal."

Senator Gleason stood. "NORMAL? Do you call the DOW taking a four thousand point dive in three days NORMAL? Think about it, Ron."

"Let's not argue about this," Bull said. "Fact is, we collectively reversed our relatively new positions on several matters a few days back, and we know what happened as a result. It's obvious to anyone with critical thinking skills."

"I find that insulting," another Representative said.

"You can find it anything you want," Bull replied, "but facts are facts."

Mary Grendel spoke up. "You all know me. And you know how intolerant I am of bullshit and truth shading. I also know each of you." She made eye contact with each person. "I'm here tonight because I've done the same kinds of things the rest of you have—for months. No one here will ask for confessions. No one here will scold anyone else. We're here to launch a corrective course of action. Tell them about it, Bull."

Bull looked over the crowd. "We all enjoy our positions in Congress, but we've violated our oaths of office. Beginning in two weeks, we're each going to announce our resignations or retirements."

That stunned the audience for a half minute. Then, the group erupted in debate. Bull let them yell, argue and whine for several minutes. Then, he said, "Let me put this in a way so we're crystal clear. Each of us has a choice. We can quietly resign or retire to a normal civilian life with no repercussions—make up whatever excuse you like. Or, I will personally out any fucker who stays in. You'll definitely be disgraced. And you'll be prosecuted. Believe me, you won't get off like John Edwards did."

"Holy shit!" Red exclaimed to his partner. "Did you hear that? It's incredible."

The crowd sat back in their chairs in solemn silence, contemplating Bull's order and the accompanying threat. A young second-term Representative stood. "Senator Bullman? If we leave en masse, won't that raise questions? You never see forty-nine Members of Congress walk out the door together unless they've been voted out of office."

Bull gave his trademark toothy grin. "Good point, young man. I've thought about that too. We'll leave in a series of roughly equal size groups over the course of two months. Since we do practically everything else by seniority, we'll leave by seniority too. The first wave will include those with the shortest tenures in Congress."

That brought an uproar among the youngest in the crowd. "How do we know you old timers won't stay after we've left?" a Representative asked.

"I'm glad you asked that," Bull said, and the audience quieted down. "I will be the last of this group to retire, but I want one of you to volunteer." He pulled an envelope from the inner breast pocket of his jacket. "In this sealed envelope, I've placed a confession of my misdeeds and tendered my resignation. I will give this letter to the person who volunteers tonight. When I retire on schedule, you will return this letter to me with the envelope sealed. Note I've put a stamped wax seal on the flap. Should I fail to abide by our pact, release the contents of this envelope to the press."

Mary Grendel said, "I'll volunteer. I'll be leaving before Bull. And I know precisely what Bull has done. Even if the paper inside that envelope is blank, which I'm sure it's not, I'll out him if he fails to perform."

One of the more obstinate and senior Representatives spoke up. "I trust Mary to do that. Folks, I've struggled with the problem I thought I alone had, wondering how to get the monkey off my back. Much as this pains me, I see no other solution than what Bull has set before us. I will tender my resignation on the schedule Bull has laid out. Those of you who have a patriotic bone left in your bodies will do likewise."

One by one, the attendees begrudgingly concurred to join the caravan of departures. A few couldn't voice their assent because they were sobbing.

"There's one matter left tonight." Bull held up a stack of three-by-five inch file cards. "On each of these file cards, I've written a date. They represent departure dates by seniority. Come on up and get your card. We won't meet again. We're adjourned."

A line formed in front of Bull. With a knowing smile and sometimes a handshake or pat on the shoulder, Bull handed a file card to each Member.

• • •

"Quick, let's get back to the car," Red told his partner. They scampered back to their unmarked FBI vehicle and proceeded to video the attendees as they left the Community Center.

Red glanced at his partner. "We hit pay dirt tonight, man. I can't wait to see the expression on Max's face."

"Me too. What a night! I've never been involved in anything so massive."

"I'll have to take my girlfriend out for something more than pizza next time."

55

Ellie May showed up ahead of time for her rendezvous with Representative Barry Sanford from California. She'd become accustomed to lounging at the Ritz and the Four Seasons hotels when a cataclysmic shift in the venues took place. Motel 6 and Days Inn were far more comfortable than the alleyways and back seats of cars she used back home, but they were a far cry from the opulence of the original properties.

She took it in stride though, noting the pay hadn't changed nor had her living quarters. Ellie May donned her fuck-me outfit, primped and waited for Representative Sanford. *Maybe he'll just drop off his envelope like a few others did last week. That'd be fine by me. One less dick to lick. I'll go mall shoppin'.*

St. John lined up several hotel reservations for the girls before she learned she had to split. She'd given the girls the dates and instructions to take their cut and leave the balance in the envelopes as usual for pick up. Little did the girls know that St. John was gone and no one else connected with their game would retrieve the envelopes. Large windfalls awaited maids in several hotels, never to be reported.

After a half hour, Ellie May became restless. Sanford was late. Thirty minutes later, she became irritated, but she focused on the money she'd collect and turned on the TV. An old re-run of The Andy Griffith Show had just started. When it ended, Sanford was still absent. She dialed St. John's cell number, but it wasn't in service.

What should I do? Don't wanna piss off Sanford. And I really don't wanna have St. John get her boxers in a bunch. So she waited another hour and then changed into her street attire and left the hotel.

This same scenario played out thirteen other times for thirteen other girls. They all figured it a one-time occurrence with their johns until it happened again with their next appointments. They couldn't reach St. John, and they knew no one else to contact, including one another. Something was amiss.

One by one, they left their residences and moved to other cities, working mostly for call girl services. Two had independently spent their time in St. John's service preparing for life after. They'd developed their own pornographic websites that offered webcam sex for a fee. Three others landed in exotic dancing bars. The dominatrix returned to Richmond where she picked up where she'd left off.

Ellie May didn't know what to do. With no connections to any other madams and little money saved, her options seemed limited. She knew one thing for sure—returning to Romney was a non-starter. Having gotten a taste of another way of living, she couldn't return to $50 lays and $15 blow jobs. She remembered St. John's counsel about what would become of her in a few years' time back home.

She quickly came to a second realization. She had to find a less expensive place to live. The twenty grand she'd saved since she arrived in D.C. wouldn't last long with a two grand a month tab for rent.

Ellie May moved to a small apartment in Laurel, Maryland—a suburb northeast of D.C. and a short drive south to the University of Maryland. She dropped her alias and resumed life as Ginger Compton. On her first grocery shopping trip, she saw a hiring add in the window of Giant Foods. A half hour later, she'd become their newest employee.

Maybe I oughta invest in myself. Start takin' some college courses. Who knows what kinda job I might get some day.

56

The FBI's list of corrupt officials had grown to forty-nine after Red's intelligence gathering operation of the meeting in Rockville. No one took pleasure in seeing the list grow, but everyone expressed satisfaction they were closing in on the Congressional figures involved in the conspiracy to manipulate the stock market.

"What we still don't know is who's pulling the strings on these people," Assistant Director Wyatt said. "It seems clear from Red's recording that these idiots were being manipulated. There's no evidence they collaborated among themselves in any way. In fact, I draw just the opposite conclusion."

"We need to get Ruddock to talk," Max said. "Let me have a crack at him."

Wyatt gave Max a long look. "You've been away for a while, Max. I, uh, I'll give you time with him. But no rough stuff. Agreed?"

"Righto."

An hour later, Max sat in a windowless FBI interview room across a table from Ruddock who appeared calm and confident. The room was wired for sound and video.

"My name's Max. Do you go by Jim or James?" Max asked.

"Are you playing good cop?"

"I could call you *asshole*, but I'd rather call you by your given name."

"You can call me Jim or Ruddock or nothing for all I care."

"All right. I'll call you Jim. ...So Jim, we've got a little problem here. When I say *we* I mean you for one and us for another. I'm going to lay it all out for you because you're going away for a very long time."

"For a B&E?" Ruddock laughed.

"Laugh all you want Jim. See if you find this funny. We've got you cold for the B&E. Attempted murder on Merryweather? Well, I can see how a good defense attorney could argue otherwise. But..."

"Speaking of defense attorneys," Ruddock interrupted, "I..."

"Shut the fuck up, Jim. I wasn't finished. ...As I was saying, an attorney might argue you carried that knife for self-protection. Maybe a stupid jury would buy it if that was all we had. But now you're in trouble for something far worse." Ruddock let this news hang in the air for twenty seconds. He saw a twitch around Ruddock's eyes and knew it was time to let the other shoe drop.

"You see, Jim, after your arrest, we recorded your voice."

"So what?"

"Good question, Jim. We wanted that recording to compare with another one. Do you remember being in Chicago recently? Tailing a pretty reporter through a park? Beating her half to death and then calling nine-one-one?"

Jim's eyes widened, but he didn't move, didn't breath. Max knew he had him.

"Well, Jimbo, newsflash. The voice print we gathered here matched the nine-one-one recording. Guess what else." Max raised his eyebrows and smiled. "The victim of that beating listened to five different recordings, one from you and four from other men, speaking the same words. She picked you out of an audio line-up. Not just from the Chicago recording but from the recording we made here too."

"That's just..."

"A coincidence? Believe me, any jury will take that to the bank. What we've got here, Jimbo, is assault and battery and attempted murder in Chicago and a B&E in Bethesda. Of course with the Chicago charges, the attempted murder in the Merryweather home becomes far more credible."

Gotcha you bastard.

Ruddock squirmed in his chair. This was real trouble. Not a death sentence, but decades behind bars. The only thing worse would be ratting out Tony.

"Now I'll move on to *our* problem. We believe you've also been involved in corrupting some of our highest elected public servants. I'll be honest. We can't prove it, but we know it. You're off the hook there, but you could do yourself some good by helping us understand the intricacies of that operation."

"What would I get out of it?" A trickle of perspiration ran down Ruddock's temple in the air conditioned interview room.

"That depends on how useful you are, Jimbo. If you help us a great deal, I could imagine a comfortable life for you in a Federal pen. Otherwise, I suspect you'll be holed up in a really bad state facility, either in Illinois or Maryland. You have personal experience with state prisons. But, hey, maybe you like being gang-raped."

Ruddock ground his teeth. He clenched fists on the table top.

"I see I got your attention. That woman you tortured in Chicago is a personal friend of mine. So if you want to try anything, do it now." He shrugged off his jacket and let it drop to the floor. "I'd love to mop the floor with you. DO IT!"

Ruddock didn't move. He pulled his fists into his lap, glaring at Max.

"Just as I thought. You pussy." Max picked up his jacket and turned his back to Ruddock like a matador, back to the bull. Facing the door, he said, "Think about what I've told you, Jimbo. I'll be back in an hour." Max walked out.

• • •

Charles and Brent, the two agents tasked to bring in Novotchin, called from GW University Hospital. "Max, we did everything like you told us," Charles said. "We used a lot of finesse."

Max had trouble understanding. "And your problem is?"

"He had a stroke as we walked out of the Capitol building. We didn't even handcuff him. He said he'd come voluntarily. No hassle. He didn't want the embarrassment."

Carrie sat across the desk from Max in the office they'd been temporarily assigned. "What's happening?" she whispered.

Max ran his hand through his white hair. "What's his condition?"

"I think he's dead."

"You think?"

"We performed CPR on him until EMS showed up. They took over and rushed him to the hospital. We followed, but they haven't yet confirmed his condition."

"Find out and call me immediately."

Max replaced the handset and looked at Carrie. "The excitement appears to have killed Novotchin. Stroke. I'll know for sure in a bit."

"I wanted that pig to squirm in court and be put away for the rest of his life to rot in some dungeon for what he did to Brenda."

Max shook his head. "There's all kinds of justice. This is what Novotchin got. At least we won't incur the expense of a trial."

Carrie nodded. "Silver lining."

57

Carrie had spent three days dialing for interviews with thirty-two politicians on the FBI's new list whom she'd not previously interviewed. The assistants she spoke with bounced her around to others who told her their Member of Congress wasn't granting interviews on anything to anyone. Finally, she'd landed four interviews.

"Now that you're all wired up," Mara Gonzalez said, "I'm leaving the room to test the system. Flip this little plastic switch to turn the mike on. I should be able to hear and record what you say."

"Let's do it," Carrie said. She switched her wire on. Once Mara was outside the room and down the hallway, Carrie said, "Okay. Testing. One…two…three. I'm broadcasting live from a room at FBI headquarters."

The door opened, and Mara reappeared. "Works like a charm. Switch it off to save the battery, and let's go."

Carrie entered Senator Forest Wickes' office and presented herself to the Senator's executive assistant right on time. Mara and another agent stood in the hall.

Senator Wickes neared the end of his first term in office. At thirty-four, he'd already made a fortune in a high tech start-up that went public—before the tech bubble burst in the early part of the century. After his company went belly-up and with his financial haul from the IPO safely tucked away, he spent the next few years cultivating local movers and shakers in preparation for a run for the Senate in Colorado. At forty-two and with his record as a congenial, can-do Senator, it seemed he'd enjoy a never ending future in the U.S. Senate.

"Good morning, Senator," Carrie said with a smile.

"It's nice to meet a superstar from the press," he said.

"You're too kind."

Carrie launched a series of soft ball questions that gave the Senator a basis to tell the world what a great job he was doing. He relaxed into the interview. Then, she said, "What say you, Senator, about the rumors that a number of Senators and Representatives are being blackmailed for their votes?"

He looked down at his hands. "Why, uh, I haven't heard that rumor."

"How about the rumor that many will be leaving office shortly?"

Wickes looked up at Carrie and frowned. "Where do you get all this wild speculation? I assure you that's not the case. When have you ever seen a mass exodus from Congress unless the voters vote people out of office? It doesn't happen."

"Do you know people have been killed in connection with this conspiracy?"

He didn't respond.

"How badly do you think people will suffer due to the stock market debacle?"

"I know all about the stock market knocking people off their feet. Remember my high tech company went under when the tech bubble burst."

"What I remember, Senator, is that you ran a company that was heavily in debt with no prospect of ever being profitable. And I recall you socked away most of your IPO money, leaving you a very wealthy man."

Senator Wickes walked to his desk and pushed an intercom button. "Jennifer, please escort Ms. Linden from my office. Our interview has ended." He turned to Carrie. "I'm sorry I can't be of more assistance to whatever you came to accomplish. You'll understand that I must get back to work for the great state of Colorado."

After lunch, Carrie and the agents moved on to her next interview. It went about the same, except the Representative from Delaware uncharacteristically swore at her, using the most foul language he could muster.

The next morning, Carrie tackled her two remaining interviews with the same results. "I've tried approaching them differently, but I'm being stone-walled. We know these guys are guilty, and I think they recognize I know they are. But I can't get them to crack."

"It was worth the effort," Mara said. The other agent nodded in agreement.

Back at headquarters, Carrie relayed to Max what had happened.

"You can't win them all. I'm surprised four of them even let you in the door. It was a long shot. Think of it that way."

"At least we got Ruddock. I'd like to face that SOB," Carrie said. "Talk to him about that night in the park." She still ached from the beating, but she was now ambulatory with the use of a cane.

"This isn't the right time to confront him. Let him stew a bit more. He's got a new attorney showing up this afternoon. We'll see what they come up with."

• • •

Michael phoned Carrie a few hours later. "You okay?"
"Much better. Out of the wheelchair and using a cane now."
"I hope you'll soon be cane-free. How about dinner tonight?"
"Fine by me. I heard you won't represent Ruddock. Why's that?"
"That would have been selling my soul to the devil."

58

"I've never seen anything like it," the defense counsel told John Wyatt and Max. "There's little I can do for him. My client wishes to remain in your custody."

Wyatt and Max gave each other a puzzled look.

"Ruddock has authorized me to tell you a few things. He'll plead guilty to the B&E in Bethesda and the assault and battery in Chicago. Says he specifically pulled his punches to ensure the victim would survive. Seems he knows something about beating people up to the point of death but not beyond."

Wyatt said, "A Chicago jury will hang him by his nuts for attempted murder."

"I can assure you I told him the same—not quite in those colorful words."

"We want him to talk about another topic," Max said. "Might help him. I gave it another try yesterday, but he's refusing to talk."

"Not going to happen. Whatever you think you can do to punish him for his crimes, he fears something far worse if he talks to you. I don't know what it is, but I can guess. I wouldn't want to be in his shoes."

Wyatt spoke. "We believe we know what *it* is. Tell him we can protect him."

"I didn't just get off the boat, you know. I told him that. Won't help."

Max clapped his hands once. "That's it then." They adjourned.

Jablonski answered his phone on the second ring. "Jablonski here."

"It's Max. I've got good and bad news."

"What's the bad news?"

"You guys won't be able to prosecute Jimmy Novotchin."

"Goddamn motherfucker. We can't let him get away with..."

"Don't you want the good news?"

"What is it?" Jablonski asked.

"That goddamn motherfucker is dead. Stroked out after we arrested him."

"Now that *is* good news. I can't wait to tell Gino." They hung up.

• • •

"Mr. President," Archibald Graystone nodded, stepping into the Oval Office.

President Stine shook his hand. "Archie, thanks for coming. Give us a report."

Graystone noted the other figures in the room. Same crowd as before, except for the addition of Great Britain's Prime Minister and the German Chancellor. "I'd like to say good day to you all, but the worldwide market has given up fifty percent of its peak value. I've talked with investment leaders, heads of major global banking and investment firms and many heads of state. We still can't see an end to the selling."

The German Chancellor said, "And we thought 2008 was a bad year. Have you looked at who is buying as the market declines?"

"There's no pattern to it. One banker suggested we close the markets to all trading," Graystone said.

"What an imbecile!" President Stine said. "Even I know that'd be dumb. I hope you put the kibosh on that."

"I asked that individual never to repeat that suggestion again to anyone. It would intensify the global panic that's set in, and it would create permanent distrust in the worldwide stock market going forward. I suggest we focus on what we can do in the absence of other information not available to us."

That launched a conversation about the role governments could play to keep the wheels on the global economy.

59

Carrie and Michael stayed nearby for dinner. Morton's in the Bethesda Hyatt Regency had been a favorite of theirs. Carrie hooked her cane behind her chair.

They made small talk during their first course. Both enjoyed a classic wedge with bacon bits and lots of blue cheese. After her first bite of filet mignon, she said, "I went to a neurologist this morning about my feet, especially my right foot."

"What did he say?"

"It was a *she*, Michael. ...All my bumps and bruises are healing up nicely, and I don't have any broken bones in my feet. But she said I have neuropathy. That's a fancy term for nerve damage." Carrie looked at her plate.

"Say more."

"The nerves in my feet are misfiring, sending pain signals to my brain when there's no reason for the pain. Diabetes sometimes causes what I have, but I don't have diabetes. So they can't treat me for that."

Michael reached for her hand, but she pulled it away. "I'm so sorry, Carrie. What can they do? What treatment can they prescribe?"

"She said nerve pain is still very much a mystery, despite all the advances in medicine. There aren't any treatments for my injury. She recommended a few other docs for me to consult. In the meantime, my cane helps relieve the pressure when I'm up, particularly on my right foot. It also steadies me when I'm suddenly hit with pain."

"Oh my. Isn't there some kind of medication you can take? Pain killers?"

"I don't want to take narcotics because I won't be able to think clearly. I'm taking Ibuprofen. There isn't anything else. Next week I go in for something called a nerve conduction study. It measures the speed that nerves carry electrical impulses. But that's not going to solve my problem—it'll probably just confirm her diagnosis. I may heal naturally over time, or," she shrugged, "I may live with this condition permanently. There's no guarantee I'll recover."

"Goddamn it! That sonofabitch!" Michael pushed his plate away.

"If you're talking about Ruddock, I know he's the one who attacked me. Did you refuse to represent him because he hurt me?"

"Oh to hell with ethics. Yes. I refused because he hurt you and because Amici likely sent him to hurt you. I can't defend that…that animal!"

Carrie chewed a bite of her filet mignon.

"I can't eat anymore," Michael said.

"You'd better, or I'm taking the rest of your strip steak home with me."

Michael gave her a half-smile. "You can still joke in the face of what you learned today. I don't get you."

"I'm not dead for crying out loud. I just hurt. Maybe it'll heal, maybe not."

"This is exactly what I was talking to you about in bed."

"I know, but it doesn't change my mind about what I want to do with my life."

Michael stared at Carrie for a half minute. "Okay. I give up. I still love you, even though *we* aren't going to work. I'd like to remain close friends."

Carrie used her napkin to dab a tear in one eye. "I love you too. I hope we can always be friends."

60

At 9 AM the next morning, the Phoenix-based FBI team showed up on the big screen in the FBI amphitheater. The balance of the D.C. investigation team plus Wyatt and Max observed the screen.

"What have you found?" Max asked.

A voice in Phoenix said, "We've been on Amici like white on rice. He can't say anything or go anywhere without us knowing what's said or what he's doing."

"That's great. Again, what have you found?" Max asked.

"Uh, nothing. He goes about his days like any bail bondsman does, even though he travels in some pretty fancy local company. The worst he does is occasionally utter a curse word. That's it."

Wyatt looked at Max. "Are you sure your surveillance devices haven't been spotted or tampered with?" Wyatt asked.

"All I can say is we used the latest micro devices we've got, squirreled away where they can't be seen, in his offices, cars and at his house. Every few hours we run an electronic check on every one of them. They're all operating."

"All right, enough of this bullshit," Max said. "We're not getting anywhere. Get a warrant to search his offices, cars and home. Pull his mail and check his bank accounts. If it'd help, run a colonoscopy on the guy, but get something we can use."

• • •

"Where did this shit come from?" Gwen asked Brittany as she stomped out of the spare bedroom and into the living room. Gwen held up a quart-sized Ziploc bag filled with roughly a pound of cocaine.

"Oh that's just a little something I picked up for us in town."

"You fucking bitch. You're gonna get us busted."

"You worry too much. Pretty much everybody in town is cool about this stuff. Let's have a toot and chill out." Brittany took the bag and flopped on the sofa, smiling.

Panic hit Gwen. She ran into the bedroom where she'd hidden the cash-filled duffel bag that served as their bank. It sat on the opposite side of the closet floor from where she'd left it with the zipper open. She screamed and ran back to the living room.

"You goddamn bitch. You fucking whore. You stole from me to buy this shit."

"I got it for you too. You said we were partners in everything."

"Who'd you buy it from?" Gwen put a hand to her mouth, afraid of the answer.

"Rosie's friend Carla—that freaky chick. She's got a satchel full of this shit."

Gwen could hear the faint sound of tires crunching on gravel. It became louder and louder. Clearly, more than one vehicle was cruising up their long driveway.

Gwen looked out the glass panel in the front door and saw six police and other unmarked vehicles pulling up to the open parking area in front of the house. She ran to the couch where Brittany had dipped a fingernail in the bag for a little snort.

"GIVE ME THAT, BITCH!" Gwen screamed and reached for the bag.

"No! Go get your own." A tug of war ensued and the bag burst, scattering cocaine over both of them, the couch and the floor.

The authorities burst through the door in time to see a cloud of cocaine erupt and finally settle. Carla took the lead, holding a Glock 17 and wearing a blue windbreaker with D E A emblazoned with yellow letters on the front and back. A dozen police and DEA officers piled into the little house. "Get your bitchy asses on the floor. NOW!" Carla ordered. The other cops spread out to search the premises.

Gwen gave Brittany an angry look and, as they got down on the floor, said, "See what you've done. We could have had a good life. Oh my God."

"That's right, Brittany, or whatever your name is," Carla said. "I've got you recorded saying you're both users and you'd both be happy to distribute for me. So I sold you enough to distribute. You bitches are in deep shit. In fact, it's all over you."

• • •

Mara Gonzalez received a call the next day from Herman Garcia, a friend at the DEA. "We found something I think you guys should see," Herman said.

"Yeah? What's that?"

"A few of my colleagues busted a couple of lesbians in Taos, New Mexico for possession of cocaine with intent to distribute. They're going away for quite a while."

"I thought that was your bailiwick."

"Right, but this is about a laptop we found in their house. The older one said it was hers. We had a techie check it out, and she located a ton of deleted files."

"Herman, don't keep me in suspense. Cut to the chase."

"About twenty percent of the deleted files aren't recoverable, but those that are include hundreds of video clips and still shots. We haven't viewed them all, but the ones we've seen involve male and female Members of Congress having sex with women. The women are very likely *not* their spouses. I asked the laptop owner how she acquired the files. She said a guy named Jeremy Blevins gave them to her."

"Holy crap! We need those files ASAP, Herman."

"I'll email them to you in two minutes or less."

"Thanks, Herman. You're the best."

61

Senator Grendel stuck her head in Bull's office. "Got a minute, because we've got a problem."

"For you, Mary, anytime."

Mary closed the office door behind her and sat in a chair across Bull's desk. "I have it on good authority that most of the folks in the first two waves have met. They won't resign."

"WHAT!" Bull jumped from his chair with his fists up in the air. "Who the fuck do those morons think they are? THEY CAN'T REFUSE TO RESIGN!"

"Well, that's exactly what they're doing. And if *they* don't go, you can bet folks in the next few waves won't go either. They've stopped meeting with their hookers. They think they can keep their heads down and ride this mess out."

"Damn it. I will butt fuck every goddamn last one of those bastards. When I'm through with them, they'll wish they'd been screwed by a real bull."

He paced the floor for a minute and asked, "What do you think about calling another meeting like the other night?"

"We can try."

"I'll set up the venue. You call Gleason and a few others to whip the group into showing up. We'll take another run at those assholes."

• • •

"And what brings my favorite FBI Director here today," President Stine asked.

Malcolm Parr gave the President a stiff handshake and handed him a file, labeled, *Top Secret*. A tall, sandy-haired fellow in his late sixties, Parr had served three consecutive Presidents from both parties after a successful career in the private sector. Known as a no nonsense guy, people in both parties trusted his honesty and had a healthy respect for his authority. Both took a seat on opposing couches.

"Mr. President, as you know, we've had a number of Members of Congress under surveillance for some time in connection with the conspiracy to undermine the global stock market. The file shows in greater detail what I'm about to report."

"What I don't understand, Mal, is how'd we find out about this mess to begin with? And why are we dealing with it so late in the game?"

"Mr. President, the answer to your first question is simple. Are you familiar with Carrie Linden?"

"The syndicated columnist?" Malcolm nodded. "Sure, I read her columns pretty reg'lar. She's a good writer and a straight shooter. My kinda gal."

"Ms. Linden discovered the plot in Congress through a former college roommate. Some time after college, the roommate became a high-priced call girl who helped corrupt some Members of Congress. She was severely hurt and ultimately murdered. Ms. Linden raised a red flag, but no one would listen at the time. Someone beat her practically to death while she investigated the matter."

"My God! That's one brave woman."

"That she is, sir. Ms. Linden finally got everyone's attention, and she's a key advisor to the FBI in our efforts to apprehend anyone involved in this conspiracy. As for your second question, the financial arms of our government suspected the stock market's rise was fueled by Congressional action, but the FBI was never brought in on the matter. Our government is, unfortunately, so big and complex, that different agencies don't always know what's going on in others. To be fair, the financial agencies may not have even thought someone was breaking any laws."

"Bull pucky! Remind me when this is all over that we need to recognize Ms. Linden in some way. I've taken this talk down a rabbit hole. What's your report?"

"Sir, we have incontrovertible evidence that fifty-five Senators and Representatives have been compromised. Actually it's now fifty-four because Novotchin died. He was one of them."

"HA! He was a prick. I imagine it'll be a short funeral procession."

"We have videos of each one having repeated congress with a hooker."

"HA! That's a good one. Congressmen congressing with a hooker. Do you really mean one hooker or several hookers servicing the lot of these jokers."

"It's several. We have confiscated computer files with date stamps that show the demands placed on each official by blackmailers, and we know for a fact they immediately complied with the stated demands. There's a spreadsheet showing a semi-monthly fee of eight thousand dollars per visit, paid by each politician to the hookers. We don't actually have evidence of money changing hands, but we do have the madam in custody on a drug charge. She's willing to testify about the antics of the elected officials and how they were blackmailed in exchange for a reduced sentence on the drug charge. You see, the computer files were on her laptop in her possession."

Grimacing, President Stine pumped a fist into the air. "Dang them."

"The other night, forty-nine of them met in a community center in Rockville, Maryland, at which time Senator Bradley Bullock ordered them to resign from office. Apparently, he's one of them, and he similarly plans to resign."

"Oh no, not Bull too." The President stood and paced silently for two minutes.

Finally, he looked at the Director and said, "Listen Mal, we gotta big problem here. The country's economy is in a nosedive. Confidence in the stock market couldn't be worse. Tens of thousands of Americans are losin' their jobs, and it's far worse in the rest of the world. Now, I'd like to prosecute every one of these varmints and put them away in some dark, dank hell hole. But there's a problem with that."

The Director looked at the President, "What's the problem, sir?"

"It's political and might become military. If we put on a big show of prosecutin' these turkeys, the U.S. will get blamed for the ills that have befallen other countries. And don't think for a minute they won't confront us, demanding compensation. When we can't pay, and we can't, bad things will happen. It won't just last a week or a month. It could last generations. Imagine trade embargoes, travel restrictions, property seizures, kidnappings and maybe declarations of war against us."

"Not a pretty image."

"If that wasn't enough, Americans have lost faith in the economy. They don't have much faith in their government and their elected leaders. But this… this could lead to anarchy. And I wouldn't blame 'em a bit. We've gotta find a solution other than prosecution, but we've also got to nail these rat bastards to the wall somehow."

"Maybe I have the answer, sir."

"I truly hope so Mal. That's why you're paid the big bucks as FBI Director."

Parr smiled. "One of our young agents dates an aide to one of the fifty-four. She innocently alerted him to the meeting these folks had a few nights ago. They're going to meet again tomorrow night at the same place in Maryland."

President Stine rubbed his face and took a deep breath. "What do ya suggest we do with that information, Mr. Director?"

62

The mechanic stepped off the Amtrak train at Penn Station in New York City. He'd taken a couple of trains cross-country from Palm Springs in order to carry his Beretta PX-4 Type F that fired a 9mm round with a 17+1 round magazine capacity. Upon disembarking, he immediately took in the comingled scent of garbage, human sweat and urine. *You would think one of the greatest cities in the world could clean up its act. The underbelly of this place is rotting. All you see above is a thin veneer of sophistication. Kind of like an old whore spruced up for business on a Saturday night.*

He hadn't been able to reach his last shooter, and that bothered him. If the ex-Seal went off the rails and took out his three assigned targets at his leisure, the mechanic would have hell to pay. He didn't care about upsetting Tony or offing the three executives, but his other employers would surely hear about the blunder. It'd sully his reputation. Maybe force him into an early retirement or worse.

Upon leaving Penn Station with his duffel bag, he walked the short distance from 3 Penn Plaza to a little restaurant on 32nd Street in Koreatown for dinner. He'd eaten there before and enjoyed their parboiled octopus with a side salad.

After dinner, he carried his bag to the bathroom and checked his Beretta. The former Navy Seal was a very dangerous man, even for the mechanic. Be prepared—that was something he'd learned in the Boy Scouts as a kid and throughout his career as a mercenary and later as a hit man.

He caught a taxi south to the West Village where the assassin lived. After exiting the taxi at the corner of the man's block, he phoned him yet again. No answer. The message system was off too. This wasn't good.

He spotted the five story red brick building and noticed neither apartment on the top floor was lit. A person walked out the entry and held the door open for him, thinking nothing about whom he might be and what business he had inside.

The mechanic eyed the mailboxes and found 'Bob Horvath'. *That's my guy.* Each of the ten mailboxes in the little lobby had three small slots that allowed an owner to peak into a mailbox without going through the hassle of opening it. Using a penlight, he peered into Bob's mailbox. *Chock full of mail. Not good.*

Hearing footsteps descending the staircase, he saw a young Asian woman a few steps from reaching the entry hall. "Hello. I do not mean to disturb you, but I am a very old friend of Bob Horvath. Have you seen him recently?"

She appeared frightened in the way people in large cities are unnerved when addressed by complete strangers, especially someone with the mechanic's appearance. "Uh, I, uh, no I haven't. No one sees him much. Never comes to co-op meetings. Kind of a loner I guess."

"Gee, too bad. He is a nice fellow once you get to know him."

"I know one thing for sure. He'd better do something about the stink coming from his unit or our Board of Directors is gonna come down hard on him."

The mechanic quickly digested that piece of information. "I completely understand. If I see him, I will ask him to dispose of his garbage." He smiled at the young woman who quickly stepped past him and out onto the street.

He bounded up ten flights to the fifth and top floor—two units per floor—pulling on leather gloves and retrieving his Beretta as he raced upwards. The unit opposite Bob's showed no light coming through the peephole or around the front door.

The mechanic quietly set his bag down and knocked on Bob's door. Waited. Knocked again. No answer. There was a definite and identifiable odor emanating from Bob's unit—the stench of death. Once you smelled it, you never forgot it.

He stashed his Beretta in his waistband and pulled his SouthOrd professional lock pick set from his bag. Ninety seconds later, he'd opened the fourth and last bolt lock on the metal reinforced door. With Beretta in hand, he knocked again and called out Bob's name. No response. He stood to the side of the door and opened it an inch. A waft of death swept up his nostrils, and he knew all he needed.

The mechanic breathed through his mouth as he entered the unit. The apartment couldn't have measured more than three hundred square feet—a tiny living, dining and kitchen area with a small bath off the kitchen, minimally furnished with a two-seater sofa, lamp, and small table with two chairs. A TV sat in a corner next to two small windows, facing the sofa. Clean. Not a dirty dish in the sink.

A door led to the bedroom, and as he stepped closer the odor became even more pungent. Standing to the side, the mechanic used his Beretta to push open the bedroom door. He took in the scene all at once—a chair, small dresser and a queen-size bed. A large black man, attired in his Navy dress blues, lay on his back on the bed with a hole in his forehead and his brains splattered on the wall behind.

Ah Bob, why did you have to go out this way? Then he saw a FedEx box on the chair. Not just any FedEx box. *His* FedEx box—unopened. He unzipped the strip on the box and lifted the flap. The $225K he'd sent Bob hadn't been touched. The mechanic put the box under his arm and took a final look at the dead assassin. Quietly, he closed the front door behind him, grabbed his bag and left the building.

Goodbye Bob, I will spend your money wisely.

63

Fifty-two Senators and Representatives attended the meeting at the Rockville Community Center. The threat Senator Bullock had issued could not be ignored. Several had banded together prior to the meeting to discuss strategies to face up to Bull and demand alternatives to Bull's plan for an exodus from Congress.

As they filed into the Center once more, they grumbled about Bull's command for their attendance. If he was one of them, how dare he require their presence? But the threat hanging over their heads had the figurative consequence of a guillotine.

"People, let's come to order," Bull intoned in a deep resonant voice. "Everyone please take a seat. This won't take long." The attendees quieted down as they sat and stared forward at a man they were coming to despise.

"I see we're a couple people short. I'll speak with them individually following our meeting. The reason I asked you to come..."

"Demanded we come," a Representative yelled. "Who the hell are you..."

Four doors to the meeting room burst open. An army of fifty men and women ran through the doors and encircled the group. They wore blue parkas with F B I across the chest and back in big yellow letters. In their hands, they carried shotguns at the ready. The distinctive chink-chink sound of shells being chambered into fifty Mossburg pump-action shotguns resounded throughout the room. Attendees craned their necks left and right, observing the display of force and wondering whether Bullock had anything to do with it and what it meant.

Once the tactical team was in place another group of four agents surrounding the POTUS entered the room and strode purposefully to the stage. President Stine broke through his escort and walked up to Senator Bullock who stood frozen, mouth agape, at the spectacle.

"I'll take it from here, old buddy," the President said. He gave Bull a pat on the back. "Take a seat, pardner."

Confused, Bull stepped from the stage and dropped in a chair in the first row.

"Well, well. Ain't this just dandy. Like Bull, here, I see we've got a couple of rats missin' from the ship. Tony?" He called to one of his FBI team. "Send teams to collect the two Senators who felt they needn't show up tonight. You know who they are. Take 'em to the holdin' place you've got set up. I'll talk with them directly."

The agent double-timed it from the room.

The President looked out over the crowd for several seconds.

"What's the meaning of this?" Senator Lyman Jeffries asked.

The President snorted. "Shut up Jeffries and sit. And that goes for the rest of you. If any one of you utters a peep during my short speech, I'll have one of these fine men and women gag you and hogtie you to your chair.

"Bull, I 'preciate you gettin' these folks together. Very efficient. Saved me a lot of hassle. I'm gonna make this short and sweet. Y'all know what you've done. More importantly, the FBI and I know all about it. We've got videos of you...most disgusting. We've got dates, places, payoffs...but worst of all, we've got dated documents showing commands given to you and you carryin' 'em out in your respective Houses. You've violated your oaths to the American people. You've degraded the Congress of the United States. You've wreaked havoc on the global stock market through your highfalutin rhetoric and actions. And if that wasn't enough, you've made people suffer and die. That's right folks. D...I...E."

Most of the audience looked down and away from President Stine. Several sobbed in their seats. Only Senators Bullock and Grendel faced him and nodded their heads in sorry assent to the charges he leveled.

"If it were up to me, I'd strip you varmints naked, wrap barb wire around your chests and use my horse to drag you through a patch of Texas cholla. That's a type of cactus. It's a might painful. ...But, I'm told I can't do that. I could have y'all arrested and held without bail for treason. Now that has a nice ring to it. Maybe after you're convicted we'd televise fifty-four hangin's. That'd make for good TV these days. Help the ratings out."

Those in the audience looked aghast.

"But, it'd also create much bigger domestic and international problems than we've got. And what we've got on our hands is a might awesome. So here's what we're gonna do. And if anyone objects...hell I might execute you myself tonight. Deal with the constitutional consequences after."

Those who'd been sobbing stopped. Everyone faced Stine and listened.

"I see I've got your rapt attention. The good news for you beasts of prey is there won't be any prosecutions." He let that hang in the air and noticed a wave of relief sweep over the crowd. "Of course, we've revoked your passports and put you all on a no-fly list. That's just so we'll know we can get our hands on you."

A few actually smiled, taking relief in the news—no prosecutions.

"But here's the bad news. Each of you will resign Congress tomorrow. Those who've got pensions comin' will renounce them in writin'. No use havin' our good, tax payin' citizens continue to support a bunch a traitors. And you'll all voluntarily make a donation to the Market Crash Relief Fund. HA! I just made that name up. Kinda catchy, I think. We're gonna use that fund to help people all over the world who've suffered the most from the global market collapse."

That brought more smiles. The President could see the thoughts registered in their faces. *Sure, make a donation. Cut back other charitable giving and put it all in the President's Market Crash Relief Fund. Yee-haw!*

"Looks like ya think that's a might good idea. That's good, 'cause y'all will each donate EIGHTY PERCENT OF YOUR NET WORTH!"

The audience began grumbling loudly and several shouted complaints.

President Stine grabbed a Mossburg from an agent and blasted a shotgun round into the ceiling. "I like the way that brings a room to attention," he said.

"Folks, this ain't up for discussion. That'll leave twenty percent—still far more than most Americans have. Now, pay attention. In a few minutes, these fine agents and their colleagues outside will put you in a bunch of vans they've brought along for this special occasion. They're gonna take you to FBI head-quarters. And you're gonna sit there until your financial advisors or spouses show up and give a detailed and true report of your assets and liabilities. You're gonna sign that report and an IOU to the IRS. HA! Kinda poetic." He smiled. "You'll have three months to liquidate eighty percent of your net worth and give it over to the IRS for our little relief fund."

A Senator in the front row stood and barked, "This is illegal. I'll have my lawyers sue for..."

President Stine chambered another shotgun shell in the Mossburg. He pointed it directly at the Senator and yelled, "WHO STANDS WITH THIS TRAITOR? IF YOU DON'T, STEP AWAY! RIGHT NOW!"

Agents in the room noticeably tensed. Attendees scattered and watched as the President stared down the barrel of the shotgun at the Senator. The man's tan suit pants suddenly developed a large, growing dark spot in the crotch area. The Senator cried and wobbled on his feet, readying himself for a shotgun blast. He collapsed to his knees.

"ANYONE ELSE?" the President hollered. "I've had enough of this traitorous bullshit. You refuse to do what I've ordered, and you'll be wettin' your pants too, right before you're convicted and hanged. Huh, I just decided to add somethin' to your penalty due to your friend Mr. Poddypants here. You're also gonna sign an affidavit givin' the Federal Government the right to garnish all your future earnings to the tune of eighty percent. Anyone else wanna add to the tab?" he asked between clenched teeth, looking each Member of Congress in the eye.

After thirty seconds of silence, Stine lowered the Mossburg and handed it back to the agent who'd given it up. He turned to the lead agent. "Get this herd into the barn and get 'em branded proper like," the President said.

Three agents escorted the POTUS from the premises as the ring of agents organized the Members of Congress into groups to be herded into awaiting vans.

No one spoke. Everyone was caught up in their own thoughts and calculations. There'd be no time to transfer wealth to offshore or numbered Swiss accounts that many had. No way to keep those accounts secret anyway. No time to re-title assets in the names of spouses or children. And, without passports and now on a no-fly list, there was no place to go and hide.

The President had indeed reduced them to livestock.

64

Three weeks passed. On a Thursday, at 4:05 PM, Archibald Graystone walked with confidence into the Oval Office.

"Howdy, Archie, my friend." The usual team, plus the FBI Director, were present for Graystone's visit. "Take a seat and give us the news. I hope like hell it's good."

Graystone eyed each advisor. "Mr. President, I won't bore you with the details of what's happened in the market. Suffice it to say, globally, the markets have shed about seventy percent of their peak value. Another way to characterize that is the market is now selling at the same level as it sold about thirty years ago."

The President punched a fist into the air. "Gol darn it, that's a generation of wealth that's disappeared."

"Yes sir, it is. The good news is we optimistic that we've bottomed out."

"I am not gonna get on TV and tell the nation and everybody else who's listenin' that this thing has ended just to find out it hasn't."

"Quite correct, sir," Graystone said. "There are reasons why my colleagues around the globe and I believe we've turned the corner—two in particular. First, the technicals or statistical trends in equity prices over the last seven trading days indicate we're bouncing back, globally. Second, tens of billions of dollars worth of currency are pouring into the market from all over the world. There's no pattern as to the source of these funds. In other words, it isn't just a few buyers or a couple of countries or a handful of brokers. The deluge is coming from thousands of sources through hundreds of brokers worldwide."

"I've got another one of my dumb questions," President Stine said.

"Mr. President, I haven't heard you utter a dumb question yet," Graystone replied.

"That's reassurin'. Here's my question. Who would know this is the right time to buy into this depressed market? Couldn't it drop further?"

Graystone looked at the other men and women sitting around the Oval Office. Then, he continued. "That's an excellent question, Mr. President, and one we've given some thought to.

"You see, the underlying assets or companies being purchased are not worthless. Although a few companies didn't survive this disaster, the vast majority did. Oh, they laid off thousands of people and maybe used up a ton of cash on hand, but they generally have the same leadership, the same market shares, produce the same products or services with the same quality, and so on. In other words, they have value.

"If some one or some group benefitted from this crisis, they probably bought in long before the run up and sold at the peak for significant profits. They don't want to destroy publicly traded companies because they still have value. So, at some point, they needed to curb their greed. We believe that's been done. They're now buying up companies at fire sale prices. We just don't know who's doing it, and there's no way to find out."

"So the market's goin' back up," the President muttered.

"Over a period of months, maybe a year, it will. Not to the peak we experienced, not evenly, and maybe not to the price point before the run up. But we believe it's on its way back up. When it levels out, we expect to see many current buyers take their profits and exit the market. We can't do anything about that either."

The FBI Director spoke up. "Mr. President, if you delivered a message about the state of the market, you might want to use the opportunity to announce your Market Crash Relief Fund. The Members of Congress who departed had a collective net worth of six billion dollars. They were all pretty wealthy, but two Members were billionaires, even after the crash. We expect to collect four point eight billion dollars from them. So far, we've collected a little over two billion. That's a drop in the bucket relative to the overall loss in the market, but..."

The Treasury Secretary interrupted. "But used selectively, we could really help a number of companies and individuals who've been hurt the most. We, and I mean this group, has met to discuss how to administer this fund to ensure money gets in the right hands without a ton of government expense in the process."

"I'll look forward to your report on that, but make it quick folks. We don't have time to dilly dally around with this. People are hurtin'."

"Mr. President," Graystone said. "This may not be the time or the place, but there is one individual who singlehandedly made a big difference in this entire saga. Her name is..."

"Carrie Linden," President Stine said. "I've heard all the reports on Ms. Linden. What she did. How she did it. What she suffered, and continues to suffer. I realize we can't chase every bad rabbit that a citizen reports, but we've got to find ways to listen more carefully to the Carrie Lindens out there. They often know more about what's going on than the rest of us put together."

Turning to the SEC Chairman and Treasury Secretary. "I want you two to establish a commission on the down low to examine what's happened and come up with recommendations for how to prevent this from happenin' again."

"If I may suggest," Graystone continued. "We need to recognize Ms. Linden's contribution in some way."

"Archie, that's exactly what Mal and I have discussed. We've got a plan to do just that. However, it's not something we can broadcast. If we did, we'd open up a can of worms. It'd lead to a host of questions and conjecture about the fifty-four Members who abruptly left Congress."

The FBI Director said, "Some of their local supporters are praising them to the heavens, erecting statues and naming roads and airports in their honor. All because they relinquished their right to their pensions, supposedly to aid our government."

"That's fine and dandy with me," the President said. "But we can't let the public know what a bunch of scumbag traitors these men and women were. This democracy is teetering on the brink, and we can't let it slip into the abyss."

"I understand, sir," Graystone said.

"So sit tight. You'll be invited to a little private event some time soon."

"I look forward to it."

65

Max sat with Wyatt in his office watching Dick Snyder on webcam. Dick was Special Agent in Charge of the Phoenix FBI Office and a former colleague of Max's.

"So here we are again, guys," Dick said. "We've been around this block so many times, I'm getting dizzy." He referred to the repeated surveillance on Tony Amici and ultimate search of his office, home, accounts and vehicles. "Nothing. That's what we've got. Nothing."

Frustrated, Wyatt asked, "Everything kosher with his accounts?"

"Squeaky clean. Nothing questionable. No loose ends. Nothing unexplained. Oh, there is one thing. He sold all his equity positions through a local Vegas stock broker right before the market crashed. Claims he thought the market was overheated, and he decided to get out. ...Lucky, huh?"

"So did I...on a hunch," Max said. "Can't arrest him for timing the market, unless we can prove he had inside knowledge."

"No evidence of that. He does employ several thugs as skip-tracers. They're all ex-cons. You've got to be a tough guy to run down creeps who skip out on bail."

"What about the floor safe you found in his office?" Max asked.

"No big deal. He had ten grand in hundreds stashed in the safe. Said it was rainy day money. No records of anything untoward. If I didn't know better, I'd say he's got someone in the FBI coaching him on when and how to evade us."

"Hmm, that's not it," Wyatt said. "He's just very slippery. One of these days, he'll forget to oil up, and we'll get him. Thanks for going after him another time, Dick, and I appreciate you including my guys on your team."

"No problema. Your guys gave us a motivational boost for the job."

"Pull the plug on it, and send my guys home."

"Will do."

Max added, "You're the best, Dick. If you couldn't nail him, no one could."

They signed off.

Later in the day, Max sauntered into Michael's Bethesda office. He could hear Michael in his conference room loudly scolding a client.

"If you violate your restraining order again, I will no longer represent you. You've beat up your wife multiple times. She's got every right to have you put away for good. Get it?"

"But I love her, and it's not..."

"I don't care about your feelings. My concern and why you're paying me is to keep you out of jail. It's time for you to man up and move on. Go get some psychotherapy, but stay away from her. If you don't, I hope they put you behind bars and throw away the key. We're done here, unless you want me to charge you another hour of my time as a nuisance fee."

Seated in the lobby waiting area, Max watched Michael's chastised client slink out of the meeting room and leave the suite of offices. Max stepped into the conference room as Michael organized papers in a file.

"Sounds like you've got a winner of a client there—a real brain surgeon."

Michael looked up with a frown and then smiled. "Funny you should say that. He is a brain surgeon."

They burst into laughter.

"What's up?" Michael asked.

"The good guys have scored a few victories and a loss."

"Tell me."

"First off, the State of Maryland deferred to Illinois on Ruddock. Illinois had the strongest case against him for the worst crime: his assault and attempted murder of Carrie. Ruddock pled guilty, and the judge gave him a mandatory thirty years with no possibility of parole. He'll be close to seventy when he gets out, *if* he survives Stateville Correctional Center. That's where they sent him. It's one of the toughest state prisons in the U.S. It's where all the creeps from nearby Joliet landed when that prison shut down."

Michael raised both arms over his head. "Touch down! Serves him right."

"And Julie White, the madam in the Congressional corruption scandal. She was sent up the river with her lesbian girlfriend for possession of cocaine with intent to distribute. They'll both do twenty years in the Penitentiary of New Mexico in a minimum restrict facility. It isn't the harshest environment, but if they screw up, they'll be sent to one. It's just south of Santa Fe—nice place to visit."

"Been there," Michael muttered.

"After that, she'll head back to D.C. to serve time for running a brothel."

"All good so far."

"Ruddock won't talk about Amici, even though we have evidence the two know each other. And Amici's made only vague comments about Ruddock.

Nothing usable. White says she's never heard of Amici, and we have no reason to disbelieve her. She said she didn't know Ruddock, until she saw a picture of him. She said his name was Jeremy Blevins. It frightened her, and she clammed up."

Michael raised his eyebrows. "Sounds like we could connect the dots among the three. How's this? Amici sets the game in motion. Ruddock manages it. Ruddock hires White, but doesn't let her know about his employer. Ruddock fears reprisal from Amici if he rats him out, and White fears Ruddock for the same reason."

Max shrugged. "You're probably right, but we can't prove any of it. The bad news is Amici's free as a bird. Despite best efforts, the FBI found nothing incriminating."

"I know he ordered Ruddock to attack Carrie. I know it from the meeting Carrie and Melvin had with him. And I know it from my conversation with him."

"I don't doubt you, but knowing it and proving it are two different things."

"Right. Ruddock's probably damaged Carrie's feet for life. ...I've got a notion to visit Amici and..."

Max frowned. "Listen to me. You're not a murderer. You killed that Arizona Sheriff last year, but it was in the midst of a struggle. Self-defense. It's not in you to commit a premeditated assassination. Either you'll screw it up or you'll get hurt in the attempt or you'll get caught. Believe me, I know what I'm talking about. Leave it alone. Time will take care of Amici."

Michael gritted his teeth. "Have you told Carrie all of this?"

"Yup. She was elated. She's planning to visit Ruddock behind bars."

"NO WAY!" Michael exclaimed.

"HA! That's what the lady said. Amazing, huh? She's thinking about writing a book about life behind bars and figures he'll give her some insights."

Michael shook his head. "I love that woman, but I'll never figure out how I could have fallen in love with her, given her interests."

66

At 9:30 AM, Wednesday November 24, the day before Thanksgiving, a light dusting of snow coated the streets in the District of Columbia. The White House looked whiter than usual as the caravan of Town Cars stopped, one-by-one, at the entry gate to show ID before proceeding.

Michael reached across the back seat and gave Carrie's hand a gentle squeeze. "You ready for this?"

Carrie looked at him. "I'm still shocked this is actually going to happen."

They exited the government Town Car and waited inside the entry doors for the others: Melvin Grimes, Hank Greenbaum, Leo Bernstein and Max Foerce. Two Secret Service agents took their winter coats and escorted them to the Green Room—a parlor on the first or State Floor of the White House, used for small receptions.

Several people already in the room and talking in small clusters turned to greet the guests. "Welcome, Ms. Linden," Malcolm Parr said. He walked over and shook her hand. "Please let me make some introductions." And he did...to the Vice President, the Speaker of the House and Minority Leader, the Majority and Minority Leaders of the Senate, the Chairmen of the SEC and Federal Reserve, the Treasury Secretary, the Attorney General and the Chief Justice of the U.S."

Archie Graystone walked in a few minutes later. Approaching Carrie, he said, "How are you, my dear?"

"I'm holding up pretty well, except for my right foot."

"I know. I hope today will be some small recompense for your sacrifice. This has been long in the works."

A man opened one of the six doors to the Green Room and announced, "Ladies and Gentlemen, the President of the United States."

Everyone turned and watched as President Mark Stine strode into the room wearing a big smile.

"Howdy everyone," he boomed as he made a bee line to Carrie. "I've wanted to meet you for months, young lady." He gave her a big hug.

He raised his arms and said, "Let's proceed. Folks, y'all have a seat. All except Carrie. Oh, are you all right to stand for a few minutes darlin'?"

"Yes, I am," she said, wiggling her cane.

"Let's you and me stand next to this podium." After ushering her into position, he said, "This is an unusual ceremony. The times are unusual as our nation and the world recover from the financial meltdown of this past summer. It's also taken us a while to rope all these folks together in one spot for this occasion. We've had an unusual event with the mass departures of elected officials from Congress. Usually, a ceremony like this is open knowledge to the public, but I trust all of you, for the sake of our nation, not to breathe a word of what transpires here today for reasons you already know.

"What's not so unusual, however, is we're here to honor the bravery and self-sacrifice of one of our citizens, Carrie Linden. This young lady follows in the proud footsteps of fine men and women before her who risked their lives for our country in the cause of justice."

He looked at Carrie. "In a moment, my dear, I'm gonna read the citation. But I want you to know that I personally thank you and our nation thanks you for all you've done to alert us to the financial crisis and help to bring those varmints to justice." With that, the President read a citation and an aide stepped forward with a box. "I hereby present you with the Presidential Medal of Freedom for an especially meritorious contribution to the security and interests of the United States of America."

Everyone in the room stood and applauded. Tears rolled down Carrie's cheeks as the President stepped behind her and clasped the ribbon carrying the medal around her neck. President Stine gave her another big hug and whispered, "You need anything young lady, anytime, call me here or back home on my Texas ranch."

By noon, Carrie and the small group she'd arrived with at the White House, plus Archie Graystone, lunched in The Private Dining Room at The Hay-Adams Hotel. The President had insisted his guests be lodged at the hotel at government expense a few nights for the presentation.

When Carrie had been asked by the President's aide what family members she'd like to attend the ceremony, she thought about her father figures, Melvin, Hank and Leo as well as her uncle Archie. Family for Carrie also included Michael and Max. She couldn't leave them out. After a lengthy lunch, each guest departed— Graystone to New York for a dinner, Michael and Max to a client meeting, Leo for a nap in his room, and Hank to return what would likely be a bevy of phone messages.

Melvin and Carrie remained at the table while it was cleared. "That Stine guy's a pretty good fella," Melvin said.

"I agree."

"How're yer feet doin'?"

"Ah, you know, left foot's pretty good. Right foot? Well, not so good. But I manage. The cane helps a bit."

"Sorry yer strugglin' with that."

"I'm really happy you came, Melvin."

"Me miss a chance to see ya git an award at the White House? Wild horses couldn't have held me back. I'm proud of ya like ya was my own kin."

"Thanks. That means a lot coming from you."

Neither spoke for half a minute.

"Guess you and Michael figgered out whatcha wanna do with yer lives."

"Not an easy decision, but you helped frame it for each of us. The result was inevitable, but we're still very close friends. I think we always will be."

"I'm glad they got that fella Ruddock who hurt ya."

"True. But they never put a glove on his employer. And you and I know who that was."

"Yup. Well, don't worry 'bout him, honey. He's gonna git what's comin' to him." Melvin winked at Carrie.

"Shall we leave?" Carrie asked.

Melvin helped her to her feet, and they left the dining room.

67

February was cloudy in Las Vegas. Cold too, but not as cold as other parts of the country. The mechanic studied his target for six days, following him in a car he'd rented with false ID. He could have finished the job in three, but, like many who visit Vegas, he decided to see a few shows in one of the world's entertainment capitols.

Jersey Boys brought him to tears one night at the Palazzo Hotel as he reflected on events in his life during the years when *The Four Seasons* grew to be one of the most popular singing groups in the U.S. Two nights later, he marveled at the acrobatics and staging in the *Cirque du Soleil* production of *KÂ* at the MGM Grand. *Great shows. Maybe I should visit Vegas more often.*

He'd begun thinking about his next project that would take him to Manila. It didn't pay as well as his current assignment, but he couldn't decline the work because the request came from a frequent client.

When Amici canceled the assignment to assassinate a dozen of the country's leading corporate executives, the mechanic had packed up his new French FR-F2 sniper rifle, ammunition and Zeiss Diavari scope and stored them in his U-Store-It unit outside Clearwater, Florida.

The go signal from Shanghai finally came in late December. The client wanted Amici gone within three months. Excited about ridding the world of a person whom he believed had not an honorable bone in his body, he retrieved his rifle, ammo and scope and headed to his favorite shooting range, nine miles from his Clearwater condo. Once satisfied with his proficiency with the weapon, he packed his gear and hopped on a Greyhound Bus—destination, Las Vegas.

Upon arriving, he'd checked into the Bellagio Hotel. The economy had been hit so hard that tourism volume was down, papers reported, about forty percent. That enabled him to stay in an elegant suite for $189 per night, plus tax—a sweet deal.

After observing Amici a few days, he decided not to take him out during daylight hours. The effective range of his French rifle was 800 meters, but he could get much closer at night. And he relished the thought of seeing the clear expression on the smug bastard's face when he caught the bullet.

The question remained, *where?*

Amici left EZ-Bonds promptly at 5 PM every night—still daylight in Vegas in February. His evening excursions took him to various dinners and meetings. However, Amici predictably went home nightly, his chauffeur dropping him curbside and driving off as Amici walked thirty-seven paces to his front door. His entry was well lit, though the straight five foot wide path from the street to the entrance was darker.

Some people believe Nevada is a big desert with little plant life and few trees. Not entirely true. Amici had planted eight Great Basin Bristlecone Pines— the state tree of Nevada—on both sides of his walkway decades earlier. Their height now exceeded thirty feet. Each had multiple trunks, covered with thick bark and bundles of needles that approached two inches in length. Enough mass to darken the walkway.

Sometimes, you just get lucky, the mechanic thought. The house across the street from Amici's had been dark every night. The owners were away, probably lying on a beach on a Hawaiian island. Their flat roof would allow him to position himself comfortably one evening and take Amici out with range to spare on his rifle. The wide parapet wall would serve as an ideal place to set his shooting tripod.

Last night, he'd set up and sighted in his rifle. Tonight, he'd finish the job. There was no need to follow Amici today, he simply needed to show up about 5:00 PM and wait for his target to appear like clockwork.

Time ticked by, and the mechanic sat on the roof with his back up against the parapet wall. Few vehicles drove up Amici's street, and he could hear each one as they approached. None belonged to Amici. Being a sniper requires a good deal of patience because waiting for the right moment for a target to emerge in the kill zone is the name of the game.

The mechanic took a swig from his canteen of lemon-flavored water and looked at his Mares lighted dive watch—7:46 PM. *Come on, Amici. I want to go to the hotel and play some blackjack before bed.* The moonless night weighed in his favor.

He heard a vehicle approach. His watch read 8:37 PM. *He has arrived. Must have eaten dinner out.*

The mechanic observed Amici's car pull up to the curb as per routine. Amici emerged as usual, closed the car door and watched the driver depart. Then he turned toward his front door and began what would be the last thirty-seven paces of his life.

The mechanic tracked Amici with his scope, waiting for the moment to pull the trigger when Amici reached his lighted entry.

Halfway up the walk, a tall dark figure wearing what appeared to be a clear plastic rain poncho emerged from behind a pine tree. *What is this?* The tall figure raised a crowbar overhead and crashed it into Amici's skull. Not once, or even twice, but eight times. *No one could survive such punishment.* The mechanic ran a finger over the pulsating scar on his head, recalling his episode with the hammer in Kosovo.

The figure bagged the crowbar as he walked past the side of Amici's house, through the back yard and onto the next street. He trained his scope back on Amici who hadn't twitched, much less moved an inch. *How to play this? The death will be reported along with the cause. My client will have expected me to shoot him, not club him to death. That is my signature.* The solution was obvious.

With his rifle on the tripod and carefully aimed, he fired two rounds into Amici's back. *Good enough.* That done, he broke down his weapon and walked a block in the opposite direction to his vehicle. Forty-five minutes later, he'd left pieces of his rifle—no fingerprints—in various dumpsters on the way to the Bellagio.

Resting in his non-smoking suite and puffing on one of his Cohiba Espléndidos, he telephoned the Shanghai number.

After the first ring, a man with a Chinese accent answered. "Yes?"

"I have completed my job in Vegas. I expect you can read about it tomorrow. I will look for the balance of my compensation in the account we discussed."

"You will have it." The line went dead.

Someone else detested Amici as much as I did. Thanks for the assist, stranger.

• • •

Three days later, Carrie's phone rang in Chicago.

"Hey, it's Michael. How's your foot?"

"About the same. How are you?"

"Good. I have news. Amici is dead," Michael said. "Shot twice in the back, according to reports, but they say the cause of death was blunt force trauma to the head at night on the walkway into his home."

"Huh. That's one less creep on the streets. They have any idea who did it?"

"*They* don't. Do *you?*"

Acknowledgments

Writing is time consuming. Even when you aren't pecking away on the keyboard, you constantly think about it—working out details, resolving inconsistencies, rounding out characters, refining dialogue, considering language and tone and pacing and sequencing. In the middle of all this, life and relationships go on, and that's a good thing. I thank my wife, Lili Montakhab, for her observations and critique of every chapter as the work unfolded. I also thank my financial advisor Mark Copeland of Signature Estate & Investment Advisors for his perspective on the global stock market. The encouragement I received from friends and family, no matter how much or how little, propelled me forward. They include, and you know who you are, Behrouz, Bill, Bruce, Carl, Christa, Christine, Cindy, Cyrus, Dick, Ed, George, Gordon, Helen, Hugh, Jerry, Jim, John, Malcolm, Margaret, Maribel, Mark, Michelle, Mike, Paul, Rob, Scott, Stewart, Wayne, Wey-Wey, Zhana. I regret if I've missed someone.

John J. Parkington

John began his career as a clinical psychologist in a West Virginia mental health center. He earned his PhD in psychology at the University of Maryland and completed a subsequent program of study at Harvard. John taught psychology at the University of Maryland and Georgetown University and spent over 30 years consulting to top management in major corporations around the world. Having written for academic psychological journals, he has penned three psychological thrillers—the trilogy: *Justice Rendered, Body Parts* and *Touch of Corruption*. He is currently at work on a new novel in the series. John lives with his wife in Palm Springs, California and part-time along the Southern California coast and has been a member of the Palm Springs Writers Guild and the American Psychological Association.